OF
SINS

BY

STEPHANIE HUDSON

Queen of Sins
The Transfusion Saga #12
Copyright © 2021 Stephanie Hudson
Published by Hudson Indie Ink
www.hudsonindieink.com

This book is licensed for your personal enjoyment only.
This book may not be re-sold or given away to other people. If you would like to share this book with another person, please purchase an additional copy for each recipient. If you're reading this book and did not purchase it, or it wasn't purchased for your use only, then please return to your favourite book retailer and purchase your own copy. Thank you for respecting the hard work of this author.
All rights reserved.
This is a work of fiction. Names, characters, places, brands, media, and incidents are either the product of the authors imagination or are used fictitiously. The author acknowledges the trademark status and trademark owners of various products referred to in this work of fiction, which have been used without permission. The publication/use of these trademarks is not authorised, associated with, or sponsored by the trademark owners.

Queen of Sins/Stephanie Hudson – 1st ed.
ISBN-13 - 978-1-913904-85-2

Queen Of Sins is dedicated to the four ladies whom I would be lost without. They keep my crazy train rolling. Their dedication, professionalism and friendship are second to none.
Thank you Maralyn, Claire, Sarah & Sloane.
Love you ladies xox

"Anything is possible when you have the right people there to support you"

WARNING

This book contains explicit sexual content, some graphic language and a highly additive dominate Vampire King.

This book has been written by an UK Author with a mad sense of humour. Which means the following story contains a mixture of Northern English slang, dialect, regional colloquialisms and other quirky spellings that have been intentionally included to make the story and dialogue more realistic for modern day characters.

Thanks for reading x

PROLOGUE

LUCIUS

The end.

I will be honest, I didn't expect it. Then again, why would I?

But well, that was the thing with hope, it had the power to cast all the dark endings into the shadows and shine its light on all the endings you were wishing for. The endings that included you stepping away from a war hand in hand with the woman you loved and raised as the victors. Raised to the Heavens, as the evils you fought were long turned to dust and the threat left dead in the battlefield. A crumbling wasteland that had yet again been turned into a fated graveyard, which would become nothing more than another story told. One that years would no doubt warp until its details were little more than a myth.

The War of Souls.

That was what they would call it.

But as for that useless hope, it had ended up as nothing more than a prayer left unanswered by the Gods, who were too afraid to intervene. A prayer that was roared louder, as one by one they all fell around me. A prayer that once more turned into a promised curse as each soul was taken. Because it was all wrong. Those that we fought weren't our enemies and each forced swing of a weapon came from the hands of who we loved. It was no longer a war against good and evil. It wasn't one fought with hatred in the hearts of men defending their home.

No… it was… *Gods in heaven*… but it was a battle of a hand forced to fight, and I felt each one tear another piece from my soul as I was forced to kill my own. And as the Tree of Souls continued to lose its leaves, so did my hope at ever seeing that flower bloom again before it too, was forced to fall. Just like that darkness had overtaken it, turning it crimson to black the first time that precious soul had died. And now, that flower belonged to another, and that heart I once owned was one I had been forced to lift my sword towards.

So, I motioned my beautiful warrior forward, and forced out the words I hated my cursed soul for saying,

"Very well, let us do this…"

"…My Queen of Sins."

CHAPTER ONE

AMELIA

MAN EATER

"Seriously… this is our ride?" I asked incredulously, now faced with a line of beasts that were being mounted by our leaving party. This consisted mainly of Carn'reau and his men. But there was also Vern, Gryph and of course Trice, and I had to admit, I wasn't looking forward to the time when I would have to say goodbye to them. Just the idea that I may never see them again had me swallowing down the hard lump in my throat at the thought of waving farewell to my three Scottish saviours, who admittedly, had started to make it seem like a full-time job in saving my ass.

"Well, I grant you, it's not a stolen 1970 Dodge Charger RT," Lucius said after taking the reins of the strange beast. As for me, I put my hands on my hips and pointed out,

"Hey, I didn't steal it!"

"Oh no, I am sorry, you just traded it for a stolen Ferrari... my mistake," he said wryly, making me roll my eyes at him and the second I saw his eyes heat, I knew why.

"Oh, no way, buddy, not happening," I said, referring of course to the promised spanking I got whenever I did roll my eyes at him. But my response only made him smirk back before informing me,

"Maybe not, but I promise you, sweetheart..." He paused so he could stride his long legs over to me in a second, before he tugged me to him and whispered his promise down at me.

"*...I am keeping count.*"

Then he kissed me, and I had to say, by the end of it I felt like taking a ride on something else. Which was why I said in a breathless way the moment it finished,

"Can I not just ride you instead?" His reply to this was beautiful as he threw his head back and laughed, and just like that, it managed to cut whatever tension and worry had been building up inside of him. Well, for the moment at least.

After my conversation with Vena, I had guessed his worry was down to what he was keeping from me.. Now, why he hadn't wanted to tell me about the witch being involved with what had just happened, I still didn't know. Was it because he didn't want me to worry any more than I already was? I mean, I could understand this to a point, especially considering all the witch had done to me, and well, that Hex had been a bitch to remove! And obviously not something I would look forward to experiencing again any time soon.

So, the witch had been the one to send the Wraith Master. Big deal, as I already knew that she and Lucius' evil brother were scheming to try and take control over the Eye and use it as a weapon. And well, it didn't take a genius to know that I was now on his brother's radar. Especially after he had seen the way I had been able to handle the Eye without becoming the next 'Miss Extra Well Done and Crispy' in Hell's beauty pageant. then

It was also obvious why he wanted me.as was the only one who could handle the Eye and survive it.

Of course, this meant that all I had now was doubts about what was going on in Lucius' head, I couldn't help but feel as if there was something more he was keeping from me. Oh sure, I had wanted to ask him and confront him about what Vena had told me. But then, to be honest, I had been scared to after knowing how much we had both endured at the hands of the Wraith Master. One who had technically killed me once already, and I really didn't think neither I nor Lucius could cope with the witch succeeding a second time by some other twisted means.

So, with this in mind, I gave Lucius a break and told myself he could no longer make any decisions without me first being in on it. No, he wouldn't do that to me again... *would he?*

"As much as I would prefer that means of travel, sweetness, I fear its only destination is back in a bed and no closer to getting you home."

"Home?" I questioned, picking up on the word, making him tense once before telling me on a smooth whisper,

"*Our home.*"

On hearing this I gripped onto him tighter, holding him in a way that told him how much I liked the sound of that. But then I had to be sure.

"Now, is that home the one in Hell or in Germany?" I asked, making him grip me tighter, and with his chin resting on the top of my head and my head tucked to his chest he whispered,

"Wherever you are is my home, Amelia."

Now, I had to admit, I liked this even better. He held me to him for a minute longer before stepping back, and I got the impression it was a painful move for him to make. The look he refused to give me directly told me as much, but it was the regret I could see in his eyes that I clung onto. Did he regret having to let me go and not having the time to hold me for longer?

Well, whatever the reason, I gave his hand a squeeze for it, making him finally smile down at me before pulling me closer to the beast, one that was obviously saddled for us as it was the biggest of the herd… if that was what you could call them.

"Erm, so what exactly is that… um… thing?" I said feeling bad calling it a thing, but after tipping my head slightly to one side and not seeing anything obvious to tell me its sex, there was little else to call it. Lucius' lips quirked up at this, but instead of laughing at my antics he stepped behind me and told me,

"It's a Manticore… *oh, and it's a boy.*" He whispered this last part after pushing me closer to it, making me reply in a cocky but still slightly strained voice,

"Mazel tov." At this Lucius chuckled before saying,

"Come on, my Khuba, you will be just fine."

"Oh, I doubt it, I mean I thought that thing was its second tail but now I know it's a boy then I'm not so sure." Again, Lucius' lips quirked at this as he led me over to the mighty beast that looked as tall as the biggest of horses, and twice as wide! But, taking its size out of it, the rest of him looked just as deadly, with the body of a lion covered in reddish coarse fur. He had a spiked tail that had metal cuffs clasped to the largest spike, one that seemed to be on the end of a scorpion's tail. Then, along its spine reminded me of a porcupine with a line down its back of needle tipped quills, that at the moment were all laid flat. I also had a feeling they wouldn't stay this way for long should it suddenly get pissed off. But then Lucius saw me looking and commented,

"Its tail is quite poisonous, along with the quills along its back that can be fired but…"

"Oh goodie, the added fear to the journey will make it go all the quicker and much more enjoyable," I quipped, making Lucius inform me,

"As I was saying, it is why it is contained in metal," he continued, making me say a quick,

"Ah."

"Yeah, 'ah' indeed… now I will lift you so you can put your right foot in the stirrup before swinging your left leg around," he told me, nodding towards the arched metal ring that was strapped and attached to the large saddle that was clearly big enough for two. It was also beautiful, like most things in this realm, as the white leather was intricately decorated with embossed Elvish symbols that were interwoven in elegant vines. As for the rest of the creature, its feet were like large horses' hooves, that stamped in the dirt impatiently, kicking up the burnt orange dust.

However, its head was another thing entirely, as it looked like a human man had been shifting into a lion before being caught frozen between the two forces. It had the flat black nose that followed down into the snarling mouth of a beast, with three rows of deadly looking teeth that I wanted to keep as far away from my body parts as possible.

Its eyes, however, were a greyish blue and were shaped like a man's, along with a long forehead and ears that were tucked under a coarse fur that made up a flaming red mane. It was unnerving the way those knowing eyes looked at me, as they seemed far too intelligent to belong to an animal the Fae race used as transport. Hell, but I half expected him to speak and tell me to lay off the donuts as I was hoisted up into the saddle.

I also wished I could have said that I had been graceful in this 'mounting of the beast', a million Pip jokes not withstanding at that terminology. Yet graceful and the name Amelia Draven didn't usually go hand in hand unless I was swinging a blade at someone's head. Which meant that I overcompensated in my 'swinging leg' and nearly went sliding right off the other side in a heap. Of course, I would have done, had it not been for Lucius saving me while mounting the beast himself and using my sliding leg as leverage to do so. which also served its purpose in pulling me back upright at the same time.

"Smooth, cowboy," I commented, making him chuckle behind me before whispering in my ear,

"I know… in fact, one may think that I had planned for your clumsy infliction to strike and counteracted its failure with a graceful move of my own." I looked back over my shoulder at him to give him a pointed look, knowing that I would find him smirking down at me.

"Yeah, yeah, cocky much?" I grumbled, at which he laughed before wrapping his arms around me and taking hold of the reins that were attached to the harness around the creature's head. Then he made a clucking sound as his tongue hit the roof of his mouth, which told the beast to move forward with the rest of the herd that had already started to move.

"What did you say this creature was again?" I asked, not recognising it the first time from any books, but then when he said the name again, something twigged in my memory bank.

"It is known as a Manticore."

"The Man Eater?!" I shouted, a little too loud considering I was currently sitting on its back.

"A little louder there, sweetheart, and I fear he might take it as an invite," Lucius teased. As for me, I refrained from retorting with a sarcastic, *'well that's all we need, a ride that eats us at the end of our journey,'* just in case it could understand us. But then suddenly that old Persian fable my father used to tell me came back and had me reciting some of it aloud.

"Truly have the Sages said that to cherish a base character is to give one's honour to the wind, and to involve one's own self in embarrassment." At this, Lucius took hold of my chin and turned my face to the side so he could look into my eyes.

"The Scorpion and the Turtle?" he asked, making my eyes widen but then of course he would know it, being that he started off his new life in Persia by my father's side.

"My fa…"

"Your father… but of course. And you are right, sometimes it is merely the nature of our being that dictates our actions, just like the nature in me to… *protect what is mine,*" Lucius said, whispering this last part in my ear on a promised growl.

"Is that why you won't let him eat me?" I teased back, making him nip at my ear before telling me,

"There is only one being that gets to bite you, pet, and it is the predator at your back, not the one you sit upon." At this, I smirked before pointing out,

"Yeah, but sometimes I get to sit on you too, so does that still count?" I was soon shaking in his hold as he boomed with laughter at my teasing.

"*Most definitely.*" This was his breathy response, making me shiver against him.

"So, getting back to the creature I am currently sitting on in a totally nonsexual way... *unlike when I am playing with the beast at my back,*" I said, whispering this last part, making Lucius whisper,

"*Behave, my Khuba.*" I grinned in return.

"So, these Manticores?"

"And not to be mistaken with a Mantyger," Lucius added, making me question him.

"They're not the same?" I asked, knowing now that many historical myths believed they were.

"No, for they are something different and most definitely cannot be tamed. Although, the creature we ride now can also be known as Mardykhor in Persian," he told me and I had to admit, that when like this, I could listen to Lucius talk all day and hang on every word. But then this wasn't exactly surprising, as combined with being a massive geek for knowledge, I was also a hopelessly in love one at that.

"Ah, but of course, *Mardya*, meaning man and *Khowr*, meaning to eat, so that makes sense," I replied, knowing these words in Persian.

"Along with the Greeks, who named the beast Androphagos," was Lucius' reply, making me snort a laugh and say,

"Which also means man eater... okay, so tell me, is there a name for them that doesn't mean it's gonna look at me as a takeout meal strapped to its back?" Lucius chuckled again and said,

"It may be the Scorpion in this fabled scenario, but there is something important you're forgetting."

"Yeah, and what's that?" I enquired in a cocky tone.

"He's not the only one you ride with that possesses a deadly nature... *and my bite is more deadly than his,*" he told me, making me feel somewhat better that I would get there with all my limbs intact and not as some tasty snack along the way.

"So, you can relax, pet," he added, making me laugh nervously and say,

"Well, at least I know for sure that one of you doesn't mind me riding you." At this he wrapped an arm around me possessively, and I knew this was in a teasing way when he growled,

"*Indeed.*"

"Besides, its stinger is contained for a reason," he told me. So I looked over my shoulder, only to find Lucius' big bulk of muscle in the way.

"Oh yeah, harmless... what you gonna try and convince me of next, that those three rows of teeth are blunt and for sucking on Fae fruit lollypops?"

"I think we already covered riding me, sweetheart, but hey, if you want to turn your attention to sucking then be my guest, but just so you know, riding one of these things with a raging hard on isn't going to make this journey a comfortable one, despite having you in my arms." At this, it was my turn to throw my head back and laugh and I had to say it made the start of the journey a comical one and surprisingly, it was down to the maneater between my legs... Pip pun most definitely intended, I thought on a giggle. A sound that got me a comforting squeeze of his hand at my side.

A squeeze that dug in harder the moment I said,

"I never thought I would say this, but I am looking forward to getting back to your Kingdom in Hell and maybe getting reacquainted with your tower, especially your pool, as I think after this journey, I will need it." This of course was referring to the dust of the dirt road we travelled down. But then I had to question his reaction, as I had expected his witty reply... However, what I didn't expect was his body to tense, his hold to tighten and his voice to be strained as he answered in a single stern word that this time was anything but playful...

"Indeed."

CHAPTER TWO

FLIPPED AND STRIPPED

That one worded reply marked the beginning of a stretch of silence between us, along with the start of my worry. Because it was as if a switch had been flipped in Lucius at the very mention of his kingdom, and now all I did was question why?

Was it because of how he would be forced to treat me again when there, or was it because it was a reminder of having me taken from his tower? This, despite him once believing I would have been untouchable there. But then, with that logic, I guess there wouldn't have been many places left where that same bitterness wouldn't follow, seeing as something bad had happened wherever I had been. Gods, but I was starting to think I was cursed, as trouble most certainly knew how to find me. I mean, was I leaving bad guy breadcrumbs or something?

In a perfect world, I would have asked him what was wrong… oh who the Hell was I kidding, in a perfect world we wouldn't even be here right now. And as for our first date, it would have gone the way Lucius had envisioned it, with him walking me to my door at the end of the night after the gala and coming inside. I would have woken up to him making breakfast and then we would have spent the day together. After that, well, I didn't know, but what I did know was that three months later it wouldn't have brought us to this point. To where we were making our way back to his Kingdom in Hell after I had died in his arms and come back as some other version of myself that was no longer fully mortal… if I even had been to begin with.

My point was that in that perfect world, we would not potentially be facing a war and the eradication of his people. An entire race of vampires that included so many I cared for, including my mother and the man I loved.

So, the truth was… *I was terrified.*

Terrified of what awaited us next. Terrified of how it would all end and when it did, asking myself if both our hearts would be left intact and unscathed. And as for right now, that terror seeped into an unknown future where Lucius could potentially be making decisions without me knowing until it was too late.

So, there it was. I was afraid. Not because I feared his anger or frustration, but more the honesty I knew I wouldn't like, or the lies I knew I would hate even more. Because whatever it was, I had to hold on to the promise he made me never to leave. Which meant that everything else I could cope with, and hope that when the time was right he would tell me… or really… *was I just being naive?*

Whichever the answer to my unspoken fears was, I tried to focus on the surrounding countryside, or what little of it I could see bathed in moonlight. Especially as we were long gone from the eternal glow of lights granted by the moat of sapphire blue flames that surrounded the castle and constantly licked at its pure white walls. A light that had offered a clear view of the road ahead for the first fifteen minutes of our journey.

However, now it seemed like an endless road of dark orange dirt that was framed on one side by fields of pale green grass, and on the other a strange forest of bleached white trees. Trees that, without the sunlight, now looked eerily like an army of ghosts just waiting to whisper words of caution and warn us to turn back. Because the further we travelled away from the ethereal Fae castle, one that had been surrounded by fantastical creatures only known to the human world as myths and nothing more, I couldn't help but feel a sense of loss. As if I was leaving behind a piece of myself, and the more distance we put between Calidad, the land of Dragon Flame, and ourselves, the more hope I seemed to lose.

Of course, when I noticed the way that some of Carn'reau's men had fallen back so they could travel behind us, boxing us in no doubt for safe travelling, it only increased that feeling of dread and doubt. Which was why, as we turned a corner, I looked back at the castle one last time before it went out of sight for good. Then in hopes of cutting through the tension, I told Lucius,

"You know, I think despite it all, I am going to miss Rivendell."

"What's Rivendell?" he asked after I had finally broken the silence.

"Rivendell is an Elvish valley in Middle-Earth and where the quest to destroy the One Ring began," I told him, making him chuckle and reply,

"Ah yes, how could I forget your little ugly friend, Gollum, that still occupies my shelf," Lucius said, making me laugh before looking back at him in surprise.

"Have we been getting acquainted with my movie figurines by asking google?" I enquired in a knowing tone.

"What can I say, unfortunately I had time on my hands when my Chosen One did a runaway act, leaving me with nothing but worry and curiosity to fill my time… well, that and hunting a little wayward mortal across the seas," he replied, making me wince.

"Yeah, yeah, I get it, I made bad decisions… geez, no need to rub it in and bring Gollum into it," was my reply, making him place a hand to my belly and pull me closer into his body. Then he growled in my ear,

"You're my precious and don't you forget it." On hearing this, I couldn't help but burst into laughter, one so loud it to shocked everyone in our group enough to turn their heads our way and stare at us. But I was too far gone in my humour to care, and jiggled in the saddle forcing both Lucius' arms to curl around me and take hold of the reins in both hands, just to stop me from sliding off.

"I take it she is well, my Lord, and not indeed having some kind of fit?" Carn'reau asked after pulling up his own Manticore beside us, making me wonder where his own frightening beast was. The one I had seen him sat upon the first time I met him, when Vern had sacrificed himself and double crossed him in that shit hole village.

"It is hard to tell the difference, I know," Lucius commented with a smirk I knew he wore even without seeing it, making me elbow him in the gut.

"Oi!" I shouted, making him release an over exaggerated,

"Humpf!" sound, and with it Carn'reau's eyes widened in surprise, most likely wondering why I was allowed to get away with such an offence. Then Lucius started laughing himself and lifted a hand to my cheek, cupping it from behind before turning my face to gaze up at him then he spoke without taking his eyes off me,

"For your sake, Carn'reau, I hope that when you are fortunate enough to find your fated soulmate, that she too is as spirited as mine." Then he leaned down and kissed me, doing so until I was breathless and as for Carn'reau, by the time it ended he was already gone, and therefore I missed whatever response he would have given to Lucius' sweet declaration. After that, it seemed to ease the tension I had been feeling, as no matter what was going on in Lucius' mind it didn't change the way he felt about me, that much was obvious. And well, it wasn't as though he didn't have enough on his mind so really, maybe I just needed to cut him some slack.

After all, his people were under threat of being wiped out, so all I could hope for was that this was what it was that lay heavily on his mind and not something else. As for the rest of the journey, I thought that we would stop at some point, however Lucius seemed determined to keep going. Then, when I started to get uncomfortable in the saddle, he simply positioned me in a different way, swinging my legs up so I was sat in his lap. After this, I had to say the feeling of finally being able to close my legs had me sighing with relief, making him grant me a warm look before telling me,

"I don't want to stop until we are closer to my own realm." This was said with regret in his tone, which was why I replied,

"I understand." Then I snuggled closer to him and, despite holding me close, when I sneaked a look back up at him, he still managed to look uneasy now all jokes between us had faded. His gaze was firmly ahead watching the road we travelled down, as if his thoughts were consumed with the danger that may greet us. Even being flanked either side by

Carn'reau's army, Lucius was still clearly anxious. It was as if he was at the ready to be attacked at any moment and couldn't relax.

I couldn't say that I blamed him, not after everything that had happened. It was also clear that Lucius had felt out of control since arriving here, meaning it was of little wonder he wanted to get back to his own realm. To get back to a place he could control, being its King.

Because, no matter how much I tried to offer silent comfort, he remained like a tightly coiled spring, his muscles almost humming with power, and I knew at the first sign of trouble his demon would consume him. In fact, I knew the only reason I wasn't sat here now against that demon, was that with his armour it would have made the journey even more uncomfortable for me.

Thankfully, I was wearing a thick dress, and my shoulders wrapped in an even thicker cloak that managed to keep me warm against the cool night. A night that I knew would last three days and longer than this journey would. However, when it started to rain lightly, I knew that unless I was wearing a large plastic bag, then whatever I was wearing would soon be drenched. Especially should the weather decide to take a turn for the worse which, given the look of the storm clouds rolling in above us, I could say with confidence I was going to get cold and wet pretty quickly.

Something that definitely seemed to be an overwhelming factor in Lucius' decision to finally stop, and I nearly sighed in relief when he called out for Carn'reau. As soon as he pulled his beast alongside ours once more, Lucius declared,

"I don't want Amelia to be out in this weather."

"There are some caves not far from here, it is the ideal place for a camp and is sheltered enough to build a fire, and one that will not be seen from afar," his general replied, and I didn't realise until then that I had been tense until hearing this, only relaxing again as my relief set in. Of course, Lucius felt this and hugged me closer to him the moment I did.

"Good, then we will remain there until the storm passes and my Queen has had time to rest." Carn'reau bowed his head before steering his beast out to the side so he could gallop ahead and get to the front of the line.

"You know, technically I am not your Queen," I said, and despite the playful tone he scoffed at it.

"A fact I will change as soon as I can get a fucking ring on your finger." At this I laughed, and replied in a whimsical voice,

"Oh, my handsome King, that's so romantic... tell me, have you proposed much because that was so beautiful." At this he laughed, tightened his arms around me and replied in a husky tone,

"That wasn't a proposal, sweetheart, it was just a fucking promise." My whole body shuddered at this and I ended up feeling his knowing grin against my neck before it turned into a kiss. Then he wrapped my cloak tighter around me and held me in a way that was as sheltered from the rain as he could get... well, that was until it became a downpour and therefore impossible. It was also strange being in the dark and not knowing what time of day it was, therefore making it difficult to know how long we had been travelling. Although, it was definitely long enough for me to feel sore, that was for sure.

But thankfully it must have only been an hour or so more of travelling before we were coming up to a series of caves. Caves, that unless you knew where they were, you would never have found without the aid of daylight and braved venturing off the road and into the forest as we had done. Because they were near invisible, and I wouldn't have known about them at all had it not been for the obvious fact that we had stopped.

Which was also why it definitely made it a good place to camp, as now the weather had taken a turn for the worst and I found myself shivering in Lucius' hold.

"We are here, sweetheart," he told me, and my teeth chattered when I reminded him,

"Thank the Gods, I can no longer feel my ass and am worried it might have been left behind on the road somewhere." Lucius chucked and replied,

"Now, would I ever allow something like that to happen? No, not when I do so love this ass of yours and have plans to take it in the future."

"To take it. Like where, on a date?" I asked laughing, which sounded weird through the cold snapping of my teeth.

"Most definitely… one you will never forget," he told me in a way that I knew was another promise, and this time when I shivered it had nothing to do with the cold. As for our herd of beasts and their army riders, they had each come to a stop at the bottom of a wall of stone where I could just make out the caves above. Large hollows in the rock face that would have been impossible for us to reach on foot. It made me silently question how we were supposed to get to them, when that answer soon came after Lucius slid off the back of the Manticore. Then, before I followed, Lucius started untying a bundle attached to the saddle, one I knew held rations of food, a skin flask of water, and what looked like rolled up fur blankets that had all been provided for us by the King for our journey.

Lucius then turned back to me and reached up, telling me,

"Swing that leg over, sweetheart, and I will catch you as you fall." I gave him a pointed look that made his lips twitch trying to hold back a knowing grin.

"Fall, eh?" I said, making him smirk this time.

"This coming from the man who spent thousands of years riding a horse... yeah, 'cause that's fair," I muttered as I did as I was told. I felt smug when I didn't fall, but ended up sat on the saddle with both legs dangling over the side facing my cocky Vampire. Although, Lucius just shrugged his large shoulders at this and said,

"Or I am just naturally graceful." I laughed once and replied,

"Way I remember it, there was nothing graceful about me dropping your ass to the floor, handsome." Hearing this he allowed his grin to show a second before he snatched out, shackling my ankle and tugging, making me fall into his awaiting arms.

"Well, would you look at that... you can fall gracefully after all." I scowled at him and as held me only an inch away from his lips, said,

"You cheated."

"To get you in my arms quicker, sweetheart, I will always fucking cheat." Then he finished this bad ass statement by crushing his lips to my own, deepening the kiss the moment I wrapped my legs around his waist and at the ready to climb him like a damn stripper's pole! But then I had to say, there was something that had to be said for kissing in the rain as it was... *beautifully wet and raw.*

However, it was the clearing of someone's throat that finally made me realise we weren't exactly alone and when I pulled back, Lucius snarled in annoyance before we both turned our heads towards the person who dared interrupt us. Of course, on seeing all those faces now turned our way I blushed scarlet, and had to say I was glad for the interruption, even if Lucius clearly wasn't.

"My Lord, the deepest cave is the one on the far right,"

Carn'reau said with an amused twitch of his lips, obviously hinting that we should head that way if we wanted to be alone whilst we made out like randy teenagers.

"Good, see that we are not disturbed… it's time to get my Queen warm," he said, making me want to bite my fingertips at the sexual intent that laced his words. Then he pulled my legs from where they were hooked at the base of his spine, but before letting my feet touch the floor, he swept them up. I quickly heard the whoosh of air as he revealed his wings and used them to fly us up to the top of the ledge that was the start of the caves.

Lucius then raised his chin as if scenting something in the air, making me ask,

"What is it?"

"Fuel," he replied, before clicking his fingers and igniting what must have been old torches left deeper within the cave, and that ominous darkness now started to illuminate with a warm orange glow. I had to say that it looked far less foreboding now there was the warmth of fire light, one that also made it easier for Lucius to walk inside and navigate his way deeper into the cave. I would have questioned how Carn'reau and his men would get up here, when I remembered what Lucius had said.

"What about the rest?"

"They will remain and set up camp below," he replied, making me look behind to see that parts of the forest had started to glow where they were already building fires. Of course, I couldn't see much more than that as we travelled further inside, and soon it was easy to see that this cave had been used many times over as its own camp. Especially when we came to larger part of the cave, as there were remnants left of a natural fire, one circled with larger stones. One that ignited with another flick of his wrist, and following a magical thought was lighting up the cavern and creating a warm space around us.

Lucius let my legs fall before setting me on my feet and walking over to a pile of wood, where he picked up a few logs and tossed them on the fire, which made sparks float up like little lightening bugs. It also made me jump and I think it was because Lucius' actions seemed so methodical, making it difficult to know how to act. But then he came up behind me and with his hand spanning my stomach, he pulled me back against him and whispered in my ear,

"Relax, I won't bite this cold ass of yours... *at least not tonight.*" I shivered when he added this last part. But then my whole body actually shuddered when he added in a stern command,

"Now strip."

CHAPTER THREE

FORGIVENESS

The moment he said this I tensed until I felt his hands pull back one side of my cloak, so he was free to slip part of my dress off one shoulder, then he placed his lips there and whispered against my skin,

"Here, let me help you."

After this his other hand snaked up my body, starting where he had his palm flat against my belly, moving it up the front so his hand lay flat in between my heaving breasts. Once there, he slowly took one end of the ribbon that was keeping my cloak in place, and started running it teasingly through his fingers as he kissed his way up my neck. I don't know why but I was frozen to the spot, not daring to move in case I broke the spell he had lured me into. In fact, it was only when I felt the quick tug at my neck and my wet cloak fell from my shoulders that I came out of my dazed and lustful state. Of course, the sound of it slapping to the ground helped as it echoed around the cave, telling me that any noise we made would surely travel, seeing as it seemed to amplify our actions.

"I don't think that's a good idea," I said with my shoulders shaking, but Lucius informed me sternly,

"No, what isn't a good idea is having my girl freezing in wet clothes, when they could be drying by the fire and I could be warming her with my body." This was backed up with actions as with every word said he gathered up fistfuls of my skirt. One that was soon resting at my hips before there was enough material in his grip to pull it straight over my head, leaving me naked. I shrieked in surprise when the cold hit my skin, but he quickly turned me around and plastered my freezing body to the front of him. Then, before I could complain, his wings shot forward and enveloped me in a blanket of feathers, making my eyes widen in shock. Eyes I raised up to his, showing my surprise as his wings closed in tighter. Wings that were large enough that they covered both of us, even reaching over the top of his head. As soon as we were completely covered, I looked to the side to see the warm glow of the fire shining slightly through his Phoenix feathers, making him look like some kind of fire Angel.

He was incredible.

"*You're... you're stunning,*" I whispered breathlessly, making him tip my face up with a bent finger under my chin, telling me softly,

"My sweet girl... now, time to warm those quivering lips." Then he kissed me, and like always it was a kiss that stole my breath. I released an intoxicated moan that echoed around the cavern, reminding me why I didn't think it was a good idea for things getting too heated between us during this little impromptu camping trip of ours. So, I pulled back, ignoring his growl of disapproval that also echoed.

"I don't think this is good idea, there are hundreds of men out there and, well... around you I can't exactly be quiet," I admitted, but then his wings started to tighten around us, and the action brought me closer to him, eliminating the small space I had tried to put between us.

"I don't give a fuck who hears us, your screams belong to me regardless," he told me with a fierce admission, before conquering my mouth again, doing so this time with a fist in the back of my hair, so I had no chance of putting even an inch of space between us this time, as he really kissed me. It was hot and heavy, and he didn't just warm up my lips, he ignited an inferno in my belly! One that naturally made me forget about all my worries of who would hear us, now being replaced with a desperate need to come, and by any means he was capable of. Seriously, one minute I was saying no in case his army heard us and then he kissed me, and I ignited for him as easily as the fire he made burn.

But that was the power of this man and what he did to me. As burn for him was exactly what I did, now moaning out my consent,

"*Yes,*" the moment I felt myself being lowered down, expecting to feel the harsh hard cave floor under me. Which was why I was surprised when I felt soft, thick furs instead. It seemed Lucius had been busy whilst his wings had been around me, as he had obviously set about rolling out a makeshift bed with his mind.

Then, as his wings released their hold on me, I soon found I was now covered with his body lying stretched out over me instead of being encased in his feathers. And as much as I adored his wings, the feel of his body was far better. But then something about Lucius was off… *different*, as if he was trying to communicate something with me that his lips wouldn't say. Because it became like an almost desperate need as his hands seemed to be everywhere. It was as though he was mapping out my entire body as if trying to memorise every inch of it and admittedly, it was the kind of passion that stole my breath, making it difficult for me to breathe. To the point that I tapped a hand to his cheek to get his attention and once I had it, I forced my breathless self to ask,

"*Hey… are you okay?*" He must have known why I asked this, as his behaviour was somewhat erratic. He was acting as if our time was running out or something and if I was honest, it was freaking me out.

He released a deep sigh before using both hands to push my hair back, leaving them there to frame the sides of my head. I couldn't help but give him a worried look in return, as his own gaze looked darker in the shadows of his body. However, his hair was almost glowing from the firelight, making it look like hot sand under the burning sun, which gave him an angelic aura.

But in that moment, he looked so lost for words. It was as if there was so much he wanted to say and just couldn't get it out. Making me question, did he feel guilty about the things he was keeping from me? If I pushed even a little, would the things Vena had told me be on the tip of his tongue ready to come out?

Whatever the answer, I just knew that Lucius was struggling with something, and I decided to help him out the only way I knew how. Meaning that before he could answer me, I fisted my hand in his hair at the base of his skull and yanked him down to me, taking him off guard with the fierceness of my kiss.

A dominating kiss that quickly took his mind to only one place, one where he didn't have to think about anything but this single moment in time. A kiss that didn't take him long before reacting, beginning with him pulling back a little and growling down at me. A deep rumble that came from his throat as I was being rough with him. Something I continued to do when I pushed against him until there was enough space between us so that I could take control, slipping my body to the side so I could climb on top. As I straddled him, he started to sit up, and I positioned my inner thighs against his hips, marvelling at the weighted length of his arousal between us. However, I placed my hands on his chest and pushed him down. Then, when he looked as though he would protest, I said in a lustful voice,

"*Let me make you feel good, honey.*" His eyes widened in surprise before he relaxed his tense muscles under my palms. So, he lowered his body down until his torso was elevated only by resting his weight on his forearms at his sides. This was so he could maintain eye contact with me as I ran my hands down his chest in a sensual way, and at the same time grinding the lower part of my body against him.

A body that was already so ready for him after just one kiss, a fact he could feel as I was soaking a patch over his cock on the trousers he wore. It was also the reason why I tugged at the waistband, after first hooking a finger there and snapping it back against his skin, telling him exactly what I wanted. He raised a cocky brow before asking me,

"Something in your way, sweetheart?" I gave him a cheeky grin in return, one that told him exactly what I wanted… which was to be in control this time. In fact, I felt myself getting high from the thought of having him at my mercy for once, yet I also knew that my sexy dominating act would all crumble the moment I tried to rip off his pants and they didn't budge. So, instead of even trying, I shifted my body down his so as I could push up his wet tunic, and kiss my way up all those delicious pale muscles. Gods, but each one revealed was like a new gift I could bestow my gratitude upon, making them tense as I lay featherlight kisses along his skin. I couldn't help but grin as I knew he was ticklish. But that wasn't all, as the moment I raised my lustful gaze to his,

I could see he was also trying to hold himself back from taking control… one he was so used to claiming.

So, with this in mind, I wanted to make it worth his sacrifice of power by allowing him to switch control over to me. Which meant that I purposely didn't lose contact with his heated gaze for more than the seconds it took me to pull the tunic I had gathered up over his head. Then, when I was close enough to his neck, I bit his ear, tugging slightly before telling him,

"Well… how can I suck it if it's still in your pants, handsome?" Then I bit his neck and grinned with his flesh still in my mouth, when I heard him suck in a shuddered breath. A second later, my grin grew wider when I felt the material between us disappear, making me smile against his neck, before whispering,

"*Good boy.*" He growled at this, and again I smirked before making my way down his body to the treat that awaited me. I also made sure, as I slid my body down, to capture his cock in between my breasts after purposely tucking my arms in. This was so it would push them together, creating a tighter seal on his length, making him groan and hiss out a,

"*Fuck!*" Once again, I marvelled at the sight of him biting his bottom lip for just a second at the sight of the head of his cock emerging from between my breasts. Then, after winking at him, I tucked in my chin and licked the head, paying special attention to the bead of cum dripping down. Then I moaned as the salty flavour of him burst across my tongue, making me sigh a breathy,

"*More,*" before going back to try and gain more with the tip of my tongue working the slit.

"*Gods, woman!*" I heard Lucius hiss as his head fell back, and a quick look to his hands granted me the sight of him fisting the furs beneath him, no doubt to prevent himself from grabbing me, something I knew he wanted to do the moment he warned,

"You're playing a dangerous game here... ahhh." This ended in a moan of pleasure the moment I swirled my tongue around him, after first raising up and fucking him again within the swell of my soft round flesh.

"You were saying?" I teased, making him growl,

"Pushing me closer to the edge here, pet." I smiled against the perfect smooth head of his engorged cock, then licked it again, and whilst keeping eye contact, told him,

"Then let's push you over it, should we?" I said in a seductive promise, before releasing hold of my breasts and dropping even lower so I could finally take the length of him in my mouth. I couldn't help but marvel at the delicious ache in my jaw, reminding me of his impressive size. And well, knowing what this particular part of him could do to me, it was of little surprise that it had me quickly moaning around his girth. I also wasn't the only one, as Lucius' head snapped back further making the veins in his neck rise with the strain.

"Fuck, Amelia!" Hearing this was when I purposely sucked harder, before swirling my tongue at the top of his cock as I brought my lips back up, keeping a tight seal. I loved seeing the reactions I got from him, they made me even more addicted. It was those breathy growls that continued to come thick, fast and heavy. It was the way his abs would tighten every time my lips went back down, doing so in a way that made sure my lips made it a tight wet pass over every inch of him. Then I would open my mouth wider and lick my way back up.

Of course, I couldn't take all of him, as I had what most people had... which was a gag reflex. However, I did try to relax my throat enough to take as much of him as I could and when I did gag, I knew it only added to the erotic moment for him. Because by the sound of his growls, he most definitely liked hearing me struggle around him, and that in itself gave me even more power. I knew this when I felt his hand palm the back of my head as he would hold me down for longer than I would brave myself. Doing so just on the cusp of what I could cope with.

But I had to confess the feeling of that masterful hand there, one embedded in my hair, well it was like a trigger to my own sexuality. I loved it when he dominated me, despite being the one in control at that moment. Because it was more about getting him to lose his own control that was the key. Something that, with every stroke of my tongue down his cock, was most definitely achieved, as his fist would tighten in my hair. Then I would use the added saliva being choked on his cock created as sweet lubrication as my lips sucked him down, making it drip down his length in a way I knew he liked.

However, I want his release and I knew teasing him would only last so long before he decided to take me. So, instead of licking the length of my tongue up every inch of his cock, I did what I knew worked best. What I knew he liked the most, which was his length as far down my throat as I could cope with, over and over again. Which I did but also now by adding something new to the mix, wondering what type of reaction I would get. So, with my free hand I cupped his heavy sack, now soaked with my saliva, and squeezed a little at the same time sucking down his length over and over again.

Oh yeah, he liked this! I knew that for sure the second he threw his head back, making the cords on his neck strain as he roared,

"FUCK!"

I became utterly mesmerised as I couldn't take my eyes off him as his growls became louder.

"FUCKING HELL… Gods, woman!" he shouted as his hand tightened painful in my hair, adding even more to my erotic kink and building my pleasure. This made me moan around his length and he shuddered when I did.

"I am… I am going to…" he started to say, making me grin around him before letting him go long enough to tell him,

"Cum, so I can swallow you down, my King." Another shudder later and I knew this was precisely what he wanted to hear. I knew this as the sound of his pleasure got louder and his hips started to move in earnest, and the thought of him now fucking my face was so hot I felt myself dripping down my thighs! I was close to coming and I hadn't even been touched yet. But then, after one more stroke of my lips down on him, he held me there as he erupted in my mouth, making me gag as I tried to take it all.

"RAHHH, FUCK, GRHHH!" He roared so loud it actually made me hope that the cave didn't come collapsing down around us from the force of it. I swallowed him down over and over, gagging at the same time as I had no choice but to let it flow slipping down passed my lips.

Gods, but the force of it!

In fact, it was only when I felt the last hot jet of semen from the end of his cock hit the back of my throat, did he relax his hand on my head. Now smoothing down the hair that he had been pulling at as I swallowed the last of him. Then I finally let him slip from between my lips, amazed that he was still hard. During this time, he continued to stroke back my hair as I took the time to clean up the parts I had missed, making him hum in contentment, telling me he liked being worshiped this way. It was also obvious this was something he enjoyed watching too, if the grin on his lips was anything to go by.

"My sweet, bad girl," he mused, making it my turn to grin before I shifted up, and just when he thought I was going to lie down next to him, I straddled his hips one more time and told him with a sexual promise,

"I haven't finished yet." Then, before he could comment, I took hold of his length still wet from my lips and guided him to my entrance before thrusting down over him suddenly.

"FUCK!" he roared again, with his hands instantly going to my hips, digging his fingertips into my flesh in a deliciously painful way, making me release a breathy,

"*Yes!*" Then our mingled sounds of pleasure echoed louder this time, but I no longer cared who heard us. Because he was right, my screams of pleasure were all his! Meaning that as I rocked my hips over him, I did so in a desperate way as I needed to come so badly, that I got totally lost in the action.

"Amelia, fuck... Gods, fuck woman!" I ignored this warning as I rode him over and over, and the moment I screamed out my orgasm he bolted up. Then he formed band of iron around my back with the strength of his arm around my waist, and he held me tight over his length as I shuddered out my release over his cock. Then, when my core had finished quivering down his length, he growled in my ear in a dark demonic growl of words.

"*My turn, my bad girl.*" Then he turned me, so now I was the one beneath him, pinned on my back.

"Now again!" he snarled down at me, before he started pounding into me in a furious motion, making me have no choice but to hold on for dear life. It was no surprise that it was only a minute later, and I was screaming again, this time with the strength of my orgasm being so powerful that I saw black spots. In fact, I felt myself almost falling from the world of sanity and slipping quickly into sexual madness. Lucius sensed this and lowered himself closer to me, before he fisted a hand at the top of my head, and with an unyielding hold on my hair, he used it to pull my neck to the side. Then he sank his fangs into my flesh, drinking from me for the first time since I had been awake. But taking from me wasn't enough as he wanted that same connection made in return. So, without breaking his feed, he placed his wrist to my lips telling me silently what he wanted me to do, making me comply instantly as I felt another side of me come awake with blood lust.

I even felt something tingling in my gums as if my canines were growing at the root and trying to push past my other teeth. In truth, I didn't have much time to think about what was happening as I was too far gone in my need. Which meant I soon bit down into his flesh, feeling it slice easier this time, before my mouth was overflowing with his blood. Then, the second it hit my tongue, I moaned around the taste of him, now drinking it down like a fucking elixir of life and sex.

Meaning that just when I didn't think I had anything left in me, I came, screaming his name as I gave way to my last release, one that hit me so hard, it felt as though it would never end and had the strength to kill me.

"LUCIUS!"

Shortly after shattering around him, he followed me, coming deep inside me, at the same time roaring his ownership over me,

"MINE… ALL FUCKING MINE!"

After this he continued to lap at my blood in lazy long licks, as his hips started to slow after he had just given in to his second release. This time, one that coated my insides in that hot and comforting way. It was after this that I must have started falling under the lure of unconsciousness, because I was confused when I felt his forehead lean against my neck and heard his words follow.

Words that had me closing my eyes to panic, as I could have sworn I heard him say…

"I'm so sorry, Amelia, please forgive me."

CHAPTER FOUR

ENEMY AT THE GATES

The next time I woke, I was surprised to find myself once more on the back of the Manticore and well on our way again. But when I focused my eyes, after first looking at my dark surroundings, I found Lucius' stern features looking straight ahead. It was only when he felt me shift in his arms that he looked down at me, and those narrowed eyes finally softened.

"I think I wore you out," he admitted, making me chuckle.

"I can think of worse ways to pass out than to be fucked into exhaustion." At this, his lips quirked.

"Where are we?" I asked, seeing that we weren't back on the road as I would have thought. No, we were still deep in a forest, although unlike when we had been searching for the caves, this one wasn't filled with ghost-like trees. Because it was the total opposite in that regard, seeing as the trees were as black as the night. In fact, if it hadn't been for the line of torches carried by the riders, then I wouldn't have even been able to see my hand in front of my face.

Although, at least the rain had stopped, and the storm had long passed. I also noticed that at some point Lucius had re-dressed me, and I was happy to find that my clothes were dry once more thanks to the fire.

"We're just coming up to the portal, we crossed over the Dark Fae lands not long ago," Lucius replied, which certainly explained why he was on edge, as we were technically in enemy territory here. This, despite having Carn'reau travelling with us, who is the rightful King of this realm. Because currently, this was where his uncle ruled, and I knew from what I had overheard that his uncle's spies were everywhere.

"Is it far?" I asked, thinking this was good to know.

"No, the portal is just on the edge of these lands, look…" Lucius said nodding ahead of him. I turned to look, to find a beautiful archway that seemed to be glowing like a beacon in the dark. It was one that was raised up from the forest floor as if it stood on top of a small hill, surrounded either side by thick black trees. But then the closer we travelled, the more I could make out, as the parts that shone were an elaborate design of Elvish symbols. They were illuminated like light shining behind glass. In fact, it reminded me a little of the doors of Durin from Lord of the Rings, in that it was carved on to a flat stone tablet. Though I couldn't tell if the design had been carved there or was only glowing when activated.

Then I watched as two of Carn'reau's men approached the pathway that led up to the portal. They swung themselves from their beasts and each raised a sword to the top of two large columns that were positioned there at the bottom of the hill, like sentinels guarding the magic. These each held a tulip shaped lantern, that only sparked into life the moment the tips of their blades touched the stone, making a lightning bolt travel up the length until it erupted into a blaze of light at the top. This set off a chain reaction, as every couple of metres or so there was a smaller version of the columns igniting into another tulip of flames that then lined the path.

It was enough that it cast a warm glow over the army, one that hadn't yet dismounted, making me wonder what they were waiting for? In fact, other than the first two, Carn'reau was the only one to slide from his saddle and start making his way up the illuminated pathway. As for Lucius and I, we continued to make our way to the front as the army started to part down the centre, giving us a clear path.

"Is the army staying here?" I asked, making Lucius tense before telling me,

"They are waiting for blood to be spilt," he replied cryptically, making me frown in question, but before I could ask any more about it, we had reached the end. I then watched as Carn'reau looked to be chanting something at the portal, before he took his blade and sliced it down his hand and placed its bloody print at the centre where there seemed to be the biggest circle of words. If I was to guess, being the type to question everything, I would have said it was most likely a rite of passage. The blood of the worthy, that type of thing. As the second he did this, he took two steps back as a rumbling of stone could be heard.

"What's happening?" I asked, making Lucius whisper,

"*The portal is opening for its King.*" I was about to ask if it only opened for him but stopped in sight of what began to happen next. As now the rock inside the glowing arch had started to crack, starting with the circle of words he'd just decorated with his blood. However, as the cracks grew bigger, instead of the loose rock falling to the floor at his feet, the stone broke away and simply fell away into an empty space beyond. It was as if it was being sucked inside the portal itself, now coming away in broken pieces like a jigsaw falling through someone's hands. Then, pretty soon all that was left beneath was a glowing blue mist, making it impossible to see what was beyond.

Carn'reau lifted a hand and signalled for his men to dismount. Then, before waiting for his men to proceed him, he stepped inside, his masterful form quickly disappearing from sight. I watched as the three McBain brothers seemed to come from nowhere, having been hidden by the trees.

"Where have they been?" I asked. Lucius nodded to Trice who looked over to us with concern, making me wonder what that had been about?

"They travelled ahead of the army to make sure there wasn't an ambush waiting," Lucius told me, and also answering another question of mine, as it was obvious now he had been giving Lucius the 'all clear'… because really, what else would it have meant?

I watched as Vern, Gryph and Trice all dismounted their Manticores, before the rest of the army followed their King's lead. Then after watching all three brothers disappear through the portal, I knew we would soon be next. So, one by one the armed soldiers passed us, adding to the dark line of bodies that continued up the pathway. This they did until they too reached the top of the hill and stepped into the glowing portal, and Lucius and I were all that remained.

I wanted to ask about the beasts they each left behind, but didn't get the chance as Lucius had started to dismount. I swung my leg over to do the same and he caught me as I slid down, lowering me gently to my feet. This time there was no playful jokes about me falling, as he was all business, and I don't know why, but I felt uneasy because of it. And, unlike last time, he also didn't bother with any supplies our beast carried, telling me we were obviously at the end of the road.

After this, he took my hand and led me up the pathway,

but the closer we got, the more hesitant I became. I don't know why but I just had the strangest feeling, as if this was a critical moment in our future. Like one of those points in destiny where you had two paths to choose from, knowing that either one could mean the biggest turning point in what would become our fate. Which meant I couldn't help but question when looking back to this point in our history, would walking through this portal be a decision we would regret, or a step we were thankful we took?

This was why I pulled back a little just as we reached the top, now standing only a few steps from the portal. Lucius looked back at me, clearly questioning my hesitation, which was why I told him,

"The last time I went through a portal I ended up in the Fae realm, and even further apart from you."

Hearing this, Lucius closed his eyes a moment as if pained by my words before they snapped back open with a flash of crimson. This was combined with a strange expression I couldn't read, it flickered across his face before he composed himself and said,

"Your hand is in mine, and by stepping through this portal nothing will change that, Amelia." I nodded, knowing this was all I needed to hear before we stepped through together and, like he promised, his hand never left mine.

However, the moment we stepped through, that hand tensed around mine as it looked like my instincts had been correct. But this time, the enemy wasn't one that came to us.

No, this time, it was one…

Waiting for us to arrive.

CHAPTER FIVE

PAINFUL GOODBYES

After stepping through the portal, we were greeted by both the army and the rolling grey field that was covered in a thick blanket of fog. I couldn't have told you what colour the grass was, only that it reminded me of an early morning frost back in my own mortal world. It looked like some valley of sorts, with mountains either side and jagged chunks of rocks that were littered throughout the landscape. In fact, it looked as if the mountains had come alive and had started throwing pieces of themselves at each other in competition to see who could throw the furthest. Beyond that, it looked as if the landscape continued on for miles and miles before anything different could be seen on the horizon.

As for our own view and current predicament, I didn't have the height that Lucius had so I couldn't see for myself over the tops of his men. But it was clear that the enemy had been surrounded, something I considered a plus.

However, Lucius could see, so I took it as an even better sign when he relaxed his hold on me.

"Lower your weapons, these men belong to me," Lucius ordered, making the soldiers split down the centre just as they had done moments ago in the other realm. This allowed him the freedom to walk down the length, pulling me along with him. At the very end we found the McBain brothers, having some kind of standoff with three other men that I couldn't see fully because the brothers tall and bulky frames were standing in the way. Despite this, I could tell that their weapons were still drawn, as the flaming arrow belonging to Vern was hard to miss, and it was poised and ready to fly at some poor bastard's head.

"Can you tell this posh twat here, to lower his fucking arrow before I shove it up his ass!" a voice said that I immediately recognised, making me shout,

"Clay!" This was when the McBain brothers separated, looking back at me as I tried to push my way through. This revealed the sight of, Clay, Ruto and Caspian and I couldn't help it, but I pulled from Lucius' grasp. Of course, being that they were part of his council, he allowed this. He also didn't protest as I practically ran into them, before trying to wrap my arms around their frozen bodies, as my overly warm gesture made them all tense. I saw Clay look over my head, which wasn't hard seeing as he was huge! But he must have received some sort of 'okay' from Lucius before finally relaxing into it.

As for Caspian, well no surprises… he just grunted, as was his way, making me wink up at him.

"So, how's that soul of yours I own, big boy?" At this, Clay burst out laughing before telling me,

"Fuck me, little bird, but I knew why I liked you."

"Yeah, and why's that?" I asked, releasing them and taking a step back.

"Because shit was boring before you came along." At this I burst out laughing too.

"Hey, badass, stab anybody lately?" I turned to the punk lad who looked more like a teenager and, as usual, was smirking down at the knife he had been tipping and swinging around his hand, as was his habit.

"No, but I died and then ate a Wraith Master's heart, so does that count?" At this Ruto's eyes grew wide, making him nearly drop his blade before his gaze shot to Lucius, no doubt to see whether this was true or not.

"No, I was the one that did the stabbing… and Amelia…" Lucius spoke as he walked up next to me, before taking hold of the back of my neck. So, I tilted my head back, as he clearly wanted my attention, and said,

"Yeah, handsome?" At this, his lips twitched once at my use of his nickname, before he dipped his head lower and warned,

"*That is the last time I hear you joke about your death… understood?*" I swallowed hard as he tensed his fingers into my neck and I nodded, knowing he was serious, making him grant me a swift kiss before growling over my lips,

"*Good girl.*"

After this, he turned back to his men and said,

"It is good to see you, my counsel." Lucius finished this by clasping Clay's shoulder and nodding to the others.

"So, what are you guys doing here?" I asked, but it was Lucius who answered,

"I sent for them."

"You did?" I asked, my tone questioning, then he told me,

"It is time to take you home, sweetheart." As soon as he said this, my mouth dropped open in shock. We were going home. I knew then that our time in Hell had come to an end, and I couldn't say I was disappointed. But then realisation started to infiltrate, and I couldn't help but look towards the three McBain brothers, to see that one in particular looked pained by this information.

It was also in that moment that Lucius didn't need to guess what my thoughts were, as he turned to see who I was looking at. However, whatever his thoughts about this were I didn't know as he said nothing of it, as really… *what was there to say?*

We all knew this time would come, as a goodbye between us was inevitable. Just as it had been with Vena, meaning again it pained me to realise that I might never see the three of them again. And Nero, who I wouldn't just miss but who I would also miss saying my goodbyes to. Gods, but it had felt like I had spent an entire lifetime here, and it was one that had been filled with making friends along the way. But Lucius was right, we had been in Hell for far too long and it was time to go home. I then wondered if this meant another journey was on the horizon?

I was jerked out of my inner musings when Lucius nodded to Carn'reau, as if relaying to him some silent command, and before I had a chance to ask, Lucius was pulling me off to one side. Again, the soldiers parted to allow us through as he walked me towards one of the rock formations that rose up from the ground, like small islands that looked as if they were floating over an ocean of fog.

"Is this what you wanted to tell me, because you know I would agree with you, it is time for us to go home," I said the moment we were alone, and some distance from the rest. But he tugged on my hand, making me sit down on one of the smaller boulders. As it was clear this was what he wanted me to do, once more acting methodical in his actions. Then he untied a small satchel that had been tied at his waist, before handing it to me, purposely ignoring my question as his next order was directed down at me.

"I want you to eat."

"Lucius, I'm fine, I just want to know…" I started to say, only he took hold of my chin and forced my head up, before telling me,

"Please, just indulge me in this, Amelia." I released a sigh before opening my mouth ready to tell him that I wasn't hungry, when my stomach took the opportunity to growl. Lucius raised a knowing brow at me, as if daring me to continue to try and deny it after my treacherous body had just sided with him.

"Fine, look see… happy?" I asked after fishing out a biscuit style bread and taking a big bite.

"Indeed," he replied in that knowing tone I was used to this word being combined with.

"Now, stay here, eat and drink, and I'll be back in a moment," he told me, and instead of making some joke about not being his breakable human pet anymore, I took note of his tense jaw and decided to cut him some slack.

"Where are you going?" I asked instead.

"I have to give orders to my men, and the army," he replied with his tone tense, and again it was as if he was waiting for something to happen. Did he fear an ambush? Maybe it was just because we were so close to getting home and he wanted to get us both there without a hitch. I mean, it wasn't as though he was being paranoid here as that damn witch had been like a bad penny!

So, I watched him walk away, leaving me to try and not over analyse that bad feeling in my gut, instead trying to convince myself it would be fine. But then, with every bite I took of the strange Fae bread, it was like swallowing lumps as it sat like lead in my stomach. Not that it was the bread per say, one that was a cross between a rich tea biscuit and a scone in the shape of a grape leaf. No, it was because it was like trying to force yourself to eat when all you wanted to do was throw up with worry and anxiety. That sinking feeling like a snake was coiling tighter around in my belly, but one that I just knew was getting ready to strike me at any moment.

Something was wrong,

I just knew it.

A few minutes later, I was brushing the crumbs from my dress and smacking the cork back into the flask after downing the contents. At least the water had helped in stopping me from feeling so nauseated and maybe Lucius had been right, perhaps I had needed to eat something. Speaking of whom, I looked up and this time found him speaking to the McBain brothers, who were looking grim.

"*Now what is that about, I wonder?*" I muttered to myself with a frown after first watching Lucius nodding his approval at them. The brothers then approached me, so I stood ready, having a feeling that dreaded time had come. In fact, it was why I had to look down a moment and cough back my emotion before looking back up to find three handsome, rugged faces each wearing the same expression... dejection.

"I guess this is the part where we say goodbye," I said, being the first one to say it and trying not to let my voice break.

"Aye lass, that wull be th' gist o' it," Gryph answered.

"I guess this means going back to a peaceful life for the three of you, especially now you don't have to save my ass anymore," I said, trying to make light of the situation, even though it felt as if I was trying to force the emotion down my throat as I could feel the tears being held prisoner in my eyes.

"Mi'lady, aiding you in your troubles has been an honour

we will hold within our hearts for the rest of our lives," Vern said, making me smile, as my vision blurred.

"I guess posh Vern is yet to wear off," I commented making him grin.

"It is indeed." At this he lowered to one knee, and at the same time swung his bow around to plant on the floor. Then he put both hands to the top and bowed his head to me.

"*Oh no… you don't…*" My protests were cut off when he told me,

"You will always have my bow and own my loyalty, Princess." Then he stood finding tears in my eyes that I still would not let fall.

"I will miss you, Vern," I told him after swallowing hard. He cleared his throat and took a step back so that Gryph could take his place. This time I didn't even try to protest as I knew this was something that meant a great deal to them, as it did to me. Which meant that just like his brother, Gryph took to a knee, at the same time swinging his massive Warhammer to the floor. I felt the power of it vibrate through the ground beneath my feet making me jump. Then he too bowed, placing both hands on the hilt.

"You wull always hae mah hammer, juist as ye wull always own mah loyalty, Princess." He said the same, only with his heavy accent I felt my lips start to quiver. He nodded once, and then heaved his large bulk back to his feet before swinging his hammer back in its holder.

"I will miss you, Gryph," I told him, making him bow a head in thanks, grinning that handsome grin of his. Then he jerked his head to Vern before nodding behind him telling him silently to give me and Trice a moment alone. I briefly looked towards Lucius to check that he was still alright with this meeting with Trice and saw for myself that he was busy. In fact, it looked as if he was writing something down on a strip of parchment, making me wonder if it was orders that needed to be taken somewhere?

However, Trice stepped in front of me, cutting Lucius off from view, and I sucked in a shuddered breath as the emotions started to finally bubble over. Because now it had come to his turn to say goodbye, and I knew this was going to be the hardest part. But then, when he too started to lower, I could take no more and stopped him as he swung his sword to the front,

"Please, oh please, Trice… you can't, you can't do that too… I won't last much longer here." He looked up at me in surprise by my admission, taking in my tears that had now finally started to fall freely. I then watched as he rose back up and after taking a few seconds to himself, he suddenly said,

"Oh, fuck it!" Then he let his sword fall to the ground and I watched it disappear into the fog by our feet before Trice then wrapped his arms around me, lifting me off my feet so he was holding me up to his head height. I was just thankful that it didn't end in bloodshed knowing now that Lucius had obviously given us this moment… although, what that must have cost him, I could only imagine.

As for Trice, he simply held me to him, and I breathed in the scent of him as if trying to draw in his essence and keep it with me forever. I never wanted to forget even a single thing about my three heroes. Because the truth was that I had come to love Trice almost like one would love a brother, I suppose, and it made me feel guilty that I knew it wasn't the same type of love he felt for me. But I also knew that one day there would be someone out there for him. Someone made for him. Someone so perfect, that he would fall fast and hard for them, more than he ever did for me. Someone who would love him back in the same way and be his fated one, just as I was for Lucius.

But most importantly, *someone he wouldn't have to fight another for.* Selfishly, I wished that someone could be Vena. Selfishly I also wished that I could have kept him in my life forever. But that would have been a cruelty that I would never want to inflict upon anyone's heart. Which was why I knew I had to let him go. Which meant that I was selflessly about to break my own heart.

So I did, doing so the moment he started with the same words his brother had.

"You always hae my sword 'n' ye wull always hae mah loyalty, and… Princess… ye wull always hae my…" It was at this point that I stopped him by placing my fingers over his lips and shook my head a little.

"Please don't say it… please, Trice… I care for you too much to hear you say it… to hear you gift it to me when…"

"When?" he asked, his voice husky and thick with his own emotion, and I knew I had to tell him.

I had to say goodbye to more than just my Scottish hero,

I had to say goodbye to his love for me.

So, I placed my hand on his heart and nodded down to it before I told him…

"When… it is not mine to own."

CHAPTER SIX

WHEN HEARTS LEAVE

"*When it is not mine to own.*" The moment I said this he lowered his head until our foreheads were only an inch away from touching. It was all the reminder I needed to know that pretty soon Lucius would hit his limit, and I didn't want that to come in the form of violence. So, I kissed the scar on Trice's cheek, making him suck in a startled breath as if barely ever feeling anything other than his own touch on his marred skin before. The thought saddened me, and I prayed with everything inside of me that he wouldn't have to wait long before feeling it again, next time from his fated soulmate.

Then I whispered,

"*I'll never forget you.*" It was in that moment that he felt the tears fall for himself, and when he pulled back, he swiped them away with a thumb. And unsurprisingly, it was in that moment a stern voice broke through our moment,

"You are needed, shifter," Lucius said, his voice as cold as ice and I knew, despite all that Trice had done for me, he would never have anything but disdain for this particular

McBain brother. I half expected Trice to put up a fight but obviously now knowing it wouldn't have made a difference to my decision, he gave me one last squeeze before putting me down.

"Try keepin' oot o' trouble this time, lass," Trice said with a wink, before leaving me to my own stern looking King. I released a sigh as I watched the brothers walk away and swiped away the rest of my tears admitting to him,

"I am going to miss them." Lucius finally lost a little of his stoic stance and released his own sigh.

"This is where they belong." I nodded, telling him,

"I know that." This was when he stepped up to me, and as he took my hand in his I knew he was ready to lead me over to his men. But I pulled back and told him,

"Thank you, Lucius." At this he looked surprised and before he could question it with more than a raised brow, I whispered,

"I know that couldn't have been easy, so thank you for giving it to me... *thank you for giving me that closure in saying goodbye.*" I lifted his hand so I could kiss the back of it, wondering why he now looked even more pained. Had watching me say goodbye to Trice been harder on him than I realised?

"You're welcome, Amelia," he replied after a long silent moment passed between us.

"What will happen to them?" I asked then and he knew instantly what I was referring to.

"They will be granted back their souls." Hearing this, I closed my eyes as a deeply rooted relief washed over me. Then, when I opened them again, I looked over to them as a grin spread over my lips.

"Well, they definitely earned it," I said, and Lucius scoffed at this before telling me in an unsympathetic tone,

"They also deserve death for taking you from me."

"Yes, well, I think they made up for that offence, honey," was my reply, and one he might have argued against had I not ended this with an endearment. One that clearly seeped deep into his heart and stayed there, as his features soon softened. He stepped into me so he could cup the back of my head and use it to pull me to him. Then he dipped his chin enough so he could lay a tender kiss on my forehead.

"*My sweet girl,*" he hummed as if to himself, making me smile as now that feeling was seeping into my own heart and staying there. Now just how long it was to stay there was anyone's guess as Lucius suddenly stepped back, putting distance between us. I frowned in question but when I watched Lucius shake his head a little, I decided to ask,

"So, what's the plan then?" His answer to this was to simply hold out a hand to me and grant me a one worded order.

"Come." So, I responded the only way I could in that moment, as I didn't think demanding much more from him just then was a good idea. Because something was clearly still weighing heavily on his mind and admittedly, I was getting close to trying to shake it from him. But then, one look at the army of men and his own council, and well, I didn't think doing that was wise. So instead, I placed my hand in his and let him pull me from my spot by the rocks. He led me back over towards Carn'reau and just as we approached, I became amazed to see a portal start to appear. Like a piece of the world was being cut through, after it first shimmered and distorted just like it had done back in the Harpy's lair. Something that soon had Lucius' brother Dariush stepping through, after creating his very own portal.

"Wow," I muttered in awe as Lucius stepped up to him, keeping me held close next to him. Needless to say, I wasn't exactly looking forward to seeing him again, not considering I had been the one who had nearly caused his execution by his brother's hand! Which is why I ended up being surprised as the moment Dariush saw me, he grinned.

"Brother, I think it's time I introduced you properly this time," Lucius said, pulling me in front of him and placing both his hands on my shoulders.

"Dariush, this is my Chosen One, my Electus, Amelia," Lucius declared, and I had to confess, it tugged at my heart with the soft and tender way he said it. Which was why I granted him a smile over my shoulder before I held my hand out to his brother, telling him,

"It's nice to meet you properly this time." His handsome brother's lips twitched in amusement before he took my hand in his. Then he raised it up to his lips to kiss, making Lucius growl and Dariush's smirk turned into a full-blown grin.

"The honour is all mine, for I believe I owe you my life." I swallowed down the hard lump, and told him,

"I am just sorry that I was the cause of it being in jeopardy in the first place." He released my hand and then used his own to wave off my apology.

"It's all fun and games in Hell, besides all brothers need a test of loyalty now and then, isn't that right, Luc?" Lucius scoffed behind me and said,

"They certainly need their asses kicking." At which Dariush burst out laughing when I elbowed Lucius in the ribs, scorning him,

"Lucius!"

"Yes, remind me to pay you back for that one, brother."

"No need, for I have a little warrior princess, who likes to keep me in check." I shot him a look that threatened to put him on his ass without words… or at least try to as I remembered back in my bedroom in Afterlife. It was when I realised that Lucius had gone easy on me all those times before. Lucius grinned down at me, whereas his brother simply laughed again.

I had to admit that it was strange seeing these two in a different light and how easy they were around each other. Telling me that everything I had witnessed before this point had been an act. It had been one played in front of their people as it was clear no one knew just who Dariush was to their King. But then, behind closed doors, this easy manner with each other was one I would have expected between brothers. A thought that made me happy and more than anything else, it made me thankful. Thankful that Lucius had that. That he had at least one person in the world to him that he classed as family. And that before I came into his life, he hadn't truly been alone in his world.

"Is everything ready?" Lucius asked, bringing me out of my inner musings. This was when I realised that the playful moment had passed and been replaced by a serious one.

"It is, but only if you are sure?" This was Dariush's strange reply, and I watched as Lucius nodded his head once telling him that he was.

"What's going on?" I asked but before he answered me, Lucius motioned for Clay, Caspian and Ruto to go on ahead as the portal was still left open behind Dariush. His council men nodded their acknowledgement to their King, before walking past us and stepping in through the portal that still warped the world like a tear through time.

After this, Dariush himself then stepped aside and soon we found ourselves stood alone in front of this door sized portal.

"*Lucius?*" I said his name in question, and for a moment he closed his eyes as if it pained him to hear. Then, without answering me, he took hold of my face with both hands and kissed me. A kiss that rendered me breathless and nearly overwhelmed me with his passion. A kiss that was so beautiful and I knew later on if I ever looked back on it, I would class it as one of the best kisses I had ever received. Because there was so much emotion. So much love and strength. It was one hundred words and one thousand feelings all told in that single moment in time.

That single kiss that became one that seared to my soul, scorched my core, and set a flame in my heart.

Something that would never be more true in the moments that followed, as I hadn't known it until I felt my skin become wet. And all from a single tear fallen. Only this time, it wasn't one of mine…

It was one of his.

But the second I opened my mouth about to ask, was when he put an inch between our lips and told me,

"Please remember how much I love you. Never forget, Amelia, never forget how much… *promise me.*" I started to shake my head in confusion, but the moment he pulled back was when I saw the next tear fall.

I didn't understand what was happening, not until he started walking me backwards, holding my hands in front of us both. He then raised them up and kissed them, closing his eyes as if he was in so much pain.

"Lucius please, you're… *you're scaring me.*" Then he opened his eyes, and I was granted with an ocean of steel blue sadness. I was met with the devastation that was yet to come for both of us.

"Don't be frightened, everything I do, I do to keep you safe. *Please remember that,*" he whispered, and the moment I tried to tear myself free, his hands tightened on mine, keeping them captured in his unyielding hold.

"Lucius! Lucius, whatever you are planning don't… don't

do this!" I shouted again trying to pull free, but he just continued to walk me back with nothing but agony in his eyes.

"*I am sorry… so sorry…*" he whispered back.

"*Lucius… please…*" I whimpered, with his name coming out like a pained prayer from my lips the moment he suddenly released me. But then being forced to watch the cruelty as he stepped away from me, I nearly crumbled to the ground. Then, as yet another tear ran down his face, I reached out to him with a shaky hand. He focused on it for only a second and just as his hand started to lift, I sighed in relief, believing whatever madness had taken him was over now. But then this was to be a mistake as he only managed to graze my fingertips with his own before he suddenly shouted,

"NOW! Take her now!"

"NO!" I screamed the second I felt hands grab me from behind. Then, just as they started to pull me backwards, he spoke, and it was the last thing I had imagined he had said after making love to me.

Just after he'd kissed me as if it would be the last time.

"*Forgive me, Gods, forgive me.*"

Only this time instead of closing my eyes, I disappeared, and when I opened them again my worst nightmare was back.

As this time…

I'd lost him.

CHAPTER SEVEN

LUCIUS

LAST SUPPER FOR SOULS

"Fuck... FUCK!" I hissed, before roaring the same curse as I turned to my brother, demanding in a furious tone,

"Seal it!"

"Are you sure?" he asked, making me swipe a hand down and tell him as I passed,

"Do it and make sure nothing gets through!" My brother looked as if he wanted to say more but wisely didn't. I already knew his feelings on the matter, just as I knew my own. Because it felt as though my heart had been ripped out and pushed through that damn portal with her gripping onto it tightly.

Meaning, I fucking hated myself!

I hated myself for doing this to her. But I had done it. I had done it despite knowing all too well the bitter sting of pain that would come with it. A bitterness felt every time she had done the same to me. Every time she had pushed me away and ran from me. Oh yes, it was a pain I knew well but right now, what other choice did I have? I couldn't foolishly be allowed to believe that I could keep her safe anymore. Not after what I had learned. Not after I now knew who was responsible for it all.

For a war to gain more power was not half as deadly as one done for the sole purpose of revenge. So, I couldn't risk Amelia's life anymore and every second she was with me, that was precisely what I was doing. But this meant I had gone back on my word. I had gone back on my promise never to leave her, and asking her forgiveness for it was one I knew I would not deserve receiving. But nothing was more important to me than her life.

Nothing.

Not. A. Gods. Be. Damned. Thing!

So, I had sent word to my brother and I had made plans, knowing that he would create a portal back to where this all began. Back to the temple of the Tree of Souls.

As for topside, I had also got word to my council telling them that they were needed in Hell and had my brother create a portal to bring them here. Because it was impossible to do so from where Amelia and I had first entered, as my blood was the only thing powerful enough to open the access point to gain entrance to the Temple. Ruto had been the only Angel in the group, but due to being one of my own, the vampire in him enabled him to access Hell with the others.

However, gaining access back into the mortal realm was as easy as mounting the stone steps that led back up to the Earth under the tree and stepping through it. Something Amelia and I hadn't been able to do at the time after she first fell. That was because of the danger above, and one that included the small army of rogues and a witch I now knew as once being my mortal wife.

I stalked back to Carn'reau and barked my orders at him,

"I want you to send any soul I own in my army to the furthest reaches of Hell and amass anyone loyal to you." He bowed his head in understanding. Because in this I had no other choice. I was forced to plan as if that switch of souls had already happened. Because I knew if I headed into battle with my own people, then I wasn't only doing so with the enemy at my front but also the potential one at my back.

"It will be done, my Lord," he answered, and I released a sigh before telling him,

"I think we both know the time for being your Lord is at an end, my friend, but I will always be grateful for your continued loyalty." At this, he bowed his head and replied,

"And you will have it for as long as either of us draws breath, a loyalty that will forever come with my sword, my... Lucius," he replied, now speaking my name as an ally and friend. Something that I would need more than ever before. I placed a hand to his shoulder and squeezed, telling him without words what it meant to me.

After this moment passed, he nodded to the McBain brothers and said,

"And what of the shifters?" I released another sigh, knowing it was time to be done with these three souls. After all, Amelia had been right in one aspect, they had certainly earned it. Even if one in particular was less so and deserved to choke on that soul. But it could not be denied that everything they had done, had been done with Amelia's safety in mind. So yes,

It was time.

"Leave them to me," I replied to Carn'reau before cutting the distance between myself and the shifters, who were clearly waiting for my orders. Of course, the moment I got close enough, Trice was the first to speak, making me question my sanity on why I still let him live... oh yes, Amelia would be annoyed.

"Where did ye send her?" Trice asked with his hand on the hilt of his sword, one that was a warrior's stance. In fact, I half expected him to tighten those fingers before drawing it from its sheath, and challenging me to a fight now that Amelia wasn't around to witness it. Fuck, but more than half of me wished that he would, because if there was one thing that would have made me feel better in that moment, it would have been getting to kill this fucker!

But then I already had broken promises on my head, and I didn't want to add to them when finally getting to reunite with my girl. Because she may not have loved Trice the way he wished she did, but that didn't mean she had not come to care for him. So, I had to respect that, even if I didn't fucking like it!

Not. One. Fucking. Bit!

"Back to the mortal realm and with her father, where she will be safe," I answered gritting my teeth.

"Aye, tis fur th' best," Gryph answered with a nod of his head, making that long plait of hair of his swing over his shoulder like a red snake bound in leather.

"The lady will most certainly be missed, for she is such a dear girl," Vern said, his own body wincing on hearing for himself what a twat he sounded. Gryph chuckled, and Trice shot Vern a knowing grin.

"I beg of you, my kin, please refrain from calling me a ninny this time, for I fear my reaction to it would be to slap you both with the palm of my glove." At this, Gryph burst out laughing making his large frame shake, as he said,

"Aye noo, that be big terrifying wurds fur such wee gentleman."

"Aye, a'm feelin' mah kilt a quaking," Trice added, making Vern give them a pointed look that even I could tell meant, fuck off.

"When dae we leave fur battle?" Trice then asked as he turned back to me, and I confessed I was surprised that this would be his first thought.

"You don't, for your job is done," I stated, making Trice frown before snapping,

"The fuck it is!" Gryph then placed a beefy hand on his brother's chest to hold him back, then he took a step towards me and said,

"Whit mah brother is trying tae say is that th' fight is not over 'n' tae a McBain, th' jab is only finished whin th' enemy is dead."

"This is not your fight," I stated.

"Are yer nay trying tae stop Hell fae bein' taken over by a fuckin' tyrant 'n' amassing an army tae dae so?" Gryph said pointing out the facts. So, I pointed out one of my own.

"You're bounty hunters, not men of war."

"Aye 'n' how dae ye think we git 'ere, after all, ye shud mind hoo we sold oor souls in th' first place," Trice snapped, and my only response to this was a short,

"*Indeed.*"

"Forgive my impertinence, my Lordship, but I believe my brother just made a perfect point, and one you will find it difficult to argue against. We are first and foremost warriors, and you hold our souls as…" At this I held up a hand and said,

"Your souls are mine no longer, for I release them." At

this, all three of them became wide-eyed and clearly shocked. I closed my own eyes for a second before informing them,

"If you wish to fight for me then let it be done so through your own choices and with it the ownership of your own souls, for I am your king no longer. If you fight, we fight as one and we fight together and we do so for a common cause, not because I command it… now kneel for the last time, brothers McBain." The moment I finished, I watched as Trice's fingers uncurled from his sword before dropping his arm in shock. Then, one by one they fell to their knees in front of me, as the time had finally come. It had been all they had been working towards since their mortal demise and from the looks on their faces now, not one they truly believed would ever come to happen. In truth, had it not been for Amelia, then that might have been so. But then that was the power of a fated queen, as it was not only their King's life they would affect but more often than not, that of his people.

So, it was time to give them back what they truly desired, and I had to say, it was a practice that I had not performed in quite some time. Unfortunately, it was also not one that would work on those that were made into my own kind. Because there was a difference between owning one's soul and forging one with my own. And only one of these could be undone. Because once they drank from my blood and became a vampire, then the effect could not be reversed. However, for the souls I owned without them being gifted my blood, there was a way to undo what had been done, and it was one I didn't fucking relish!

Especially when doing so took me back to only one time…

The Last Supper.

It had been Jesus' goodbye to his Apostles and one that had been unknown to them all at the time, other than myself.

Of course, I had begged him to tell them and let them in on our plan, doing more than just hinting at it. But he didn't want to make sinners out of his Apostles... *all except me, that was*.

The biggest sinner of them all.

But as for the others, well, he didn't want to make liars out of their grief and their accounts would be needed for his plan to work. And for the most part, he had been right, for each of them spread the word until it continued to stretch to the far corners of the Earth.

It forever changed history and ensured one particular God's power into being of the eternal kind. So, I gritted my teeth, held out my unbound hand, keeping the Venom of God firmly at my side, for who knew what horrors would occur should the two ever meet.

After this, I recited parts of the words found from Mark 14:22. Words that had the power to summon forth what I would need, feeling sickened at the thought at what I would soon hold in my hand.

Being once again forced to drink to my own betrayal.

"And now, I bring forth thy that is needed to grant the souls their redemption... 'Take it; this is my body, this is my blood of the covenant, which is poured out for many'." After the last words were said, that same chalice I had drank from, started to emerge. The very one that touched my lips the day of the last supper and when the son of a God drank from his own Holy Grail. It matched his, being that it was a plain wooden cup, carved by his own hands. And as I looked down at it now, I suddenly saw myself there that day. Each had received one as a symbolic gesture that would bind that moment in the history books as being significant. For the memory of one man's actions had the power to change the world, and the word of God would live on through each of them.

But there would be no power in good, without first the evil being that of a dark canvas for the bright light of Gods to be painted upon. Jesus knew this as well as I did, for what I was to receive in return would have been worth selling my own soul for. And I did, just unknowingly at the time, to the evil, not the good I had first intended.

Which was why that image was now so fucking clear in my mind, the power actually forced me to take a step back as my legs failed me. It was why I landed on my knee, being forced to place my leather-bound hand to the ground to hold me steady. A ground that started to shake from the intensity, making me ignore the gasps of shock that were whispered as a wave of horror.

The cup in my hand then started to shake as if the force of being here in Hell was a power I could barely contain steady.

"Luc!" I heard my brother call in worry but I steadied myself and held my hand out to stop him.

"No! Stay back!" I warned, before using all my strength needed to gain back my stance.

"Fuck, it cannae be true…" Trice uttered along with his brother Gryph,

"Is that really…"

"Gods in Heaven," Vern then whispered, following suit of his brother's astonishment, making me order in a demonic tone,

"SILENCE!" After this everyone followed my command, for this was not a power meant for Hell, but one only summoned here by its owner. For this had been my own Holy Grail. The very cup I had drank from that day and one I remember slamming down at the table after hearing Jesus' words of warning that there was to be a traitor at his table. In truth, my actions had only helped in sealing my fate much before my wife had her hand in it.

I pushed these thoughts from my mind as I had a fucking job to do, and thinking upon a painful past was not going to get it done any quicker! So, I made the sleeves of my tunic disappear and lifted the inside of my arm to my lips. Once there, I allowed my fangs to grow before using them to tear into my own flesh, doing so deep enough to cut through the radial artery that supplied oxygenated blood to my arm. Once done, I lowered my hand and held the cup so that the blood could flow freely down my arm and fill a holy grail of my own making.

"Brothers of the McBain clan, each of you sold your mortal souls to a noble cause. Therefore, let it be known that on this day you earned those souls returned, for your debt to me as its keeper has been honourably fulfilled. Drink now from the Hell's own Holy Chalice of souls, and reawaken as the keepers of your own fate," I said as I passed the rim of the cup to each of them so they may drink my own sacrifice, one that, unlike all others, wouldn't gift them with my essence as a vampire. No, it was a symbolic awakening that had the power to release their souls once the ritual was complete.

Which was why I held it out in front of Trice who knelt in between his two brothers and told him,

"You are the first to bleed, shifter." His eyes widened a moment before acceptance took its place. Then he unsheathed one of his daggers strapped to his chest and used it to slice open his hand. After blood gushed from the deep wound, he held his fisted hand over the cup and let his own blood flow inside. I nodded when it was enough, before gesturing with my head for the other two to follow their brother's actions.

Once all three of them had bled into the cup, there was only one thing left to do, and that was swallow it all back so my own soul could recognise the sacrifice. So it could latch on to those I summoned and free them to the surface, something that made me fall back to my knees from the force of it before I tore my head back and I opened my mouth to let loose a silent scream.

It felt as though someone else's beast was inside my vessel, now trying to tear its way free of me! So, I freely let it, now allowing it to go back to its original host, where it was to be reunited and reborn back into its fated life. A burst of white light knocked us all back with the force of not one soul, but all three leaving me at once. My own Holy Chalice then fell from my grasp and disappeared as soon as it hit the ground. Going back to where it had been summoned from, sealed away in my largest vault back at Blutfelsen.

It was a powerful weapon in itself, just like the Eye of Janus, only this was one of my own making. Which meant that as I picked myself off the ground, I couldn't help but think of that weapon and the immense power that was now in the hands of the enemy.

In fact, my only solace was that Amelia would soon be safe and in the hands of her father. Because, in reality, he was the only one who could protect her now. He was the only one that was surrounded by his own men and those loyal to him. No one but her mother had been infected with what I was now considering a disease of the Gods…

My venomous blood given to only one other being alive.

Still to this day I had been unsure how she had survived it, as even a drop would kill the strongest of my kind. Which was why I had learned to keep it contained. It was why my arm remained the way it was, a charred Hellish limb that had the power to destroy and kill all it touched. A piece of me that was concentrated evil I kept covered.

Oh, it's power had killed in the years since it had

consumed my hand, but only one had ever survived it, and it was only now I was questioning why? Was it because Amelia had been born with a small part of it or was there some other reason? She had bitten it that day and it had possessed the power to drain her of her supernatural side. Had that been the only way she had survived it, because of what she had been prepared to gift it in return of keeping her life? Of course, as a child she would not be aware of such, but the Fates most certainly would.

Had they intervened that day?

And why was I only questioning this now? Well, years of refusing to believe she was my Chosen One could answer that. Because up until the time I stole part of her life, I had once considered my blood as a gift, but ever since that day it had seemed like nothing more than a fucking curse!

Like falling in love with a girl I couldn't protect. One that had died in my arms. No, I couldn't allow that to happen again and would do anything I could to prevent it, even if that meant breaking her heart… *one I had only just managed to fix.*

No, I had done the right thing, as Dom would know what to do. Which was why I told my men that even if they had to tie her up and carry her back to him, then that was what they must do. As for me, I would only return to claim her once this was all over and I had eliminated the threat.

Once I had dealt with my… fuck… *my wife.*

The very word felt like acid across my tongue just thinking of it. Hell, but since hearing that damn name of hers, I had thought of little else. I had questioned excessively how it was all possible, and yet I knew there was only one being alive that would know. A single soul that would have any answers for me, which was just another reason added to the endless fucking list of why it was best Amelia was not here.

Because it meant going to the one place in my past I knew I couldn't trust.

The place of my rebirth.

My father's realm.

The Tortured City of Souls.

CHAPTER EIGHT

BETRAYAL AND FIRE

I shook the lingering sensation that felt as if my brain had been rattled in my skull after gaining my feet once more, getting sick of this being knocked down shit. Then, before I could think too much about my actions, I offered Trice my hand as he was still on his ass from the power of gaining back his soul. He looked at it in surprise, making me roll my eyes and snap,

"Just fucking take it, shifter, before I use it to knock you on your ass again for being an asshole." At this he burst out laughing and clasped his hand to my forearm so I could pull him up. Then he shook his head and rubbed a hand across his chest as if the new feeling was settling inside of him. Yeah well, having your soul merged back into a vessel will do that to you, I thought wryly. Speaking of which, I looked back at my own brother, and knew it was time to get this next shit over with.

"I… I don't ken whit tae say," Trice stammered for words making me tense.

"Coming from you, the less the better I can imagine," I

responded dryly, making his brothers laugh as they joined us after getting their bearings once more.

"Ain't that th' truth," Gryph commented

"It surely be, brother," Vern said, making me look at him.

"That shit going to disappear soon or are you going to turn up on the battlefield sounding like a posh twat?" I asked, making Trice grin this time before he slapped a hand to Vern's back and said,

"We wull be ready."

"Aye, fur lucky his aim is still true even wi' his wee posh balls." Vern rolled his eyes and flipped them both the middle finger.

"I heard if yer stick it up yer ass, that wull help in bringin' back yer accent," Gryph replied, making me grin before I turned to walk away, stopping only when Trice asked,

"Wait!"

"I have little time, shifter," I informed him after I paused long enough for him to speak.

"Why?"

"Does it matter?" I asked in return before looking back at him over my shoulder.

"Aye, it does tae me."

I released a sigh and told him the truth,

"Because my Queen makes me want to be worthy of being her King."

He nodded to this, understanding it due to his own feelings, and I swear had those feelings not been for my own girl then I might have felt sorry for the bastard. Perhaps matchmaking him with the shy little Fae girl wouldn't have been such a bad thing after all.

I shook off these thoughts and started to focus on another, one that would aid me better in what I needed to do next.

Because right now there was only one person that could

help me, and as much as I hated it, I was left with no other option than to deal with the bastard, as this went much deeper than I once thought, because the roots of rage reached much further than just a few centuries in the making. No, in fact, they started back to when I drew my first Hellish breath. Possibly even further and beyond my resurrection, back to a time where my name didn't mean the sun.

Back to a time where my name was only ever remembered as meaning one thing…

The great betrayer of all time.

Judas.

Meaning only one thing, it was time to face my past once and for all… and to do that I needed one thing.

"Create me the portal," I snapped as I tore the rest of my tunic off and with a single thought, brought forth my usual plain black, Vipera skinned clothing.

My brother turned my way at my approach.

"Inside or out?" he asked, knowing exactly which realm I meant to travel to.

"Somewhere on the outskirts, for I will make my way to the Castle myself," I answered, looking down at my bound hand and exchanging the leather for a demonic, clawed gauntlet.

"Are you sure about this?" he asked with a sigh.

"You ask me that now, after it feels like I just ripped out my Chosen One's heart?!" I snapped, making him shrug his shoulders and say,

"Hey, it was better than taking her with you to the fucking Wolves… besides, I didn't say it was a bad plan." I ignored this and nodded to the space where the portal once was. Now trying to get the fucking image out of my mind of Clay grabbing her from behind and pulling her through forcefully, because what else could I have done? Amelia would never have listened and that girl, Gods, but she had a power over me like no other!

Which meant I knew that, given the chance, she would have convinced me of all manner of other options. None of which would have ensured her safety like the one I was forced to choose. Because time had proven only one thing to me and that was, despite all the power I possessed, I was still always powerless to stop someone from taking her. I was powerless to protect her from all manner of things befalling her. And the worst part was that not all of these were just from being in Hell. No, the painful truth was it had been ever since I had come into her life. I had been the target all along, and she had been the metal lightning rods stood behind me bearing the brunt of every hit against me.

Well, I refused to stand helplessly by and watch her die once more! I refused to be the cause of anymore pain. She asked me why I had created that memory of how I had wished things had gone the night of the gala, and I had told her the truth in my reply. Because if I had the power to go back, that was how it would have happened... minus forcing her to eat a fucking big steak for breakfast that was.

But I would have changed it because she deserved nothing less, and because I felt ashamed of myself that I had failed to recognise that until it was too late. Just as I had selfishly kept her in my life for as long as possible, despite knowing of the dangers. Because I was an arrogant fool who believed myself capable enough of protecting her.

Well, I would not fail her again.

So, I asked for her forgiveness, knowing that I would have no choice but to send her on her way back to her father. Then I prayed to every God out there that he had the ability to do what I could not. However, the pain I was forced to witness in her face when she realised my betrayal, was all the punishment I could take, for despite all my reasons, I still felt like the biggest bastard alive!

So, I had written two letters, one to her father explaining all that had happened and all that would happen in the coming days. I told him to prepare for war, and if he had to lock her away in that fucking tower I knew he had, then so be it!

As for the other letter, that was the one that cut me to my core just having to write it! The letter written to Amelia was one where I had tried to explain my actions and the fucked-up reasons behind them. For it was simple.

It was fear.

Fear of losing what was most important to me. Fear that she would be taken from me again, and this time that fear spread to a place where I knew I may not have the power to bring her back again. Fear, that was now so much more than just a word. So much more than even a feeling. Because now that fear had a place. It had a smell. It had a touch and a sound. It was an office. It was her blood. It was her cold skin and the sound of the last breath she took.

That fear was now my biggest weakness, and one I knew had the power to consume me should I let it. It was also one that had the power to make me lose this war and that, I could not afford to do. So, I asked for her forgiveness, not being ashamed to say, I near begged for it. But then my letter was also much more than that. Much more than an explanation, and much more than a means to get her to forgive me. Because I had to ask myself, if it came to it, what would be the last words I would say to her if I could? If I was defeated and slain, what would I have said to her with my last dying breath?

That was what the letter contained.

My goodbye.

It held, in that single page, the words I never had the

chance to tell her as she lay there beneath me, dying. No, all she had heard was me demanding that she live. Demanding that she came back to me. But that had never been my goodbye. So, this time, she would know. She would know, despite her feelings being one of betrayal and the heartache that I had inflicted upon her with my actions, she would still know how much I loved her. She would know it always, and that my love for her would be what was spoken with my dying breath.

That I would love her in death just as I did in life.

That I would love her eternally.

I clenched a fist thinking back to that letter and shaking the sight of her pain from my mind. Then I released a deep sigh and nodded to my brother.

"Let's get this shit over with."

Dariush didn't comment, but instead simply created a portal, one that was red and glowing and unsurprisingly a foreboding sight considering what lay on the other side. Well, foreboding sight or not, it was one that after nodding farewell to my brother, I stepped through. Yet when I heard another presence behind me after making it to the other side, I turned to find Dariush had followed me.

"What are you doing!?"

"What does it look like?" he replied, cracking his neck.

"Something foolish is what!" I snapped, making him smirk and say,

"Yeah well, you're an idiot if you think I'm going to let you do this alone."

"The Kingdom needs a ruler, Dariush," I reminded him, making him scoff.

"Fuck the Kingdom… besides, you and every other vampire might be dead soon, so I was thinking… if that happens… of becoming the next King of Lust, filling it full of pussy and retiring a happy man," he said, making me laugh before throwing back,

"Yes, but then whilst you're wishing, you may also dream of owning a bigger cock or all that pussy will feel is a stick in the wind." At this he grunted a laugh and said,

"I get no complaints, asshole. Anyway, if I was fucking wishing for anything right now, it would be to fight in a war I helped my brother win... speaking of which... shall we?" Dariush said, making me grin as in that moment, I could not argue against this sentiment. So, instead of arguing further about him being here, I clasp my hand to his shoulder in thanks, telling him without words how much it meant to have him by my side. And in that single nod was all it took to express so much between us. Because we didn't need to say more, not when we had our loyalty to one another, one that went beyond words.

One, I will admit had been tested recently, this was true, but it didn't change what lay ahead. And right now, that was the sight of our father's formidable Kingdom in the distance. The sounds of agony that carried along the wind like a siren's song of death, and one that never stopped singing.

"Gods, but I fucking hate it here," my brother commented, and I had to agree with him. But then it was as you would expect my father's realm to be. He was Hell's jailor, its torturer, its King of Kings, and the Angel of Death. Ironically, the stories of Hell and Heaven being at war with one another were just that, a misconception, just like angels were all good and demons were all bad. But good and evil needed two rulers, and Lucifer may have been a fallen angel, but what the stories didn't tell you was that it was by choice on both sides.

Lucifer was God's favourite child, so he made him King of his own world. Being a sadist by nature, it was the obvious choice to rule over demons and a place where the dark hearts of men could find their own Afterlife. It was why there were so many different realms of Hell. So many levels because it wasn't all just black and white. It wasn't good or bad. It was much more complex than that, just as Heaven was. There were levels of evil just as there were levels of good, and naturally for Lucifer, well he was ruler over the most heinous of souls.

He fed from the cruellest of hearts and grew more powerful from the darkest and most rotted souls, which meant that the land surrounding us was literally a sadists' playground. But it is also the very heart of Hell, which meant its landscape was at its most harsh, resembling that of a volcano that had already erupted and would never quite cool down. A combination of black sand covered wastelands could be seen in the far distance, and surrounding his castle were platforms of floating islands on a river of fire. One of flowing magma that generated so much energy, it could have powered all of Hell itself. And at the centre of it all, like a dark black heart, was of course… our father's fortress.

It reminded me of Edinburgh Castle in the way it was situated. Being built up at the highest point of the city so that whoever ruled at the time could survey over their domain. One built so high upon black bedrock, that when stood even a mile away, you would have to look straight up to view the top. It was also covered in a grey ash that looked like snow. The rumours were that this ash was actually the remains of charred bodies of the cremated souls that had rained down from the mortal realm. Those that had lived their lives in sin and didn't get to escape Hell any more than the others. Not when new bodies were found for them to be tortured in place of their own.

As for the castle, it looked as if parts of it had risen from the mountain itself. Ironically, it was also similar in design to many of the cathedrals seen back in the mortal world, as it was a series of giant spires. Spires that rose up like giant demonic fingers topped with spiked pinnacles attached to flying buttresses.

Black carved flanking towers with red spiked tops sat between the curtain walls of the castle, gleaming as if they were made of glass. Tiered pillars stood like giant redwood trees and connected a series of covered parapet walkways, that became the best means of navigating your way from one side of the fortress to the other. Crimson lights glowed from beyond the hundreds of arched stone framed windows, making it look as if the whole castle had eyes watching the entire realm. This matched the red lightning that constantly erupted from the clouds above. A ceaseless storm that circled the land, making it look like blood filled veins were lighting up the dark sky.

Finally, at its centre was the largest building, and one you would have called the keep, however there was nothing conventional about it. In fact, it looked as if the very top of the mountain had been carved smooth into a square building and its roof left jagged, surrounded by smaller towers and then the battlements and curtain walls had just been built around it, with the six colossal towers situated at its corners.

"Where is his army?" I questioned, used to seeing the sight of them training on the largest of the hundreds of islands that surrounded the city. This was because our father liked to have them at the ready to fight, or at the very least seen as a force of strength.

Yet now they were gone.

"I have no fucking clue, but I know that I don't like it," my brother replied.

"It seems my caution wasn't for nothing, but at the very

least it will save time if you create portal and take us closer." My brother's reply to this was to warp the space in front of us and create a portal, this time one big enough for us both to step through at the same moment. This meant that I was soon looking up at the imposing entrance that was framed by two round towers you would have expected to see on most castles. Yet the difference was not only the colossal height, but also the battlements at the top that were consumed in flames.

"*Fire Demons,*" my brother hissed, nodding above to where movement could be seen in the flames. Of course, the name wasn't exactly original at all seeing as these demons could withstand any amount of heat. Unsurprising, being that they had been born from the river Phlegethon, which literally translates in English to the word 'flaming'.

They were half beast, half man, standing at nine feet tall, thanks to large flat horns that reminded me of a cross between a scythe and a vechevoral. The vechevoral was a sickle shaped sword from the 19th century that originated from India, and like the Fire Demons' horns, they were thicker at the very top and curved into a deep concaved arch before ending in long sharp points.

The horns were anchored to a wide flat forehead that looked like a helmet of scorched bone and covered most of its face, other than the two rows of slits for its six eyes. Eyes that even from this distance could be seen glowing hot like the flames they stood in. The body of a man that was bulging with sweat dripping muscles and the moment we moved closer, they used these to raise their mammoth weapons at us. A twin sided scythe that joined in the middle with a straight dagger, glowing hot as though it would soon be at its melting point. However, the demon that wielded it, was also the one who made it from their very essence, meaning that it would continue to glow like lava without ever losing its shape.

A deadly weapon for an even deadlier foe.

"Well, at least we know the bastard hasn't gone completely insane and left himself defenceless," Dariush commented dryly, and I grunted an agreement, not daring to take my gaze from those living flames that stood guard. It would only take a handful of those fuckers to take down an entire legion of demons, as they could produce fire as easily as breathing. Hence why they were so rare and why our father had every one of them at his disposal.

There were two giant torches lighting the way at the top of the entrance towers, acting as a beacon for the lost souls that were lucky enough to go free and roamed these lands. After all, not everyone received an eternity being tortured and some were sentenced to remain here for a period of time. However, there were also those that could not cope with life outside their prison walls, just like in the human world. Meaning that in Hell, there were also those who actually craved the torture. Craved a life of servitude, even without the delivering hand of their cruel master. These were usually what were named 'the condemned' and became willing servants in one capacity or another.

For if they showed strength and skill, they became one of Lucifer's army. If not, then they would serve in a different way, as Lucifer was many things, but wasteful wasn't one of them. Which was why the condemned were represented by the two tortured souls either side of the entrance. Two giant horned demons that once breathed life, and reminded all who approached just what happens when you anger a God of Hell, as all that remained now were their skeletons.

They were also the size of skyscrapers which were crouched over as if praying to their Master and had simply died that way. Their flesh had long since withered away from the bone that remained and was decorated with golden cuffs gleaming at the wrists. These were attached to giant chains the size you would expect on container ships when dropping their anchor. Each chain was then connected to the drawbridge, and I knew that, had those praying hands been up towards the sky, then the drawbridge would have been up, denying us entrance.

As good luck would have it the drawbridge was down. It was also large enough for one of those dead giants to walk across and I had no doubt that from above, Dariush and I looked like ants as we walked down the centre.

We passed another statue, this time one that was kneeling in the river of Phlegethon that surrounded the castle like a flaming moat. Its demonic head hung down in what looked like eternal prayer, and out from its eyes two lava waterfalls flowed. A pair of endless streams of molten liquid glowing bright as it poured from its remains, feeding the river below. The heat was incredible and scorched our throats as we walked past.

As for the colossal crimson doors ahead, these, like the drawbridge, were already open, as if waiting for us.

"Looks like a welcome to me," I commented, looking up at the living gargoyles that clung to the arched entrance and snarled down at us as we stepped over the threshold.

"Yes, it's almost like the old man is expecting us," my brother replied, as we granted each other a knowing look. One that was both cautious and telling the other to be at the ready. Because this was the case with the King of Hell, he liked to keep his favourite sons on their toes.

Speaking of which, the moment we entered the bailey, I rolled my eyes and groaned,

"Fucking great… just what I fucking need."

"Well, it looks like we found Dad's army," Dariush said, pointing out the obvious as we had walked straight into an ambush. Which was why I looked down at my hand and summoned my sword before swinging it around and into position.

Then, I corrected my stance, getting ready for the first wave and motioning them forward, telling Dariush,

"Best not keep our bastard father, waiting then."

CHAPTER NINE

WELCOME HOME

The inside of the bailey was as it always was, a Hellish reminder of who owned this castle and a clear warning to those who wanted to enter it and survive. Because the rules were simple, kneel and cower to the overlord of Hell.

Well, that was unless he was your father and demonic maker, as I would never bow down to that fucker again! No, not now I was his equal in power, and the bastard knew it! Hence why we faced what we did now and why he had been ready for us.

So, I glanced my knowing gaze around the space, one as big as a football field. It was sectioned off into some warped version of a courtly garden, with the entrance-way being lined either side with a ten-foot-high arched wall. This pale grey stone framed a wide walkway that was currently filled with our father's men. Some of these arches were open and entwined with thick deadly vines of soul weed, and others were filled in and held a wall of spikes the length of my forearm. Spikes which currently held the broken remains of bodies, both human in nature and demon. Half rotted corpses held there like displayed insects, limp and unmoving. But then, just because something wasn't moving, it didn't necessarily make it dead... this was my father's realm after all.

A glance at the opposite side and I could even see a pair of wings impaled there, which had obviously been torn off one our father's unfortunate victims. Just beyond these 'decorated' arches, enormous, pale, dead trees could be seen, and their only purpose seemed to be that they offered a place to hang large cages from. Cages made of twisted, thorny iron which held tortured bodies within their grasp, some barely recognisable as being once a whole body.

"So, was this the welcome home you were expecting, brother?" Dariush asked with a smirk.

"Yes, although I thought there'd be more of them," I replied with my own grin in sight of the guards all now stood in their square formation. Our father had lots of different regiments in his army, and each with its own purpose. For example, the one in front of us now told me only one thing, Lucifer was clearly getting more paranoid as the years went by. But, considering what I now knew about one of his recently discovered sons, then I couldn't say I was surprised.

I had, however, expected to see his royal guard, not those of the dead souls of Samurai that had fallen on their own swords in hopes of regaining honour to their family name and bloodline. Seppuku was the name for this Japanese ritual of suicide by disembowelment, and had originally been reserved for Samurai and their code of honour. But then Lucifer had been more than happy with the influx of these fallen Seppuku warriors, as he had named them. Something that happened when the ritual was also practiced by other Japanese people during the Shōwa period. A way to restore honour for themselves and their families, particularly by officers towards the end of World War II.

But the Seppuku wasn't always used voluntarily by Samurai to die with honour rather than fall into the hands of their enemies. For it was also offered as a form of capital punishment for those who had committed serious offenses or brought shame upon themselves. Hence Hell being their final resting place thanks to Lucifer's keenness to own them. And seeing as it had been death by ceremonial disembowelment, I wasn't surprised to see the symbolic choice used for where to keep their weapons.

The hilt of which was sticking out of their abdomens where they had originally inflicted the deadly blow. A short blade that looked to be what was traditionally known as a tanto, and one used to plunge into the belly and drawn left to right to slice deep enough to sever the aorta to cause rapid death by great blood loss.

After all, if you were forced to kill yourself or decided this to be your only choice, then most would choose a quick death, honour or not. And speaking of honour, it made me wonder if they still had any left after working for the Devil, as they each drew their short blades from their stomachs. Blood seeped out with the movement, but then floated in the air as though it had been dropped into clear water.

The lost Samurais' souls of those that had committed suicide, now once again found themselves fighting for a new master, making me wonder if they feared a new death. I knew them to be incredibly skilled, hence why Lucifer had wanted them. A real Samurai also had two blades, so with their side arms already drawn from their insides, they pulled free their katanas in one swift motion. After this, they held both crossed above their heads in some sort of homage to their master, and stayed that way as if waiting for some silent command from the being himself.

As for the long blades of the katanas, each were made from Hell's black steel, and decorated with a red line down its sharp edge, running all the way to the tip. This gave them the appearance that it had already drawn blood from its enemies.

They were a sight to behold, as they were dressed in select pieces of typical 16th century armour in black and red. A black hitatare robe along with dark hakama pants were worn underneath a dou chest plate, with kusazuri, which were leather plates hanging from the front and back of the dou. These protected the lower body and upper leg but like the rest of their armour, this was all for show, as no doubt Lucifer wanted them to look the part.

What completed the look were the overly large shoulder plates known as sode, this time made from iron that connected to the kote, which were armoured gloves. The only part of them that didn't fit their past lives were the missing kabutos, the famous samurai helmet. No, instead their heads were covered in floating crimson sashes, making only their eyes glow white beneath their new veils of death.

But fallen Seppuku weren't a new fighting force I hadn't encountered until now, for I had fought them before. Although granted, it hadn't been for some time. Hence why I rolled my shoulders and cracked my neck to the side, knowing this would require at least some effort on my part. This was because they were fast, cunning, and could swipe their blade across your flesh with a mere whisper of movement. But more than anything else…

They were in my way.

"Well, this doesn't look too difficult," Dariush said wryly, and as if they had been waiting for the perfect moment to prove him wrong, the fallen Seppuku separated, revealing what we were really there to fight. Oh, and but of course, it was as far from a Samurai as you could fucking get!

"And you were saying?" I replied in a dry tone as the four-legged beast emerged from the gates behind with a bone rattling battle cry.

"Fuck me, that's ugly," Dariush commented with a grimace, a statement in Hell you heard all too often when faced with what was clearly another of our father's demonic experiments. You see there was a difference between those he classed as his sons, and creatures like this fucked up soul... his sons were gifted his blood and fuckers like this, *they were not.*

"Looks like someone has been playing God again."

"Yeah, with his fucking eyes closed!" Dariush replied with a shudder, before the beast raised all four of its oversized weapons and charged at us. It looked like a pair of conjoined twins attached back-to-back, with their limbs being double jointed so they could run in any direction. One that was currently barrelling our way with an angry scream.

In fact, it looked as if one of my father's experiments had sat up halfway through and decided to run for it, as it looked only half completed. Both its torsos were riddled with thick crude sutures in X shapes, and stitched diagonally across overdeveloped bodies. Their large stomachs bulged in places that looked as if it had swallowed bowling balls for breakfast. Its grey, wrinkled skin was sagging off the flesh beneath, hanging in places that looked as if it was dying in patches. Its arms were huge and grossly oversized compared to the rest of both bodies. These thick trunk-like arms also looked far too heavy to even lift, especially with the spiked hammers that had replaced the need for hands.

However, to overcompensate for this oversight in weight and size, metal cuffs had been forged and fused to the flesh, held to their wrists with thick, spiked iron pins. Connected to these cuffs were chains that then attached up to heavy collars, that both heads had locked around their necks. This meant that they couldn't lower their arms past a certain point, because if they tried, it would pull the chain taut after first making it rattle.

As for the ugliest part, which was of course its faces, these both looked like a patchwork of other creatures that had been used in their making. Different skins were all sewn together with only half of them taking root with its new host, as the other half hung like flaps of limp, dead leather. Eyeballs were barely held in place in eye sockets that had been stapled open and its mouth was a combination of a mismatch of fangs, metal barbs and pointed teeth in endless rows that reached down their throats and out of sight.

"Wow, it's a bit like a harpy had angry sex with a…" My brother's insult ended abruptly when he was knocked aside, after not ducking in time before this twin creature's first swing. I, however, did, and rolled his way before kicking to my feet and offering Dariush a hand.

"You were saying?"

"Well, now I will say they had sex with a fucking rock, as Gorgons don't hit that fucking hard!" he grumbled with a shake of his head, before we were forced to separate as it charged us once more. It threw one arm my way, and they just kept fucking coming one after another as the twin bodies turned full circle. I managed to dodge three of its arms as they hammered out chunks of the arched wall, when the last one caught me in the chest making me fly backwards with a grunt.

It snarled my way before turning its attention to my brother, mistaking the fact I was down and believing I would be staying that way. I released growl of frustration and punched a fist to the ground in anger as I got up, calling forth the rest of my demonic amour and feeling it envelop the rest of my body by the time I straightened. Then, just as it made Dariush go skidding along the floor, I rolled my sword and walked past him growling down to where he lay,

"My turn."

"Yeah, be my fucking guest," was his ragged reply, making me grin. Looked like my brother needed more practice. And speaking of practice,

"Hey twin fuckers, let's try that again," I said, letting it come at me this time and now knowing what to expect, I accounted for it. So, as it threw its weighted weapon at my head, I ducked, and sliced under its arms, doing so four times in quick succession. It staggered around as it had been cut deep by its ribs. Then, just as I was about to do the same again until the fuckers were in pieces, I watched as pieces of flesh started to unravel themselves from their stiches.

"What the fuck?" I muttered as these four patches slithered down as though they were alive and covered the slices my blade had made, reattaching itself in seconds.

"Well, that's a new one," Dariush commented with a raised brow as he came to stand next to me. Meanwhile the army of fallen Seppuku hadn't moved an inch.

"We will have to fight this as one," I shouted, having little clue as to what the fuck this even was, having never fought one before but then I doubt many had survived before us and lived to tell the tale.

"Or we fight it in two," Dariush said with a knowing smirk as he summoned his own sword, this time one more suited to the task than his usual, shamshir.

No, this time it was an Indian staff known as a tabar. The tabar, was an elegant battle axe and its fine grey steel blade was curved in design. This was attached to a long shaft with a carved scale pattern, topped with an ivory demonic claw holding a black glass sphere. The blade itself was the length of my arm, and one I knew powerful enough to do the damage that was needed to defeat this conjoined monster. One that was far quicker than it should be, given its size.

"I hope you have a plan, Dariush," I said, making him wink at me the second the twin beasts just start spinning around, turning quickly as they raised up their meaty arms and their heavy weapons. Once again, using this method as a way to lash out at us over and over again without any reprieve. Fuck, but it was like fighting a never-ending stream of demonic hammers coming at you one after the other. But hit after hit I counteracted with my own blade as the rest of Lucifer's army looked on, unmoving like ghosts of a Samurai.

"This is getting old real quick, brother!" I shouted after being knocked down again.

"I just need to get one good shot at it, but wouldn't you know, the fucker just won't stop and let me do it," Dariush said with a grin, as if the crazy bastard was having the fucking time of his life!

But then the second it threw all four arms backwards and roared at us, I got an idea. I narrowed my gaze on the four chains attached to its arms and the links that rattling on theirs hooks. Because its fury was causing tension and strain to the collars around its necks, making me wonder if it would be enough. Well, there was only one way to find out.

"I have an idea," I told Dariush, after he had rolled out of its charging body before it barrelled into part of the arched wall, knocking half of it down into rubble.

"Yeah, you want to fill me in?" he asked after hitting a fist to his chest, coughing.

"Try and get him in the middle, over there," I said

pointing to the only place this was going to work and making him roll his eyes at me.

"Great, fucking love being the bait," he grumbled before I raised my arms wide, walked backwards and said,

"Naturally, brother, for you are so good at it!" He flipped me the middle finger in response, making me chuckle as I took my position off to the side to wait for my opening. Then I watched as Dariush did as I asked and started to coax the ugly fucker into the centre of the courtyard in between the two walls of spikes. Then, when he was in the perfect spot, I moved in, whilst the beast was busy spinning around trying to hit Dariush who was moving too fast for him to get a hit in.

"Now what!?" he shouted, as it was clear he could only do this for so long.

"Be at the ready for this fucker to fall!" I said flipping my body upwards, and with four swift and calculated hits, I sliced through the weak links that severed the hooks by its neck. Then, as I suspected, all four limbs fell to the floor, becoming too heavy for the twin beast to hold up without help. The hammers crashed to the ground and smashed through the stone slabs, effectively pinning the creature in place as it tried in vain to lift its own limbs.

"Yeah, that'll do it," Dariush said before spinning into place and hammering down his axe like weapon, which severed the two beasts in half and right down the centre of where their backs were attached. Then, after only giving the creature enough time to part, Dariush created a portal in front of us both, telling me his plan with just one word,

"Constantinople." My grin was all the reply he needed after he reminded me of the good old times at war and how we used to fight as one. So we both stepped through with only one destination in mind. This was in between the two severed beasts before they had a chance to turn and fight us once more. Doing this meant we had the element of surprise on our side before we lashed out, kicking their backs at the same time with enough force to send them both hurtling forwards. Then, with a precise spin, we both cut through their arms so as the weight of their weapons wouldn't prevent them from continuing their forward momentum. This meant that they continued headfirst into spiked walls and became impaled there.

"You know I don't remember it going quite that way back in Constantinople," my brother said, making me reply,

"No, that's because you got us thrown in a jail cell." He grinned then and as we both turned around, we found the army now facing us, we drew our weapons up and he said,

"Ah, now this I remember." I gave him a wry look in return and said my usual,

"*Indeed.*"

Then we both stepped forward and faced the Fallen Seppuku, engaging them in battle. One that lasted only ten minutes before we were walking inside the once gated doors to the keep. Doing so with the last of our father's men falling to his knees just after his severed head rolled from his shoulders and landed with the rest of the pieces of the Samurai.

"You know, that was quite satisfying," Dariush commented before rolling his wrist and making the tabar disappear, knowing now, as well as I did, that our father wouldn't waste anymore of his men. Not when we had passed his test.

Which meant that his royal guard didn't even flinch as we made our way into the colossal entrance hall. One with a main theme that was black and death, for the floor was a polished black stone, that matched the walls. These were adorned with dark mouldings and carved figures that looked like souls were trying to make their way out of the stone. In fact, the only reason they were seen in the first place, was thanks to the strip of red flames that framed the entire room, casting crimson shadows upright and against the phantoms trying to escape the very walls of the castle.

As for the rest of the room, down the centre was a long, rectangular pool of black water. One that held flashes of white moving just under the surface. This mirrored the walls, for they looked like hundreds of pale ghosts and trapped souls. All of which were trying to escape the surface, only to be teased by being mere inches away from freedom, one I knew they would never reach.

This dark pool was no higher in height than that of a brick and was lined by our father's personal guard. Imposing figures of great height and strength that were each armed to the teeth. Armour that was shadows of black to match the room, with only their red burning eyes alerting you to their presence.

There didn't need to be any orders given, for they already knew who it was that we were here to see. However, my surprise did come at not being led into his throne room as I would have thought, but instead to a place that neither I, nor Dariush had ever been in before.

Lucifer's personal wing of the castle.

A place we approached after some time spent navigating our way through countless corridors, which were one depressing place after another, before arriving at an entranceway that was heavily guarded. I glanced at the two oversized warriors that held giant swords in front of them, and thought back to my own castle. Back to a time when Amelia had teased me with her obvious appreciation for the impressive male forms of the two statues. Ones that guarded my own personal space back at blood rock.

I shook this memory from my mind and stepped forward, telling them both of my intent and daring them to challenge it. However, they merely stood back and allowed us entrance as the door opened, telling us both that they must have had their orders to allow us inside.

Then the moment we entered, only two words came out of my mouth at the sight that greeted us…

"Hello, father."

CHAPTER TEN

HELL FREEZES OVER WHEN THE DEVIL IS IN LOVE

"Do they still have such a thing in the mortal realm as a twilight zone?" Dariush muttered next to me, making me raise a brow at him before telling him in a dry tone,

"I believe so."

"Great, good to know there's a trend starting," he said sarcastically with regard to the vast modern space we now found ourselves in. Especially considering the seemingly endless Hellish hallways of the castle we had only moments ago found ourselves in. Indeed, it was vastly different to the last time I was within its walls. But then again, the last time I was here was to aid him in recovering his own Chosen One. A fact he had clearly achieved, for not only was she also in the room with us, but she was clearly the reason for such a distinct change in his usual demonic space.

Because, in the place that usually depicted upon its walls the tortured souls of Hell trying to escape the eternal flames, there was sleek walls and modern furnishings... which wasn't what I nor my brother expected. But then again, I never expected I would end up with a collection of kid's toys displayed in my living space either but well, shit me, that had happened... and fucking quickly.

But gone was the constant reminder of death, and in its place was some luxury apartment you would have found in some Metropolitan city in Earth's realm. One that would have set you back in the millions, especially with the view that was being conjured up outside of the entire wall of glass. A view that strangely looked like Paris at night.

As for the rest of the interior, a black marble floor, veined with white flecks and polished to a high sheen, lay out in front of them like a watery blanket of oblivion. A stark white leather sofa faced the windows and curved around the stylish floating fireplace that hung from above. The whole thing looked like some kind of art exhibit with its black twisted metal that dripped down into a large tear shape, one that had a fire burning in its clear glass centre.

Beyond that, the room was sectioned by raised platforms that had a few steps leading up from the sunken living space. The first of these held a sleek dining table made of stone and metal, with high backed chairs to match. On from this, a few steps led down again into an open plan kitchen, that held an island in the middle bigger than most queen-sized beds. This too was made up of even more black marble contrasting against the white countertops of the kitchen.

I knew instantly it was all an illusion, and clearly one done for the Egyptian goddess that currently stood at that countertop mixing what looked like pancake batter in a bowl. She was also wearing something that made her look like some kind of pin-up girl from a 50's housewife magazine thanks to the frilly pink apron.

Pythia had taken many forms over her entire existence,

but what I was seeing now was what I knew to be her true self. Raven dark hair that was currently pinned up in rolls, artfully arranged over her head and interwoven with a pink bandana that was knotted at the top. Her sun kissed skin complimented the pale pink of her dress, with its dark pink underskirt giving the stark colourless room life. But nothing was more striking than that of her olive-green eyes that were speckled with branches of gold around the irises. A pair that Lucifer clearly allowed himself to get lost in if the illusion of the room was any indication.

However, the sight of both apartment and Oracle was nothing in comparison to the shocking sight of our father. It actually made me wonder if he had mirrored his outfit on Hugh Hefner, a soul that was no doubt happily enjoying his resting place in the Realm of Lust.

In fact, I knew for a certainty the famous playboy, who gave birth to the name, would be finding an invitation to another dinner party. For I could imagine he and Asmodeus would soon become good friends, if it hadn't happened already, as they most certainly shared a lot in common.

As for Lucifer, well he too looked as though he would have found himself on the guest list, as he now wore a red velvet robe with black collar, and a pair of lounge pants that made it look as if he was revelling in a lazy Sunday! All he was missing was the damn sailor hat and trademark pipe that the millionaire was known for. The tartan slippers were a nice touch though, though they did fuck all to aid him in looking like the bad ass ruler of Hell he was usually known for being.

Although, one more glance at his Chosen One, and it was of a little wonder why he chose not to give a fuck about appearances. As for his own vessel, this was one he'd kept for the longest time. The reason for which, I could very well imagine being the same reason he was now sat reading what looked like a fucking newspaper in a modern-day apartment...

Pythia.

Because he had known when he first formed his addiction to the girl, that if he had any hope of recreating the same in return, he would have to maintain the same vessel to build a familiarity with his image. So, what faced me now was the same sharp authoritative features he'd kept since the day he first laid eyes on her. High defined cheekbones, a long nose, and pale aqua eyes that changed depending on his mood. His dark hair was currently cut short and styled back from his face, which was combined with a smooth shave to match this clean look of his. As for his build, he had always maintained the impressive stature of a God, being he was the towering height of seven feet tall and a powerhouse of large muscles that encased the entirety of his body.

An impressing figure to be seen by a mortal, and one that would leave them in no doubt of who and what he was. Now, as for his true form, well that was for most, the stuff of nightmares. One I was unaware if Pythia had yet to encounter. But Pythia was an old being, older than myself and for as long as I knew of her, our father had been encroaching on her dreams. Hell, for all I knew he had been doing so for just as long as her very existence.

So naturally when doing so he'd always maintained the same vessel, creating a strong sense of his being in her mind. For no one, not even Dom, had waited for his Chosen One for as long as he had. And to make matters worse, Lucifer had known who his intended bride was to be for the near entirety of her being. In other words, a long fucking time in waiting.

Gods, but I could barely imagine it, for I had been nearing my limit after only the eleven years since I had first saved her that night, knowing without a doubt who she was to me. But for the Devil, well he had the torturous wait unlike any other, for he was unable to claim her and was powerless to do anything else but control her dreams.

An advantage he used to its fullest, meaning that the girl had no doubts to whom she belonged to from the very beginning. I almost felt sorry for her, despite the fact that she clearly wasn't here against her will any longer. Now just how long it had taken for him to convince her of that fact, I did not know. I only knew that when she first arrived here that she had been the first being who ever managed to escape him. I didn't know how, only that she had the power to flee her captive and somehow make her way out of Hell. An impressive feat in itself, for no other had even come close to evading him.

Hence, why I had been the one he had called to hunt her down. Not a task I had relished, by any means. One made even more difficult considering my disdain for the Fates, as let's just say, we hadn't exactly always seen eye to eye.

But now those times were clearly far behind us, as nothing about this scene indicated that she was here unwillingly. Well, other than the distinct black and gold collar around her neck that was inscribed and forged with the Devil's mark.

I also believed that this charade Lucifer had created was obviously meant to aid in that fact, as he clearly didn't want her going anywhere... *again.* Which just proved the level that even the Devil himself would go to for his Chosen One, for in truth we were all simply slaves to the hearts of our Fated.

A heart that even now felt the bitter twinge of agony within my chest, knowing that I had deceived my own Fated. No amount of knowing the selfless reasons why, done with the sole purpose of keeping her safe... nothing eased the pain. Nothing fucking mattered! Not when my own betrayal still weighed heavily in my gut as if it had been put there by her own fist.

I shook these thoughts from my mind, knowing they wouldn't serve me any purpose in churning them back up again. Besides, what should I have done, brought her here with me? Oh yes, I could see it now, 'please, sweetheart, sit on this wall whilst I just cut this freak fucking demonic plaything of my father's in half, before impaling it. Then be a dear and enjoy as I slaughter part of his army before I introduce you to my father.' Yeah, fuck that!

It would have been too dangerous, because Lucifer may have been my father, but he was also first and foremost a cautious King, and with this caution came the growth of paranoia, for you do not maintain that throne over the realm of Hell without being vigilant of those that try to overthrow your rule. And no other like me had the power to do just that. Which meant the only card he had left to play was the woman held over me as a weakness in the name of my own Chosen One. One I knew he would have no qualms about using to his advantage.

He was a bastard like that.

Which meant that bringing her here would have been like waving that red flag in front of his face. Or at least, that was what I always thought, yet now seeing him like this, I found myself not as sure as I once was. Because after being forced witness this strange side of him, then maybe I had been wrong in my decision. As one look at Pythia, and I now knew we were again once on equal grounds. Because, fuck me, love changed a person, whether you were the Devil or the Vampire King he created. That fact could never be denied, and the proof of that was staring me in the face in this surreal twist of events… because there was no denying the question…

Could the Devil actually be in love?

"Ah, but my prodigal sons have returned, not like I have to ask the reasons why," he said smoothly after we entered the room. Then he calmly folded up his newspaper and rose from the head of the dinner table, where he had obviously been awaiting whatever culinary delights his little wife was making him. Speaking of which, she turned her head and the moment she saw me, her eyes widened in fear. Then she dropped the bowl with a clatter to the counter and gripped the front of her apron so hard her knuckles turned white. I released a regretful sigh as Pythia had always been afraid of me. Which was of little wonder really, seeing as I was always the one charged with hunting her down. Her fear had been of Lucifer's own making, but the fucker failed to recognise this, as the moment Lucifer saw her fear of me, he growled low in the back of his throat.

"Come here, my Sarratum," Lucifer ordered, using the name for Queen in the ancient language of Sumerian. He also did so in a stern tone, obviously feeling discomfort at seeing his Fated One looking distressed by my arrival. However, when her body seemed frozen and unable to move, he clicked his fingers and the collar around her throat started to glow, calming her instantly. This obviously snapped her out of the fear that gripped her. Once it did, he said another name for her, shocking both me and my brother to our core.

"My Arammu and Ziana of mine, come do my bidding now, little one."

"*Gods!*" Dariush muttered in utter shock, as the meaning was an undeniable one. And I too was shocked after deciphering its meaning, for its translation meant he actually loved her! Something I didn't think possible for such a being. But then the proof was right there, even in the softly spoken way he had called her, his love and his heavenly life, which was what Arammu and Ziana meant. It was then of little wonder why Dariush shot me a look of astonishment.

The Devil was in love!

As for Pythia, her fear evaporated instantly, and she granted him a warm, affectionate look in return, before doing what he commanded of her. It even made me wonder if that collar didn't hold some kind of enchantment on it or had she, in fact, come to feel something for her captive? After all, he may have been the King of Kings in Hell, but he was also her Fated One in return. To be honest, after all I had witnessed these past few days, then really, nothing should have had the power to surprise me anymore… but this moment became the icing on that fucked up cake!

Dariush even shrugged his shoulders at me when he watched the insane and unlikely happen, as Lucifer grinned when she started to get closer to him, as he seemed almost… *fucking giddy?*

Then, the moment she was within arm's reach, he snatched out and grabbed her, tugging her towards him in his rush to touch her sooner. One thing became clear, that even after over a decade together, his need for her hadn't yet been sated and from the looks of things, nor would it ever. It made me think of my own obsession and I knew from experience, that I too would most likely end up being the same, for I couldn't imagine a day where the sight of my Chosen One walking towards me wouldn't have me reacting in the same way. Although, I had to admit, I was most likely better at hiding my reaction than he was.

She sucked in a deep breath as if his dominant behaviour still surprised her, and his hand collared her throat over the band of black and gold that seemed unbreakable and permanently locked around her flesh. Once again it started to glow beneath his palm, and she closed her eyes and released a deep sigh as she became compliant in his arms.

"That's it, my innocent one, relax now," he practically purred down at her, before then telling her,

"I'm afraid your delicious pancakes will have to wait, for I must speak with my sons on a matter of some importance. But I can tell you are feeling tired, my Arammu." At this, she released another deep sigh before it turned into a yawn, making him grin down at her.

"I am feeling a little tired," she admitted in a soft, sweet voice, that seemed to have a power over Lucifer as his eyes heated to a white glow, before it settled down enough for him to reply,

"Then go, my good girl, go lie down and wait for me, for I crave something far sweeter than syrup, which means you will need to rest before I make a meal out of you." At this she shuddered, clearly now thinking of something she knew was to come.

"Go now for your Sarrum commands it of his Sarratum," he said, tipping her head back by hooking a finger under the collar at her throat until it was tucked under her chin. As for Sarrum, that meant King in the old language just as Sarratum, its counterpart, meant Queen.

"Very well," she muttered lowering her eyes.

"Tut, tut, come now, you know how I like to hear it," he chastised making her blush, before a mischievous glint took form in her eyes. A pair that was soon framed with laughter lines at the corners, before she looked once to us and then said,

"I'm sorry, I meant very well, *my cuddle monkey.*" At this Dariush made a sound as if he was choking on a fly and as for me, well, my mouth dropped open like one was now welcomed to fly in it and rob me of my own breath! Was the woman in-fucking-sane!

But then Lucifer smirked down at her and instead of punishing her like his famous wrath would have prompted, instead his grin grew in size, before he playfully tapped on her nose and said,

"Oh, my sweet innocence, you'll pay for that later, and continue to pay for it until I hear you screaming what it is I crave to hear from your lips. But I'll ask you to remember the last time I did this, as I fear you were starting to enjoy your punishments a little too much... for I am clearly corrupting you." At this she blushed, despite her witty reply,

"You, Mister, corrupt me as much as I turn you soft." At this he laughed once before telling her,

"Around you, fucking impossible, my Ikkibu Ilati! For my cock has not yet seen a single day without knowing the weight of rock between my legs and nor does it remember a time before I stole you away and made you my imprisoned Sarratum!" This time he really made her blush, and I wondered if this was being told about his constant hard on, something I too sympathised with in regard to my own queen. Or perhaps it was being referred to as his forbidden Goddess, that Ikkibu Ilati translated to.

"My Arammu," she murmured softly in return, as she was clearly embarrassed after giving him a shy look, before then glancing shyly our way. This made him growl before yanking her harder into his much larger frame.

"Now, that's what I fucking wanted! You bless me, my Fated, and in reward I shall go easier on your punishment and grant you my cock to worship sooner than intended. Now go before I blind my sons just so I may take you upon this table and find better use for this syrup."

"*Ah, shit just got weird again,*" Dariush muttered, now

looking at the floor, which was when I decided to intervene before the crazy bastard tried to make good on his word.

"Yes, please go, Sarrat Irkalli, for I like my eyes where they are and have great use for them when gazing upon my own Queen," I said, using her official term as Queen of the Underworld and hoping to get this fucking meeting started, as like I said, I liked my fucking eyes where they were!

At this she smiled at me, making her possessive husband growl in jealously this time and demand in a hard demonic voice for a kiss,

"*Nasaqu, now!*" At this she simply tamed the demonic beast by placing a gentle hand to his cheek before getting up on tiptoes to kiss him. A kiss he turned into something that was borderline on being pornographic in seconds when bending her over his arm and biting, sucking, and plundering her lips, neck and jawline in a possessive display of sexual need.

"Fuck me, but I am close to asking if there is some kind of fucking waiting room," my brother commented, making me drag a hand down my face and snarl back,

"Yes, well, while you wait, I will go and fucking hunt down my own Fated, for I am now only reminded of my foolish decisions." At this he scoffed a laugh as we were forced to stand there and wait. Thankfully, only moments later and with a snarl of annoyance and frustration, Lucifer pulled her back to standing, smacked her ass and told her,

"Go, woman who enchants me, go now before I make good on my word." She smirked and shrieked when his palm made an echoing sound against her flesh, then he grabbed her hand back and promised,

"*...and you'd better be ready for me this time, or I will not be pleased.*" She nodded and before he let her go completely, he told her,

"…And Pythia… *keep the apron on.*" At this she blushed again, bowed her head once and hurried off, running through a door opposite. Lucifer then nodded to a corner in the room, as if giving some unspoken order to someone keeping himself hidden. No doubt to one of his personal guards to ensure his queen do as she was told and get back to their room without problem.

It also must have been someone he trusted beyond all else for such a task to be granted, as I knew from experience that my father didn't trust Pythia's security with many. I also had to wonder if he still didn't trust her, even after all these years? For his fear of her running from him again and going into hiding, was one I could unfortunately also sympathise with, already tasting that bitter pill for myself.

Of course, witnessing such love in his eyes when he looked at her and watched her until she was out of sight was another first, and something I'd not thought possible.

Which was when I knew…

Hell had officially frozen over.

CHAPTER ELEVEN

SILHOUETTES OF RUIN

The moment Pythia left the make-believe apartment was when it started to change. It evaporated with a wave of his hand, transforming from its expensive modern space into one more fitting for what you would expect from the overlord ruler of Hell. Even more confirmation, that the unbelievable had happened.

Lucifer was officially in love.

Because that was the only explanation there was to purposely hide a part of yourself and the world around you. An illusion created to make the other half of your soul more comfortable in the same space. He was protecting her from the darker, more sinister side of his world and transforming it into a place she would want to stay. Of course, he could simply have made her his prisoner, something I suspected she still was… but naturally, she just hadn't yet received the memo on this one.

Yet, what was the saying, if you love something set it free and if it comes back to you, then it is yours but if it doesn't, then it was never yours to begin with. Well, for the Kings of the supernatural world and the rulers of the many races that lived within it, this was not something any of us would leave to chance.

For the concept of letting something as important as our Fated Ones go was not in our collective natures. Take myself for example, Amelia had run from me and despite her foolish beliefs which made her do so, she had left and not returned of her own free will. A fact that still haunted me… and not one I would forget anytime soon.

Something I knew I now shared with my father, for he too had also felt the bitter sting from such knowledge. One which proved that just being someone's fated soulmate did not automatically mean that they would then be locked to your side forevermore of their own free will.

An unfortunate discovery to be sure, but none of us wanted to make slaves our of our queens, because other than the obvious sexual benefits…

Where was the fun in that?

So, as the world around me started to change into something far more demonic and fitting for this King of Hell, I released a sigh, feeling once again as if I had committed the greatest sin against my own soulmate. I knew that her trust in me was one I would inevitably have to earn once more, because despite writing her that letter explaining my reasons, I knew that until the girl was in my arms again, my words would have been perceived as empty. But then, what other options did I have? For right now there was no other place in all the worlds and all the realms safer than within the confines of her own home. One her father had ultimate control over. Yet, despite this logic, it still didn't make it any easier to swallow, as the bitterness felt thick enough to choke on!

As for Lucifer, this change naturally started with the man himself, with the clothes he wore igniting into a burst of flames. The scorched material sizzled away to nothing as he stepped out from the merest memory of a robe. What was left was the same vessel I had first seen that day. The very one that had made me who I was now, my second chance at life… and one which had led me to Amelia.

I had to admit that even during my years as a mortal I had never known a love like it. Meaning, it was hard not to believe in the Fates when they clearly believed in me, by blessing me with such a gift. I couldn't help but look down at my hand still covered in leather, one that I had lost nearly 30 years ago, which for a being as old as I, honestly felt like no time at all. But then, as the room continued to change, I knew it was almost symbolic for what lengths I myself had gone to in trying to cement Amelia's life so firmly within my own.

Oh yes, ourOnes, made slaves out of their kings alright, and without even knowing it.

The large open space, once transformed, still held at its centre a huge fireplace that now dominated the room in a different way. For long gone was the sleek metal and glass design that had hung in a teardrop from the high ceiling. No, instead, flames ignited within the enormous demonic skull, one with a mouth that was permanently open in a horrifying pose, as the fire burned with a raging crackle inside. A single twisted horn above its head acted as its chimney as the roaring fire inside its crying mouth created the smoke to bellow up inside and be funnelled above. Smoke that also escaped the tiny holes along the ridged horn and was sucked like a vortex around the structure.

Directly above, a chandelier of metal hoops circled the horn, holding a channel of oil that was set alight to created three rings of fire. The flickering light from the flames made the rest of the room glow, for the once plain white walls now dripped with crimson paint that most likely would have been blood. There were also demonic fur hides now stretched out and pinned at the edges on the floor that replaced the once lush and thick pile grey rugs. These broke up the dark stone floor that looked as if it had been made from slices of cooled lava.

Everything in the room had changed into some demonic Hellish version of itself and as Lucifer walked towards us, he passed a large vase that had once been made from pale marble stone. Now it was black volcanic rock that still held the shape, only before where it held large blooming flowers, now it only held death. For each one had died and had already started to crumble away to nothing before the vase itself started to shake. Then, a whimpering moan echoed from inside at the same time as a hand snaked out of the top, as if trying to free itself. Lucifer barely stopped long enough to run a single fingertip along the edge before it instantly set alight. Flames erupted around the now desperate and burning fingers as an agonising scream was heard from within. This lasted only seconds before the flames consumed the poor cretin inside. However, my sympathy was short lived after Lucifer told us,

"Serial rapist that left his victims to burn in the desert." It was after this that I believed the punishment of a fitting kind, if perhaps a little too easy for such a being. Although, I had the impression that being burnt alive over and over again was to be in his foreseeable future.

"Ah, but my Maru, I wondered how long it would be before you graced me with your presence," Lucifer said, using the term for son in his preferred language of ancient Sumerian. Thankfully though, he stuck to English, for my conversational Sumerian was rusty at best.

"As you know, I had other more pressing matters to attend

to… and well, your welcome party kept us busy," I replied with a growl, making him laugh, as I knew it would.

"Ah yes, I take that by your being here, my latest addition didn't make it?" Lucifer said with utter glee burning in his eyes at the thought.

"Um, how should I put it…" I paused long enough for Dariush to add,

"We severed that fucked up delight before impaling it." I granted him a knowing smirk, and agreed,

"What he said."

Lucifer laughed as he walked our way and said, "Excellent."

"You're happy we killed your new toy?" Dariush asked with surprise.

"Yes of course…" He took a pause next to us and said with a distasteful tone, "It made a mess constantly shitting on itself."

Then he continued walking past us, giving me chance to exchange a knowing look with my brother, who commented dryly,

"Yeah, that won't be a problem anymore."

"Ah, but the loyalty of brothers, fighting side by side," Lucifer said with a roll of his hand, as if this was all so very amusing to him.

"Yes, and it looks like it was just a warmup, considering I have another brother out there who is intent on destroying me and for some unknown reason, I'm pretty much certain it has something to do with you," I said, cutting through the bullshit that I didn't have time for, and his sadistic grin told me he liked this about me.

I was always direct, even with him.

"Very well, come along then and we shall discuss the way of things." After this, Lucifer led us through his home once more, only this time our destination was a part of his fortress both my brother and I had seen many times before... usually, *on our knees bowing to the bastard!*

His throne room, like the rest of his castle, remained the same, for there was obviously no need for this space to have been changed. Although it did make me wonder if Pythia had seen this as it was now, for if she had, then it was little wonder why the girl had run from him. It was almost something you could have classed as being cliché when belonging to the ruler of all of Hell. Because the enormous space looked like a hollowed out section of a mountain and, unlike my own castle, this time its platforms weren't filled with modern day luxuries... o*r Star Wars figures, I thought with a hidden grin.*

Its entrance was a colossal set of double doors made of stone and opened by none other than Cacus, a giant that once lived in a cave in Italy, on the future site of Rome. Cacus lived on human flesh, breathed fire and would nail the heads of victims to the doors of his cave. He was eventually overcome by Hercules and cast down here to do Lucifer's bidding, which right now included being the giant figure of a man that was half naked, covered with lashes from a whip, and strong enough to open the throne room doors.

Then, once it was done, he snarled at being chained to the mechanism that aided this opening, before a bellow of flames came from the back of his throat, setting fire to an oil filled pool. These flames then travelled throughout the throne room, lighting sections of the cavernous space with an echoing thunder from the giant's rage.

We followed our father through the decorated archways that were each carved with images duplicating his rule over the underworld. This pathway led to a bridge wide enough that you could fit a freeway down its centre and still have room. Of course, either side of this bridge was the ominous pits of Hell as they had been described since literature had begun. A time where the written word of the Devil had been spread throughout the mortal world, with most religions having their own version.

In truth, it was like being in the centre of a volcano, as lava flowed into the river of Phlegethon below. Though this was the centre of Lucifer's castle, which was indeed part of the mountain its towers, walls and turrets had been raised upon. The very foundations had been carved into its rock face and built up around the centre of its highest peak.

Around the cavern were massive columns, topped with the skulls of the many demonic creatures that roamed his lands. Their empty eye sockets only useful to the waterfall of fiery liquid that poured below in a never-ending stream of molten tears. Directly in front, the bridge led to two more levels, one higher than the other. The first of these was a hexagon shape that held a flaming symbol of the Devil's own sigil upon its floor, one Cacus had set alight upon his master's arrival. From this point, steps led up to the last and highest platform, where the Devil's throne sat waiting for its master.

Unsurprisingly, his throne was like most belonging to the rulers of Hell. Just another demonic statement to all who were in the presence of such a king. Although, even I had to admit it was an impressive sight, for there weren't many who could claim killing such a legend. The Ninki Nanka translated into Dragon Devil, and was dragged back down to Hell by Lucifer himself after he found it broken free and hiding in the swamps of Gambia. Now nothing more than a folktale and a way for parents to scare children into behaving, threatening to take them to the swamps should they continue acting out their wicked ways.

However, as for the Dragon's Devil, it was actually

named such when a mortal witnessed Lucifer take down the massive beast and drag its dead carcass back to Hell to use its remains as the ultimate trophy. The bones of which were currently still staring us in the face as a reminder of that mighty feat of power.

The enormous, winged creature was now displayed creatively into a throne, with its spine curled fifteen feet in the air ready for the back of its master to lean upon. Its ribcage was still open and spread wide from where Lucifer had done so with his bare hands, before embedding his sword within its black heart. But its bones hadn't been the only part kept as a trophy, as its skin remained, now being used as decoration hung over its own remains.

As for its head, this was given pride of place and mounted to the wall behind, being more than just a bleached bone, dragon skull, but as a cruel reminder not to fuck with the one who possessed enough skill to kill it.

Either side of this throne were four arched doorways, one of which was a portal that was swarming with trapped souls writhing around in what looked like agony. As for the other doors, I knew at least some of them led to other parts of his castle. Yet, it was also said that each one held a portal. One that led to a different level of Hell, which made sense considering in the centre of each archway there was a large keystone, with a carving at its core of each of his presidents that ruled these realms. Kings in their own right, that were depicted in demonic skulls and edged with Sumerian text either side of their ruling sigils.

We continued to follow Lucifer towards his throne, and I found myself both impatient to get to wherever the fuck it was he was taking us and thankful that we did so in silence, for I was not in the mood to entertain Lucifer any more than my being here already was. Lucifer was the master puppeteer and he prided himself on controlling the elements surrounding the lives of others so that it would lead to the outcome he wanted. Something I had the impression he was doing now.

However, I pushed these suspicious thoughts to the back of my mind as we made our way up the steps, towards the last platform where his throne sat. Then we veered off to the right and through one of the largest of the four doorways that was sat on either side of his raised throne. This led us into a gallery of sorts, and a place I had never been before.

"*Gods.*" I heard Dariush mutter next to me and I confessed to share the sentiment, for had I truly known of the full extent of my father's madness, then I might have tried to put a stop to it eons ago. I sincerely had to wonder just how far he was willing to go to in his private quest to mimic his own father's power of creation.

As for myself, I often wondered if this was the reason that I had been chosen by Lucifer, if it was our similar circumstances that led us into power. Lucifer had wanted to rule Hell, but felt wronged by the God that created him when he was forced to do so without being granted equal power for creating mortals. So, he had set about trying to beat his father's creation with one of his own that would be made in their imagine but stronger. The perfect being. Although, it was true that over the years, that vision of his had clearly been warped along the way.

As for the Gods, they realised evil must be contained and Heaven had no place for it, but like most realms, even in their infancy when they are nothing but a seed planted, everything eventually outgrows the hands that first nurture its roots. Hell was one of those seeds and its rapid growth was the reason a ruler was needed. One soul that was sacrificed with the promise of power, which in itself would grow a bitter darkness and one that only thrived on the very evil it was sent to rule over.

Lucifer was this sacrifice.

Just as I too had been sacrificed in the name of Jesus.

Lucifer's quest to create the perfect being had clearly been bordering on obsession, and far beyond just one of life's diversions. For now, in front of me and my brother, was the proof of this and it was nothing short of deplorable. Of course, I knew there had been attempts made in the past but this, well, it was like discovering a mad scientist's gallery of failures and mistakes.

At the start of this large open space was a pool of eternal blue flames running down the centre, similar to the entrance hall. The mirrored ceiling above reflected the blue light, adding dark blue shadows to the walls, and aided the demonic show and tell Lucifer had brought us here for. Then, with a click of his fingers, that show began, and those blue flames ignited in sunken wells set deep beneath the floor and below each scene.

Silhouettes of each depicted failure danced back and forth, like puppets moving against a white background, with Hell's blue flame now licking at their ankles. There were creatures I had never seen before, and those that I had heard of as nothing more than a myth. Even Adam's mighty beast, Abaddon, was among them, naturally being the largest of them all.

His representation was a flickering shadow of destruction starting with his birth in the deepest bowels of Hell. Then following on to the way he emerged in utter rage and one that, until Pip had come along, had never been contained before. It showed him destroying parts of Hell before being contained in the deepest pits of his prison with a tiny figure of Pip being thrown in there not long after.

His personal storytelling ended with his silhouette being merged with his mortal counterpart, Adam. And well, I never realised it until this moment but this was the reason that Adam had always seemed more like a brother to me than simply a friend. Because one look at Dariush and I knew this was true, as my sentiments were the same. After all, Adam's inner demon was the creation of Lucifer, just as my own was and Dariush could claim the same. So, it was of little wonder then why I made Adam my second-in-command and out of everyone in the mortal realm, why he was the one that I felt most at ease with when being myself.

My most trusted friend.

Of course, getting back to the show and on the opposite wall, before the creation of Adam, came the Keepers of Three. A shadowed depiction of their dark tale, and one I already knew. I did wonder at Lucifer's decision of why he made them the Keepers of the Tree of Souls but before I could ask this, we came to the next failure, one Lucifer stopped at.

The moving shadows were a silhouette of puppets that told the quick and brief story of a King who ordered three warriors to fight. This was before he ordered the death of another shadowed puppet, ensuring it was ripped in half by first being tied to two chariots. After this, all I could make out was the brief life of a tyrant king before he turned his back on any holy monuments or temples built in homage to the Gods. The very last of his life was of a God's mighty fist shaking in the sky before lightening split the clouds and struck a large house. Beneath this scene was a figure of the tyrant king falling into Hell with shadowed flames consuming him.

However, despite his brief tale of ruin, my eyes took me back to the beginning, back to the three warriors he had commanded into battle. I narrowed my gaze and looked back to the keepers of three and their own tale of immorality.

"Ah, I see you are connecting the shadows, my Maru," Lucifer said with a knowing look.

"Could it be?" I asked dumbfounded, making him grin this time, for I was rarely rattled about anything in his presence, and for good reason… this very reason in fact. For it meant that he held power over me and right now, that power was knowledge.

Something he confirmed when he told me,

"He started life as Tullus Hostilius and then, after having his rival Mettius torn in two, I granted him a new name, so he would be forced never to forget the sin that put him here…"

"And that is?" Dariush asked. However, I no longer needed it, as I now knew exactly who it was that had made it his mission to eradicate me and my people from all the realms.

"*Saint Matthias,*" I snarled, making Lucifer look positively gleeful, whereas my brother openly looked beyond shocked.

"Wait, you mean the guy who…"

"The apostle chosen to replace me when my name was Judas Iscariot. A replacement soon after Jesus' death and that of my own… yes…"

I paused before finishing with a growl,

"*…That bastard.*"

CHAPTER TWELVE

DEVIL'S DISTRUST

I gritted my teeth and turned to our father with a growl.

"I think now is the time you start to explain what the fuck is going on, Lucifer." His reaction didn't help cool my anger when the bastard leaned back against one of the pillars and grinned.

"It turned out he wasn't a gift of God after all, despite the meaning of his name, nor was he to be the prince I renamed him once I gifted him my blood," Lucifer mused as if we had been talking about the fucking weather!

"Again, this is the part where you start explaining what the fuck is going on," Dariush snapped this time, making Lucifer sigh,

"Ah, but as impatient as ever, my Marus."

"Yes, well, when your people are turning into mindless rogues that you're forced to hunt down and turn to ash at the end of your blade, then I would say, as their King, my impatience is more than fucking warranted!" I snapped, making him wave a hand as if batting away a fly and nothing too important.

"Yes, well, there is always one threat or another when you're a king," was his vague as fuck reply.

"That's true but I would think the eradication of an entire race would have taken precedence over much else you face as king!" I barked back, making his grin widen, which was finally when I started to get it.

"You fucking want this, don't you?!" At this he rolled his eyes and told me,

"Don't flatter yourself, kid!" I gritted my teeth at that, hating when he referred to me as such. But then again, wasn't that precisely why he did it.

"Fuck flattery, old man! You know the size of my armies and you are not foolish enough to ignore my increase in power," I stated, laying it all out on the fucking table and making Lucifer's expression darken.

"Luc, I wasn't planning on this being a suicide mission," my brother muttered in warning.

"I would heed your brother's words, my Maru." I gritted my teeth and took a step closer, feeling my brother's hand suddenly appear on my shoulder, now holding me back. But I turned back to him and said,

"Trust me, brother, for I do not intend to die this day." After this he released me and held his hands out in a 'be my guest' gesture that he no doubt would have added, 'it's your funeral' had he dared.

"Look, I am only going to say this shit once and I don't give a fuck what it takes for you to believe it, but I suggest you hear my words and understand them, for they will not change." At this Lucifer looked undecided between ripping my head off for the offence of disrespect or looking intrigued by it. Either one, I couldn't have cared less for, as he could fucking try and fight me, but he would find himself fighting an equal, that was for damn sure!

I was not what I once was.

I was no longer what he made me.

However, if I was to choose one option simply out of ease, then it would have been for him to allow me to finish what I intended to say and be done with it. So he could believe me, and we could move on to more important shit, like what the entirety of Hell was I about to face! Because one thing I was sure of and that was whatever this Matthias had planned, it went far beyond simple revenge.

No, this was all about power.

"Very well, my Etlu Maru, tell me what it is you wish for me to know so intently," Lucifer said, now calling me his warrior son, which I took as a good sign as it was a damn fucking sight better than being called kid!

"Only this, my power may have increased, along with my armies but understand me now when I say that I have no interest in becoming the next ruler of Hell, even if such a thing were possible. Even if you asked it of me yourself, my answer would now and forever be, no." At this Lucifer's eyes widened, clearly surprised by my lack of ambition for something more than what this second life of mine had already granted me.

"You're serious?" he asked, dumbfounded.

"Deadly so. In fact, if it was in my power to do so, I would rescind my rule here and I would ask my brother to take my place permanently," I replied, nodding to Dariush who had no problem ruling in my place and I had to confess, he did a damn sight better job of it than I ever could, seeing as I fucking hated any time spent in Hell.

"Why? Why as the first true son of mine would you give up what is your new birthright to claim?" he asked, doing so in such a way as if the idea was beyond all reason.

"Because being a King in the mortal realm is enough for

me and the only Kingdom I am interested in ruling." His face said it all, which was why I pushed,

"You believe my words untrue?"

"Words can be empty, Etlu, just as threats can be idle, but sometimes, they can also be loaded and full of hidden meaning. So do not believe me fool enough not to suspect that your words could be the same," Lucifer replied, pushing off the pillar he had been casually leaning against. Then he walked closer to the shadow puppets still casting their show high above the cut-out figures that portrayed his past failures.

"Then your distrust will be your undoing for we will all need to be on the same side if we are to succeed. For make no mistake, Father, a war is coming, and your knowledge of the past is what may tip the scales in our favour… that and your trust in our loyalty." Lucifer turned away from the shadow scene still playing its tale of creation on an eternal loop. Then he raised a brow and asked,

"You speak of loyalty, yet what assurances do I have that it is one in my favour?" I released a sigh and told him,

"Because, despite whatever you may believe, I am thankful for my rebirth and never more so than now, since it has granted me a gift from the Gods greater than the eternity in Heaven that was first promised to me."

"And that is?" Dariush was the one to ask this, and unsurprisingly Lucifer was the one to answer it, as he turned fully to look at us both and said,

"His Chosen One." I inclined my head telling him that he was right, although after seeing him with his own, I was not surprised.

"Speaking plainly, you created me to do a job and for over 2000 years I have done it. I have turned the vampire race into something pure and powerful and cast its memory of unruly, mindless creatures into the shadows. Vampires that are now bound to me with their very souls, but being their king is enough for me." He scoffed at this and asked,

"You think being a king ever ends?" I released a sigh and wanted to nod to those depicted in his misguided past to remind him that it ended for some of them. But instead, I told him the truth,

"No, but your control over me ended a while ago and you know it. Which means that by my being here is of my own choosing. For I come to you not to beg for your help or to place myself at your mercy, despite what you may want to believe. Nor did I come here to challenge you for your throne."

"Yes, you made that quite clear," Lucifer added in a dry tone.

"Good, then you won't be surprised to hear that I am here to seek an alliance with you, and one you will unquestionably need because this other son of yours, he's not out to seek his revenge against me but in fact against us all, and included in that is you, his maker." Lucifer laughed once without humour, and protested,

"Your words are lacking, son."

"How so?" I asked with a frown, now crossing my arms over my chest in a defensive way.

"You speak of an alliance, but tell me this, what need do I have of you on the battlefield if your army has already fallen into the hands of the enemy and being used against you. For do not think me ignorant of the facts, as you're not the only who knows when the Tree of Souls weeps. For the blood in your veins is connected with my own... or did you forget that?" At this point I wanted to roll my fucking eyes as it was hardly something I would ever fucking forget! However, I did think it prudent to refrain from arguing back, and instead decided to remind him of the facts in greater depth.

"That maybe so, but it is my blood who binds their souls, not yours and seeing as the army you think will fall from my grasp is greater than your own, then I'll say that you'll need all the help you can get to prevent him from beating you on the battlefield… for I am hardly without my uses, Lucifer, or *did you forget that?*" I said, using his words back at him and making him grin knowingly before replying nonchalantly,

"Perhaps."

"Perhaps, my ass!" I snapped, prompting Dariush to take my place in trying to convince him of facts.

"Make no mistake, Father, for two sons stand before you that have no interest in taking your place by ruling over Hell. But ask yourself, can you honestly say the same for the son you cast out, and the very one that now seeks revenge against us all?"

"And you believe yourself powerful enough to stop him?" This was Lucifer's reply, and one aimed at me.

"That is an answer you will only receive once I meet this asshole on the battlefield, but I think you know me well enough to agree that I am no coward and have never walked away from a fight. For as long as I still have breath in my body and life in my veins, I will stop at nothing before this fucker is dead by my hands!" I told him with a vicious growl, for I could feel my demon speaking on my behalf.

"Spoken like a true Son of the Devil," Lucifer said with a wink and a grin, that made me again want to roll my eyes at his egotistical need to claim my words as being one of his own making.

"Besides, as you have heard by now, I am sure, he has much to live for," Dariush said with his own grin, and one I wanted to punch off his face as I didn't relish the thought of my girl being brought into this.

"Ah yes, finally being granted a fated Chosen One certainly does change things," Lucifer agreed smirking.

"That it does," I gritted out, making him boom with laughter before I snapped,

"Now tell me of the bastard I wanted to kill as Judas, and the one I now…"

"…Vow to kill as Lucius."

CHAPTER THIRTEEN

BLOOD MAP

Lucifer led us from the gallery and into a room that acted as a private office, despite its ominous décor. Another cavernous room carved from the mountain itself, and one that became a contrast of the elements. With its smooth walls, that were white and stark compared to its harsh rocky floor filled with stalagmites. The only way to navigate through the jagged space was via the carved flat pathways that led to different areas.

I briefly looked up, seeing what I expected to find, which was a ceiling full of deadly looking stalactites, that matched those below. As for the furniture in the room, it used the clusters of stalagmites that grew from the ground, with armchairs and small tables that were cut and carved straight from them. But these mounds of mineral deposits that grew from water dripping onto the floor were different shades of red or black. This was thanks to the Hellish minerals that seeped from the rock. Obsidian was the main one, that seemed to liquify in the heat of the mountain and then re-form in these large glass-like shards.

A large collection of these made-up Lucifer's desk, where a smooth black countertop of glass was laid on top of the spikes, with some piercing through the surface. These corner spikes also served a purpose, for they were used as a way to anchor large maps in place for viewing. One of which was currently laid out with jagged shards torn through the paper, preventing it from curling back in on itself.

One glance at it, even from a distance, told me all I needed to know...

Lucifer was preparing for war.

In Tartarus.

Or should I say, in what remained of Tartarus, for it had been all but obliterated after the Blood Wars. But it was at least clear that Lucifer knew more than he was letting on, and that map laid out on his unconventional desk was proof of that.

I shook all the new questions from the forefront of my mind and filed them away for later. No, that conversation would come after I had discovered all I could about my enemy, one unknown from my past. So, I tore my gaze away from the desk and its over the top throne that sat behind it, one made from where the black stalagmites and stalactites had joined to form pillars.

Lucifer led us to the seating area that was as far from comfortable looking as you could get. Pyrope, the blood red mineral, ran like veins in the obsidian, giving the large armchair sized seats the appearance of a black heart pierced by nature's swords. A right angle had been cut out of the thickest part of the cluster for you to sit in, with the arms and back framed with a collection of black and red veined spikes, all reaching different heights. There were nine in total, and all carved in a circle, with Lucifer naturally taking the biggest chair at the head of this spiked ring of seats.

It was then, in this sitting area, that Lucifer told us the life of one Tullus Hostilius and how it connected to the Keepers of Three. Triplets that Lucifer admitted had been yet another failure,

"I soon realised where my past mistakes lay, for I had once believed that strength in battle would also mean strength of heart. Something needed to lead the next generation of vampires, who admittedly, before your rule, had been thorn in my side since their own creation... something, I will add, I did not have a hand in," Lucifer offered freely, when looking at me.

"Why not just eradicate the entire race yourself then, and save yourself the bother?" Dariush asked and I had to admit, it was an answer to a question I too wanted to know, and had since the day he turned me. However, it was also a double-edged blade, for it was one I wasn't entirely sure I wanted to know, given its implications. For we were all Lucifer's creations in a sense, and no one wanted to hear how expendable they were, no matter that the proof of such was currently being rubbed in our faces with the tales of his failures.

But then he surprised us both.

"Because the Gods that create life and then eradicate it when it is not to their liking, is no God worthy of the name!" Lucifer snapped, making me frown in question before asking,

"Is that not what you do?"

"No, it fucking isn't, for if it was, then your second in command would have died centuries ago as a mortal man and without his beast, and your fucked up brother, Matthias, and his mangled Keepers of Three would have been dead the moment they proved themselves unworthy!" Lucifer answered with a bite of anger, and I had to say I was astounded. Perhaps because I had always been under the misconception that Lucifer was the very last God to have morals of any kind, or hold some form of concern for the souls he created or ruled over.

But then, it was undeniable, for Lucifer had kept these failures living. In fact, his solution had always been to cast out those that didn't serve his purpose. Yet still, they lived none the less.

"So, the Horatii brothers sold their souls to you to win the fight their king was too cowardly to fight himself?" Dariush asked, only knowing half of the tale and getting back to the point we were here now, which was to learn more about the enemy we were soon to face.

"Oh, make no mistake, for Tullus Hostilius was no coward. In fact, it was his torturesome actions against another ruler that led him to me in the first place. This was shortly after my failing with the Horatii brothers. A misconception of mine in trying to merge three souls into one, believing this would be enough to make them the strongest of my creations yet."

"*More like the most fucked up,*" Dariush muttered, making Lucifer concur.

"Yes, yes, I think we can all agree that it went wrong," he said impatiently, with a dismissive wave of his hand.

"Yes, and I think they'd agree with that every time they look in a mirror," I said dryly, making Dariush scoff a laugh and add,

"Or tried to wipe their ass… or is it asses?" I gave him a wry grin in return before turning back to the reason we were here.

"I know of the story, what I am yet to discover is what happened next?"

"Indeed," Lucifer answered with a knowing grin, one that made me grit my teeth at the mockery. But well, so long as it got the bastard talking then I didn't give a shit. And thankfully, I got my wish, as after this, he went on to explain more of the tyrant king, Tullus. One whose name literally translated into the word 'hostile', unlike his predecessor Numa Pompilius, who was known as the king of peace, Tullus was known as the king of war. This was a massive contrast from the peaceful king, who promoted above everything the wealth and agriculture of Rome. Someone who had spent his entire rule working towards a Roman way of life where they would not need their swords.

Which meant that as soon as Tullus took the throne, he soon undid much of the good work Numa had put in place. This was because Tullus believed the more peaceful nature of his predecessor had weakened Rome, so as a result, he quickly seized crafting tools from Roman hands and gave them back their weapons. Meaning that Rome became well versed in both the arts of war and peace.

"King Tullus commanded the Horatii to fight, then found out how it was possible for one man left standing to defeat all three of their counterparts, the Curiatii triplets. Of course, when he discovered they had sold their souls for victory, naturally this knowledge made an impression enough to stay with him until such a time when it was needed."

"Well, I think I can see where this is going," Dariush muttered sarcastically, now leaning back in the stalagmite chair as if no more of an explanation was needed. Of course, he was right in some regard as we had both heard of this tyrant king thanks to the Keepers of Three and the research we had both done over the years. But our interest had always been centred on the Horatii and therefore we had no reason to go beyond their victory.

It seems now, however, we were wrong.

Lucifer went on to explain that after the Alban dictator

Mettius Fufetius, lost his fight with the Curiatii triplets, he then had no choice but to enter into a treaty with Tullus. One that would still ensure he would be king to his people, but on the condition that the city of Alba Longa would have no choice but to accept Roman rule. This also meant that should the time arise, and war were to break out from an Etruscan invasion, Mettius would lead the Albans into battle to fight alongside Rome and Tullus as its King of Kings.

However, disappointed by the outcome, Mettius Fufetius later schemed with the Etruscans, having provoked the inhabitants of Veii, convincing them to attack Rome. He did this by making them believe Rome's defences were weak and Tullus' army would be easily defeated with the aid of his own army. But then, when the time came for them to head into battle, King Tullus reminded Mettius of his duty to Rome and demand that he honour the treaty made.

However, unbeknown at the time of his scheming, Tullus went into battle believing it an easy win, for Mettius would bring his men. Yet what he didn't know was that on the day of battle, Mettius slowly withdrew his army and headed up a hilltop to watch the battle commence without his forces, breaking the treaty.

His cowardly intentions were to simply wait until it was over and if the losses were great enough against Rome, he knew fighting the weak would ensure his own victory, meaning he would then charge his army into battle to kill the remainder of the force in his way, so he could claim Rome's rule for himself.

In short, the guy was a fucking snake and the type of spineless ruler I loathed!

Now, as for the outcome, well, history would have told a very different tale that day… had King Tullus not remembered how a single Horatii brother had gained victory against three others. Because like that brother, King Tullus now faced unbeatable odds as his army was outnumbered and close to being defeated. So, making the decision, Tullus renounced his faith and his belief in his Gods, especially that of Jupiter. Then like the Horatii, he sold his soul to Lucifer. when he realised he would surely lose in battle.

"Of course, I accepted this soul of his, for I confess, his connection with the Horatii intrigued me, along with his determination to win his victory. However, it was in his revenge against Mettius where I really took notice, and foolishly believed once more that he may be the one strong enough that I had been searching for." Lucifer went on to explain the continued reign of Tullus and what eventually became of him.

This included his revenge again Mettius Fufetius when he consequently betrayed the Romans in battle. For this treacherous act, Mettius was torn in two by chariots running in opposite directions, tearing him to pieces. The result was naturally fatal and after displaying his remains for all to see, it became a clear warning to all future allies of Rome not to betray its rule again.

Added to this threat, was when Tullus then ordered his forces to destroy the city of Alba Longa after forcing all who lived there to move to Rome, to increase its population. After all, more women, meant more fucking, and more fucking meant more sons to be born and grow with a sole purpose in mind. To become strong enough to hold a weapon in their hands and fight.

"So, he was a brutal tyrant, yeah, yeah, we get the picture, I still don't see how that brought him to you if he didn't die in battle," Dariush commented, making Lucifer grin, as after all, death was his favourite part.

"He sold his soul for a victory, which I granted him in

defeating the Etruscan invasion. However, in his success he became cocky and snubbed the Gods even further, angering them by flaunting his alliance with me," Lucifer said, running a finger along the length of a single black shard close to his carved armrest.

"Hmm... I bet they just loved that," my brother said ironically, and he was right, for this inevitably sealed his fate. Because the God, Jupiter, brought forth a mighty storm after being disrespected for the last time and struck only one place with a bolt of lightning.

The home of one King Tullus.

"It was said that as his home burned to the ground and he was forced to watch all he cared for being destroyed as the flames consumed him, that he cursed the Gods. Cursed them even further, telling them with his last dying breath that he would rise again and challenge them, for his family were also the ones to suffer the wrath of these supposedly Heavenly Gods," Lucifer said with a condescending grin, before adding,

"It was quite touching really."

"Great, so he's a bitter fucker who you thought would make a great addition to the fucked-up family tree," I snapped with a roll of my eyes.

"I am the Devil, Lucius, therefore I am not exactly in the habit of coming into possession of fucking saints," Lucifer replied and well, I guess he had a point. However, I couldn't help but point out,

"Well, the joke was on you then, because he turned into one," I said in a snide comment he laughed at. Because the obvious tale ended with Tullus becoming Matthias after Lucifer got his creative hands on him.

"So, once you turned this bitter bastard, what then?" Dariush asked.

"Simple really, his body rejected my blood and instead of creating what I did in the both of you, I ended up creating something more evil in its place," Lucifer said with a shrug, as if this was an everyday fucking occurrence!

"*Wonderful,*" I muttered sarcastically, whilst my brother pointed out the obvious,

"And there it is… hence the fucked-up family grudge." Lucifer laughed and said with mirth,

"Oh no, that came later, forty-one years later to be precise, and the reason I had him cast out, for he may have been evil, but he wasn't bent on genocide, at least not back then," Lucifer told us with a casual flick of his hand.

"Oh, I have a feeling I am going to regret asking this question, but where did you have him cast to?" Dariush asked, making me look towards the desk and sigh in response to my brother's question. Because I too had a bad feeling I knew the answer.

"Tartarus."

"But of course." I then groaned with a rub of my forehead.

"Why?" Dariush asked, and for the first time during this explanation of historical events, Lucifer looked furious.

"Because in his continued quest for power, now leading his armies under a new name, he had heard of a way to foresee if his conquests would be victorious or not," Lucifer said, gritting his teeth, and when I opened my mouth to say a single name, he stopped me with a hand held up and a clear demonic warning,

"Do not speak her name, for it is mine and mine alone." Of course, he meant Pythia, who was known back then as the Oracle of Delphi. Which meant that the resurrected Tullus had made a fatal mistake, as, unbeknown to him, his father the Devil had long before staked his claim on Pythia. Which

139

meant old daddy dearest didn't take too kindly when, in a fit of rage, his new son had attacked Pythia and nearly killed her.

"Dumb fuck," Dariush commented with a shake of his head after hearing this. And it was true, for even without knowing of her connection to Lucifer, you didn't attack an Oracle. Of course, Lucifer responded to this by dragging him back down to Hell himself, imprisoning him in Tartarus for five hundred years and stripping him of his powers by taking his blood back. Something I hadn't even thought possible.

But it had been too late for Tullus, his actions had led to his demise after laying his hand on what belonged to the Devil. For what she had shown him had been that very thing that kick started this vengeful chain of events. A slice of his future, one which ultimately led him to... Well...

What led him to me.

"Of course, my sweet little Pythia hadn't known at the time what this vision would cause or that he would steal the gift I had made for her," Lucifer mused, now grinning once more when thinking of his Chosen One. As for me, I frowned before asking,

"What gift?" This was when his grin turned cunning, and he spoke with satisfaction at being able to shock me to my core...

"Why, the gift you yourself recently had in your possession... The box, I created for her."

"What the fuck!?" I shouted, before he added with satisfaction,

"Along with a blood-soaked map that would..."

"...Lead me to you."

CHAPTER FOURTEEN

SAINTS AND SINNERS

"You created the fucking box?!" I shouted, before I could stop myself from giving Lucifer what he wanted, which was of course, my reaction. His sadistic grin told me as much.

"I created it for Pythia as a way for her to communicate with me should she ever need anything she couldn't ask me for in her dreams. The origin of my blood is the only thing that can unlock the box, so I would leave it open for her and if she needed me, I would find it closed," Lucifer explained.

"And how exactly was she to communicate with you, it's not like paper was invented back then, and we all remember what papyrus was like to draw on?" Dariush asked, pointing out the first loophole.

"Yes, but as you know, the invention of paper didn't exactly come from Cai Lun, who was about as original as he was human, for where do you think he discovered the modern-day necessity?" Lucifer reminded us, making me sigh,

"The desert marsh lands."

This was a unique place in Hell where the land was a strange mix of wetland and dry barren desert. However, these swamp-like marshes were made from the demons that inhabited the land, known as Afreets. A demon that would eat continuously for months, then when all they needed was absorbed into their body, they then spent days vomiting vast amounts.

This meant that these marshes consisted of a vomited mixture of bark, a plant similar to hemp that grows in the desert, and its own skin that it sheds before eating. This is all mashed into a pulp from the three stomachs and then regurgitated in vast amounts. These giant Afreets were better known from Islamic mythology and in folklore, and were identified as powerful demons or spirits of the dead. Creatures who had the scaly torso of a man, head of a horned lizard and the tail of a snake that had the ability to split in two and become legs. Something that only occurred if they were strong enough after coming to the end of this feeding cycle.

If any of them ever managed to escape into the mortal realm, they were often found inhabiting desolate places such as ruins and temples, yet their true habitat was this desert marsh land in Hell, known as,

AzagKur, which translated meant, the great serpent land.

As for where the paper element came into it, this was discovered after the Afreets would drag the vomited pulp from the swamp. Then they would roll over it with their bodies until it was flat, and all the moisture was sucked from it and absorbed into their skin to keep from it from cracking. After that, it was then left to dry in the scorched heat of the ground before it was used as a nest for the Afreet to call home.

"So, you left your girl dry vomit to write on?" Dariush asked, making me smirk, for as I did, he too knew of these creatures, having killed his fair share of them.

"Well, I certainly didn't leave it for her to fucking eat!" Lucifer growled, making me laugh this time, as pay back was fun when it meant watching Lucifer react to shit thrown his way.

"And Tullus… or Matthias, or whoever the fuck we are calling this guy?!" Dariush snapped, making me scoff.

"Tullus died that night with his family for his crimes against the Gods. After which, I did the same as with all my sons, I renamed him. This time Matthias, as a reminder of the King he had ripped into pieces… for I confess that I thought the exact name would be too cruel," Lucifer said, making me laugh once and mock,

"Too cruel for the Devil, come now, Lucifer, don't tell me becoming a father made you soft?" He grinned at this and said,

"And tell me, just how soft did it feel when I hammered my fist inside your chest and made your heart beat for the first time with my blood in your veins?" Dariush burst out laughing and hit me on the back in jest.

"The old man has you there, Luc!"

"He did the same thing to you to, asshole, or are you forgetting?" I threw back, making Dariush shrug his shoulders and comment,

"For me it tickled."

"I'm sure it did… now, if we could please get back to the box," I replied, letting disbelief coat my tone after first rolling my eyes.

After this, Lucifer went on to explain that the night before Matthias arrived, Pythia dreamed of his future demise. How he was to be eventually cast out by Lucifer, stripped of his bloodline and his demon side, and imprisoned in Tartarus for what should have been eternity. She then saw another vision, and this time it was of me. She knew instantly that I was the one Lucifer had been searching for, the one who would be strong enough to accept his blood the way it was intended.

So, she woke and used the box, first drawing a map of what she had seen in her mind, knowing Lucifer would use his blood the way the box had been intended. But she also wrote down a single name before she sealed the box ready for him.

However, what neither one hadn't intended, was that Matthias would seek out the famous Oracle and ask her about the outcome of an upcoming battle. Although, Matthias got a lot more than he bargained for and when she refused to show him, he took matters into his own hands.

He beat it out of her before weakening her enough so that he could claim the memories for himself. However, he only had access to the future regarding himself, and was cut off with only the merest hint of his replacement being mentioned. This was when he let her go, before he could rid her of her final breath, believing he had already killed her. Then he stole the box, knowing from Pythia's thoughts that with his father's blood, he too could discover who was to be his fated replacement. And thus, what kicked started the fated events that brought us to this point. As Matthias opened the box and discovered the contents.

However, he couldn't understand the map, as he didn't know how to gain the hidden information as Lucifer did. But, he did have my name… and so it seemed that's all he had needed. That, and time. For it was hundreds of years before my mortal birth, as I was nothing more than a mere whisper of the Fates. A future both Lucifer and Matthias would be forced to wait for.

As for what transpired shortly after his attack on Pythia, Matthias put back the map, believing it was useless. Then he destroyed the single piece of paper produced by the Afreets that held the name *Judas Iscariot* inscribed on it.

A name he would never forget.

However, his actions soon caught up with him, for Pythia was not dead as had believed and, although badly beaten, she was only unconscious. Lucifer learnt of the attack, became enraged and discovered who was to soon face his wrath thanks to Pythia's nightmares.

"When I learned who it was that had committed the crime, I had him hunted down by the one I knew was strong enough to bring him to me, so I could drag the fucker back to Hell myself!"

"Let me guess, used to go by the name of Arsaces and be known as the King of Kings in Ancient Persia?" I asked with a knowing grin.

"The one and the very same," he replied.

"So, Dominic drags his sorry ass back to Hell and you throw his beaten remains in Tartarus?" Dariush confirmed.

"That is precisely what happened, for the moment I found the box on his person, he could not lie about having knowledge of the attack anymore, as the proof condemned him."

"So, this box led you to me?" I asked, now knowing of its significance.

"It did, for Pythia still had the name of you burned to memory."

"And Matthias had five hundred years to curse that same name and plan his revenge," I added, clenching of my jaw.

"And the box?" Dariush asked.

"I gifted it back to Pythia," Lucifer replied, which prompted my next question.

"Then how exactly did it end up in Connecticut, two and half thousand years later?"

"Ah, but this was my very question to her after discovering recent events."

"And her reply?" I asked with a roll of my wrist, eager for him to continue.

"She hid it, knowing of its importance, as I had made the box indestructible. Eventually, after years of constantly moving its hiding place it remained undetected until New Haven, Connecticut. I believe this was when Pythia attended Yale University there in one of her quests for a taste at normality," Lucifer said with a dismissive shrug, as if the thought that she should even try was a ridiculous one.

"And by no coincidence, this was then found by Dominic Draven?" I added, knowing the whole thing had been fucking set up from the start, and by the fucking Fates themselves for all I knew!

"I believe that was the start of events that were orchestrated to lead to this very point in time," Lucifer said, taking the thoughts right out of my mind and giving them words.

"So, let me get this straight, this witch who is working for Matthias, gets word to Dominic Draven that there is something hidden, knowing that when he retrieved the box, the one place he would take it to, was his own daughter who is an expert in deciphering ancient text," Dariush said, making me bite my tongue on the other possibility. One that led Pythia to plant it for the events to happen as had been intended, getting Amelia and I working together and therefore finally starting our fated relationship. After all, she was a conduit for the Fates themselves and as their Oracle, if she was asked to do something by the Gods, she obeyed without fully understanding why.

"This then kickstarted the chain of events that eventually brought you both here," Lucifer stated, and I knew he wasn't talking about myself and Dariush this time, but instead as I had feared, he meant Amelia and I. Meaning we had been played from the fucking start. But then, if that was the case, why had the witch seemingly been intent on stealing the box back, if she knew that was what would eventually lead us both here?

I was missing something.

"But why and to what end?" I asked, instead of voicing what was truly on my mind.

"Ah, but this is where it gets even more complicated, I'm afraid," Lucifer said and for once, he didn't look full of glee at the fucking idea of even more shit from the past to throw at us.

"But of course, it does," Dariush muttered with a roll of his eyes.

"After five hundred years imprisoned in Tartarus, unbeknown to me, he escaped using the help of my enemies who wish to see me overthrown. After Ba'al Zəbûb aided him in this, Matthias took possession of a new vessel and situated himself in your mortal life. Seen but truly unknown."

"Basically, he became my new fucking stalker," I growled in response.

"And cue his fucking with your life, brother," Dariush said, making me give him a wry look before I turned my anger to Lucifer, knowing he'd had this information all along.

"Now is the time you explain what else this son of yours meddled in. For all I know of Matthias, is as a fucking saint who took my place as the next apostle… after I caught him fucking my wife and being the lips behind the whispers to the other disciples as to why my head found itself on the end of a fucking noose!" I all but roared this at him, feeling my blood boil with every word, for this was who Matthias had been to me, nothing but a snake lying in wait for the opportunity to take my place. Of course, I had never known his true purpose other than his desire for my wife and that of my position.

Oh, how fucking wrong I had been!

"Alright, my son, but don't say I didn't warn you, for you will not like the account of loathing I am about to tell you." Lucifer's reply didn't exactly inspire confidence that I would come out of this conversation unscathed. For I would no doubt end up festering on a new depth of murderous rage. One that could possibly cause my demon to take over completely in the height of my fury.

"I would be surprised by anything you have to tell me that wouldn't send me into a rage," I commented understatedly, And to give the Devil his due, he wasn't wrong when he said I would not like what he had to say. No, if anything, he was downplaying it, and to say I was murderous was too light a word by the time he was finished.

Especially when I ended up discovering that revenge for being born meant I was to pay in blood and for once, it didn't start with my own.

No, this time, it started with…

The Death of my Daughter.

CHAPTER FIFTEEN

THE ROOT OF ALL DEADLY MISTAKES

It all started when I was mortal, and back in a time I shuddered to even think about. Back to when the name Lucius had not yet risen from the ashes of a Hellish resurrection.

When I bore the name of Judas Iscariot.

In truth, it was a time I barely even remembered, which wasn't surprising considering it was over 2000 years ago. Back when I was just a man, one made from flesh and blood and bones, and believed in something greater than myself. Back when I had put all my faith and trust and loyalty into the one who I thought would really make a difference in the world.

However, stripped down to its bare bones and left with an honest truth I couldn't deny, even now, *Jesus had been my friend.*

He had helped me through hard times. In fact, before Lucifer, he had been the only one who had ever believed I had been destined to do great things. However, I doubted those great things included his vision of me becoming a king of a demonic race of Vampires.

But getting back to mortal times, one where the Romans had been intent on wiping out Christianity, even in its infancy. A time where we both knew that there was only one way to prevent it from happening. Because we knew that the power to make a martyr out of a man was far greater than the power the man possessed himself. A memory could be everlasting and could travel distances of the likes that feet could not take you. Whispered words and legends told would carry along the wind far and wide. But none was more powerful than the tale of injustice and sacrifice. One that spread throughout the world like no other religion before it.

It was in this that I had recognised my calling and believed my sacrifice was worth the reward. Especially after the events that led to that final day. Because I had known the bitter taste of betrayal and found I had little else to live for after what my wife had done. But then, I was soon to discover, she hadn't exactly acted alone.

However, as for the name of Jesus, he would eternally be known as the Son of God, who gave his life for all of humanity and the very meaning of the word sacrifice. And as for the name Judas, well that would become the very meaning of the word betrayal. But then, if I had been granted what had been promised to me by Jesus, then I knew it would have been worth it.

Nevertheless, it was not to be and because of what I perceived as a bitter betrayal, I turned my back on Heaven and all that I had come to believe in. Instead, I put my faith into the Devil who made me. Yet despite knowing the truth of who Lucifer was, I never lost that sense of my true self, even long after I was turned. I knew the difference between right and wrong. I didn't kill women or children and even in war, I tried to spare as many as possible. I did not relish murdering innocent people or punishing those willing to steal to feed their families, for I too would never forget what it felt like to be hungry. I was neither a tyrant nor a dictator. Not like the bastard I had killed in Germany, who wanted to commit genocide against the Jewish people for some sick and twisted personal reasons of his own.

But more importantly, I was nothing like my brother Matthias, when he had been known as Tullus. This, Lucifer explained, was what had been missing in all his other failures before me. That shred of mortality that wouldn't leave my soul, and instead strengthened the part of himself Lucifer gifted me when giving me his blood. It was this that was morphed into something powerful and pure. Something that could be passed on and do the same with the seemingly soulless demons of the Vampire race.

But it was also why, as soon as the deed was done, I gave up my throne and went in seek of another King that I could pledge my loyalty to.

Dominic Draven.

But this was my side of the story and one I already knew well enough, despite the years that had passed since. However, the part I was here to discover was when Matthias broke free from Tartarus.

Lucifer then explained how he had believed Matthias may have been the key, being that Matthias had turned his back on the Gods, just like I had done with my own dying breath. However, the difference between the two of us was that my heart was not black and bitter and filled with the roots of rage. Matthias had a growing hatred for mortals, that in the ended prevented him from accepting Lucifer's blood in the way that it was meant to be accepted. Oh, it gave him power but not one over the vampire race like Lucifer intended.

Matthias knew this, and grew bitter at the thought of his father seeking out another to take the place of his latest disappointment. A bitterness that only grew and grew, doing so as a poison in the very grounds of Tartarus. A place that would only ever nurture his hatred and help form it into something deeper... something with purpose. A poison I had unknowingly released while sacrificing my hand and using the Venom of God to keep the Titans imprisoned.

This was what had infected the Tree of Souls.

Matthias' power had been drained in Tartarus by Lucifer, as a way to keep him imprisoned. Literally the roots of Tartarus had been dug from the ground by Lucifer himself and wrapped around Matthias' body. Once secured there, those roots had kept him bound for five hundred years and continued to suck the dark essence from him, rendering him without power. A power he wanted back more than anything, and after what I had done that day to save the world from the Titans, it meant I had inadvertently given him a way. For I had unknowingly released this darkness into the very roots of the Tree of Souls, and given him a means of claiming what was once his...

That, and more.

Because five hundred years was a long time to plan for revenge. And with time on his hands, he merely had to wait for when the moment was finally right, before breaking from his infected prison with only one thing on his mind... *a way to darken my soul.* Because after what Pythia had shown him, he knew the reasons why his turning had been a failure in the eyes of his maker.

His soul was rotten.

Which was why he believed all he needed to do was pull the strings of my fate enough that my soul would be beyond saving. Because Matthias knew the very moment he had reached that point and what it took for him to turn his back on everything that had once made him human.

The death of his family.

"You knew of all of this and you didn't once tell me?!" I roared, now getting out of my seat in the mist of my anger, and knowing I now had more than that of my wife's memory to place the blame to my greatest loss.

"I discovered this, yes, but seeing as his actions backfired and this served my purpose, I felt no need to tell you… not until this day." Lucifer had the audacity to say, and I swear, had my brother not then got to his feet to hold me back, I would have most likely died trying to strangle Lucifer to death!

"Not until it serves your own purpose once more, you mean!" I snapped.

"It is true, but this Matthias has become a far bigger problem than I ever envisioned him to be."

"You can fucking say that again!" Dariush growled this time, for words now failed me. Then he pulled me back and I allowed him, knowing that putting space between us was a wise decision seeing how close to the edge my demon was from trying to tear Lucifer's fucking head off!

"Luc, I know you want to tear into him right now but doing so would defeat half the reason we are here," Dariush warned.

"Yeah, and what the fuck is that!?" I barked back.

"Convincing him we were not here to challenge him," he said pointing out facts.

"Yes, well that was before I discovered he knew all these years WHO KILLED MY CHILD!" I roared, with my demon erupting for even a split second as this was directed at Lucifer, someone who looked completely unfazed.

"Yes, and I think we both know that the best way to get

revenge on the one responsible, is to discover what his next play is going to be and what he intends to do with the Eye of Janus," Dariush said calmly, but it was at this point Lucifer sat up straighter and took greater interest.

"So, he has in his possession the Eye of Crimson?"

"Yes, and I believe his plan is to use the Eye to transfer not only the souls into his possession, but also now the power that was taken from him in Tartarus… something I am thankful to say, he cannot do without my blood," I stated after getting myself back under control and shrugging off my brother's hold. Lucifer regarded me for a moment before adding even more fucking shit to the Matthias pile!

"No? Then ask yourself, if that is the case then why is he so intent on getting your Chosen One?" Lucifer's question suddenly had my veins filling with ice, but then I took a deep breath and told him,

"It matters not, for I have sent her back to the mortal realm where her father can protect her."

"Wise choice indeed," Lucifer replied with a smirk.

"Great, now that's all sorted, can we please just get on with finding this fucker, so we can cut his head off already?" Dariush growled.

"Matthias cannot leave Hell for long periods of time, but seeing as my hunt for him has been unsuccessful all these years, it leaves only one place left," Lucifer replied with a frustrated sigh, obviously pissed that he hadn't yet been able to get his hands on him.

"And where in Hell would that be?" my brother asked after slapping his hands to his knees when retaking his seat.

"Somewhere caught between the mortal world and Hell, and there is only one place I can think of…" Before he even had time to say it, I was roaring a curse, load enough this time that stalagmites cracked and fell from the ceiling, crashing to the floor.

"FUCK!"

Then this time my veins didn't just turn to ice, my heart actually felt like it had frozen, before then shattering into a million fucking pieces!

Because it was like Lucifer had said, there was only one place like that he could hide. A place forbidden to both mortals and Demons.

And unfortunately for me, it was also the one place that I had just sent my fucking Chosen One to…

"The Tree of Souls!"

CHAPTER SIXTEEN

AMELIA

BETRAYAL

"*Forgive me, Gods forgive me.*"

That had been the last thing I heard before Lucius had literally pushed me from his life, making me scream out in both heartbreak and anger,

"NO!" I shrugged out of the hold of whichever lackey Lucius had ordered to aid him in his deception. Then I hit my hand out against the cave wall where there had been a portal a heart-breaking second ago.

"DAMN YOU! DAMN YOU! Damn you, Lucius... *damn you!*" I cried at the end, letting my words trail off with the depth of my hurt. One that seemed to carve deeper into the very core of me. Then his other words started to seep through from memory, and I winced again in pain.

'Please remember how much I love you. Never forget, Amelia, never forget how much, promise me.'

"Hhhow... how could you... *how could you do this to*

me?" I asked the stone wall when Clay approached me from behind.

"Amelia."

"Don't… just don't!" I snapped after pushing away from the wall, only now seeing where it was that we were.

The fucking Tree of Souls!

The cause of all this fucked up mess!

I looked up at the colossal tree and grimaced as two leaves fell and turned to ash before they hit the floor. Two more souls lost, and yet that single flower was still there… *surviving.* The single rose that represented the part of me Lucius had stolen all that time ago. Well, now it just felt like another betrayal, only this time one he had been in control of.

But then wasn't this our pattern?

A pattern that I myself had started that very day when I had been the first to walk away. Gods, but why did it have to be this way? This push and pull, this give and take that seemed to be a constant in our relationship. I looked back to that tree, seeing the portal there that had started my Hellish journey, one that felt like a fucking lifetime ago!

The portal he had begged me not to step through. And what had I done… I had made that first step that led our lives down that ruined path! Fuck, but I didn't know who to hate more, him or me! Was that the reason he hadn't given me the chance to beg him in return as he had done to me that day? To beg him not to do this. Beg him not to cut me out and carry on without me.

Because I had known exactly what that kiss had been, for it was not only a goodbye for now… no, but it was also something far more heart-breaking.

It was an eternal kiss goodbye.

It was the kiss that said that he would always love me. The one given in case he didn't succeed, and all was lost.

Which I now knew included not only his life, but my own. For my soul was eternally entwined with his and it always had been from that very first moment I tied myself to him. My soul was his and always would be until the day I died. Something he thought he could protect me from by casting me through this portal and tricking me.

Well, fuck that!

If he thought that I was just going to leave from here and let him face this alone then he was wrong!

"Fuck this!" I snapped before walking over to that same portal which had started this, only to find myself blocked by about 200 pounds of raw power wrapped in a sexy black man's package... *his body that was.*

"Get out of my way, Clay!" I practically growled.

"Yeah, that's not gonna happen, Princess," he answered quickly, making me want to snarl like a damn cat back at him.

"You don't get to tell me what I can and cannot do," I told him.

"Actually, that's where you're wrong, as it's our asses on the line here, and I am not just talking about what Luc would do to us if he found out you walked back into to Hell," he informed me in that sexy deep voice of his.

"Oh, and who else are you..."

"Your father," he stated, making me gasp.

"My father?" I questioned in shock.

"Look, just do me a favour and read this before you decide to get our asses kicked by doing something rash when you are obviously hurt and not thinking straight," he said, pulling a rolled-up piece of parchment paper from beneath his leather jacket. He then nodded down to it when I didn't take it, still too shocked to act. Lucius had called my father?

But of course, he had. After all, knowing Lucius, he

would no doubt believe that being back at Afterlife would be the safest place for me.

"Go on, little bird, go ahead and take it," Clay said, as I was just staring at it as though it was an emotional bomb he held in his hand. One I knew would go off and blow up in my face the second I read it. But despite this, I did as he asked and took it anyway because I knew what he said was true. Any decision I made now was one I would be making in an emotional state and if the past had taught me anything, then acting on heartbreak was never a good idea.

So, I nodded, taking it from him and then turning around and finding a small rock to sit on whilst I unrolled my fate.

One that read...

My Amelia,

My love, my soul mate, my very reason for living, please know that writing this letter is one of the hardest things I have ever had to do. One I know that will shortly take second place after I am forced to say goodbye and let you go. Because asking for forgiveness when you don't yet forgive yourself is like a tainted hope. But nevertheless, I will ask it of you anyway, because as you know, I am a selfish being when it comes to you, my sweet, troublesome little princess.

So, I ask of you, Amelia, please forgive me.

You have to know that I had no choice but to say goodbye this way. I know you are hurt and most likely feel as though I betrayed you, but you have to know that was never my intention. I would never betray our love, but I will always put your safety first.

This, even more so after all we have been through, because I know with a certainty deep into my bones, that I cannot watch you die again. I cannot lose you, for I would not survive such a loss. I can barely survive the memory of it, one that will forever haunt me. A ghost I need to rid myself of and the only way I know how, is to eradicate our enemies once and for all. To kill the threat and win this war. Which means, my love, going somewhere you cannot follow.

So, you may hate me, you may damn me or curse my name, but Amelia, I promise you with every breath I take, that I will do everything in my power to come back to you. And when I do, I will spend the rest of eternity gaining your trust once more.

But until then, I have no other choice but to entrust your safety back to your father and as much as it pains me, I know that if you remained by my side, I would only be putting you in danger. So, I ask you, Amelia, in fact, to hell with my fucking pride, for I beg of you not to let my painful decision to let you go be in vain. I ask of you to go with my men and let them deliver you to the one man I trust with your life. The one who holds enough power to keep my heart safe, for you take it with you always.

Please, do this for me, and reward my love for you with proof of your own by keeping that love alive long enough for me to claim it once more.

For I have never loved until there was you.

I have never allowed my heart to beat until it beat for you, and I have never taken breath before there was your beauty to steal it.

I love you and will forevermore until the end of days and beyond.

Yours eternally
    Lucius.

Ps... I am coming back for you.

As soon as I finished reading his letter it wasn't surprising that my face was wet, and I had tears appearing faster than I could wipe them away. It also meant that when I was looking down at Lucius' words, they started to blur as those same tears landed on the proof of his love, showering them with my own.

"*Oh, Lucius,*" I muttered on a sigh, now gripping the letter to my chest, knowing that despite being angry, I also understood his reasons. After all, I had done the very same when trapped in that nightmare world and was afraid of him seeing what I may become. I had wanted to spare him the pain of failure should I not have been able to contain the darkness and prevent it from consuming me.

Because the truth was, that the things we do for love weren't always so black and white. It was not as simple as choosing between right and wrong. It was about doing what was in your heart at the time, and that sometimes means acting on your emotions and on your fears. Which was precisely what Lucius had done. He had been terrified of losing me again, and he was now doing what he thought was the only way to prevent that from happening again.

It hurt.

Fuck me, did it hurt!

But when the decision was made out of love, then it certainly took the sting out of that hurt. So, it was at this point that I knew I had to get up and do what Lucius had asked of me. Otherwise, what good was all this heartache, one I knew was affecting us both.

Which meant I needed to trust in his decision and believe he was doing the right thing, despite how much I hated it.

Because I wanted to be fighting by his side and see this through together, right to the very end.

But I also knew that Lucius could potentially get hurt or lose the fight if he had me to worry over. Because back in the King's office when fighting the Wraiths, it had been his concern for me that had kick-started the deadly chain of events. In fact, it had been our concern for each other. He had taken his eyes off the threat and I had reacted without thought when throwing that blade. Now, if we had been working together as a team, then maybe it wouldn't have turned out that way. But then again, that age old saying the Fates loved so much, was that everything happened for a reason?

And speaking of Fates, I couldn't help but look up now and wonder where the Keepers of Three were. So, I folded up his letter, knowing nothing could make me part with it, and tucked it into the pocket that was hidden in the folds of the skirt to my dress. Then I located Clay who had moved closer to Ruto and Caspian, obviously to give me space.

"Where is my father?" I asked after walking their way. Clay jerked his head to the side, gesturing behind him before telling me,

"Luc got word to him to wait by the tree topside, warning him of the potential rogues."

"So how did you guys get here?" I asked, curious to know.

"Dariush created a portal and basically told us that Luc wanted our asses in Hell. Besides, I never even knew this fucking place existed but from what Dariush told us, you can't get down here without Luc's blood, so your father should be waiting at the surface."

"Right," I said taking a step in the right direction, only one look back at the portal in the centre of the Tree and I felt suddenly torn. Just the thought of Lucius fighting against his brother, one he hadn't even known he had until recently, and I paused in my steps. But then, as I was looking around the colossal space, one dominated by that weeping tree, I started to get a bad feeling creeping along my spine.

Because there was still something missing, and that answer wasn't as obvious as my boyfriend. No, it was the eerie quiet that struck me as odd, seeing as the four of us were here inside this sacred temple with the Tree of Souls, and yet its Keepers were nowhere to be found.

"Err… Clay"

"Yeah?" He too paused, and looked back over his large shoulder and down at me.

"I don't suppose since having my freak out, girly moment, you happened to come across the Keepers of Three, did you?" He frowned at this question, one I believed important enough to ask.

"Who?" That in itself was answer enough.

"I think we might have a problem," I stated as that creeping along my spine turned into a full out shiver.

"Why do you say that?" he asked, now looking back towards the tree as if expecting to find something there watching us.

"Erm, well, let's just say that if you had met them, you would know exactly who I was talking about, as they're somewhat unforgettable, if you know what I mean," I told him, now looking around the cavernous space and trying to listen out for their distinct sound of fate-filled ramblings. One that usually ended in a murmured slur of words you could never understand. Clay motioned for the others to come closer, not having to say anything but flick two fingers to the side, telling them to split up and look.

But despite the protection they offered, the moment I heard an echoing clap and knowing thunder of laughter, I knew that we had been too late. Because this hadn't come from the Keepers of Three.

Which meant that Lucius hadn't saved me from the Hellish wolves like he believed.

No, this time…

He had mistakenly thrown me to them.

CHAPTER SEVENTEEN

AN ANGEL CAN BLEED

"*It's a trap,*" I whispered to Clay, who gritted his teeth.

But then, this soon became obvious as Matthias walked out from behind one of the colossal pillars, still clapping. I couldn't help but inwardly shudder at the sight, knowing he was the one responsible for it all. Well, him and his witch, I thought, wrinkling my nose and wondering where she was.

As for Matthias, well, he stood tall and proud, with that air of arrogance to him that spoke of power. He wore a dark red, long-sleeved tunic style jacket that had a wide V shaped panel down the front of black metal. I suppose this acted as some protection across his chest, and also held numerous belts and straps across his muscles.

His torso tapered down at the waist thanks to the thick belts he wore that held weapons, one of which that looked like a spearhead that extended from thick rings and plates of silver. Underneath the long tunic jacket that reached his knees, were a pair of thick, dark trousers and boots that were plated up to his knees.

I followed the lines of thick leather straps covering his torso that led to a large shoulder piece. It was a silver-coloured leather armour that looked inscribed with demonic symbols and runes. Attached to this were armoured sections running down the full length of his arm until they met with a black gauntlet-covered hand. And well, there was one thing for certain, *he looked ready for war.*

Attached to this strange-coloured leather armour was a hood, that cast parts of his face in an eerie shadow, although I could see more of his features this time. A face that looked aged, not just with time, but through the knowledge of being an obvious outcast from his father. His greyish beard was trimmed to a point, and speckled with black. He had a prominent nose, high cheekbones and dark eyes that were hooded under a prominent brow. It gave him the appearance of a knowing look, as if he had delved into all of your secrets and could read your mind.

"I must say, I was sceptical when Dalene told me she could get you back to the Tree of Souls, but here you are, just like she promised. But then again, Lucius is nothing if not predictable." I sneered at him as he approached and said,

"Ah, and let me guess, this is the part in the movie where you talk smack about my boyfriend, tell us your evil plan and then we fight, get away, and then stop your psycho ass at the end with minutes to spare... that sound about right?" I nudged Clay who had his massive arms folded and with a nod, said,

"Yeah, sounds right to me, Princess."

Matthias obviously didn't take too kindly to my smart mouth as he scowled back at me, as if he was a busted vein away from possessing the power to drill a hole in my head. But then, I was annoying like that, because what these egotistical bad guys wanted to see was us cowering in fear and begging for mercy. But what he got in me was a smart mouth and an army of three stood by my side.

Though I couldn't help wondering what we must have looked like, as we stood in a line facing the enemy. There was Ruto, who looked like a teenage punk, dressed all in black and looking more ready for a rock concert than a kick ass fight. He rolled his slim shoulders and as always, his fingers worked a blade in between them as was his habit. Yet his bright turquoise eyes didn't seem to miss a thing as they homed in on the enemy, just waiting for him to make the first move against us. He even tapped one of his studded army boots impatiently on the cracked floor. One where you could just see the black infected roots beneath that had lifted and cracked the stone slabs above.

As for Caspian, as usual he looked unimpressed, with his unnerving white eyes ringed with black and the dot of his pupil in the middle, making you sense the danger within him. His hair was like metal wire, pulled back from his forehead and held at the base of his skull in a twisted man bun. High cheekbones and features filled with metal piercings gave him the bad ass appearance, tattoos and metal, like the bar at the bridge of his nose, ring at the centre of his lip and silver balls either side of his chin. He had the height of Ragnar and the muscle to go along with it.

I confess, I always wondered what he was, questioning whether he was like Ragnar and one of the great Devourers. They were known to be exceptionally large, so it would make sense. As for what he wore, black strips were wound around his hands as if he was about to step out of a club into an alleyway, ready for a dirty street fight. These matched the thick leather cuffs attached to his forearms, and a black Tshirt with a faded grey skull in the centre, along with a pair of dark jeans and biker boots completing the look.

Clay, on the other hand, was stood in the middle with his arms folded, just waiting for Matthias to make his move and looking bored whilst doing it. Of course, this didn't detract from the fact that he was still the most gorgeous black man I'd ever seen, and with those unusual navy-blue eyes of his, he could quite literally melt the panties off any girl they chose to grace with their gaze. A strong square jaw and chiselled features combined with a body that looked as if it had been crafted from the Gods themselves, made him any girl's wet dream. It made me wonder if, on a normal day, these guys just lived in a gym, or did they inhabit a vessel and turn it into a contestant for the sexiest man alive competition overnight!

Well, whoever ended up with all that tall, dark and gorgeous would be one lucky girl, that was for sure. As for me, I would be a lucky girl if I got out of this alive and made it back to my own tall, blonde, and handsome in one piece. After I kicked his ass first for pushing me through that portal to begin with... oh yeah, I was putting him on his ass for that one!

But there was still yet one thing about these three that I didn't know, and that was their supernatural sides. Of course, I had seen glimpses of the strength and power in them when fighting back at Transfusion after the first attack. But I had a feeling I was about to get a lot more than just a glimpse this time.

Speaking of things to come, I couldn't help but question how Matthias knew we were coming here.

"Ah, but I can see that question playing in your mind, girl," he mocked, making me want to bare my teeth at him at the term 'girl' being said like an insult!

"It is simple, you are his only weakness." I frowned before snapping,

"Or I am his strength?" At this, he laughed before he cast a hand and said,

"Then, if that be so, why are you here? For surely he would want to keep that strength with him, not cast it to what he foolishly believes is safety." And this I couldn't argue against, and I fucking hated it!

"I knew my brother would believe this the one place safe enough for you to return to the mortal world. After all, it was proven that not all portals could be trusted."

"Because you found a way to control Dariush," I said, knowing this to be true. Again, he grinned that sadistic smirk of his.

"He most certainly had his uses and well, seeing as you are here, I would say he still does." Clay was the one to growl this time and remind him,

"And she didn't come alone, asshole."

"Oh, but neither did I, Geryon," he sneered, making me shoot a look to Clay, silently asking if this was what he was?! He shrugged his shoulder at my response, as if being the grandson of Medusa and the nephew of Pegasus was no big deal. Of course, what I knew of the mythology was that Geryon was the son of Chrysaor and Callirrhoe, and was known as a fearsome giant who dwelled on the island of Erytheia of the mythic Hesperides, in the far west of the Mediterranean. Oh, and he was often described as a monster with either three bodies and three heads, or three heads and one body, or even three bodies and one head… basically a combination of lots of heads, arms, or bodies and well, you get the picture.

"But bringing you here was ironic really," Matthias mused with a grin, making me want to roll my eyes.

"Yeah, and why is that dickhead?" Clay asked, purposely keeping his tone even and to the point of sounding almost bored. Yet I knew differently, as I could see the navy-blue material of his long-sleeved Tee, straining around his huge biceps. Even the stone washed denim around his thighs looked close to splitting, making me wonder just how far away he was from erupting into his other form.

"Well, seeing as he believed this the safest place for Dariush to bring you, when in actual fact he was walking you straight into the place I call home. But I must confess, it was quite touching seeing your little display of love and loyalty... I especially liked it when you broke his heart and walked through the portal," Matthias said, making me snap and as I took a step forward in my anger, I felt Clay's large hand at my belly stopping me.

"It was you! You were behind it all!?"

"But of course, and I must say what easy strings you both had to find and pull on. Like I said, predictable really," he said with a knowing smirk as he knew his words were getting to me.

"Of course, the Keepers of Three were very useful in showing you what I wanted you to see. It being enough to send you on your merry way into Hell and exactly where I wanted you."

"They showed me Lucius' past, asshole, not something you planted!"

"Oh, indeed, but they could have showed you so much more. However, it must be said, my dear, you played your part exceedingly well. Impressive really, it was almost as though you were following a script you did not know that I'd written." This time when I took a step closer I did so with the intention of hitting the bastard, which was why Clay banded an arm around me and held me back more forcefully this time, making Matthias start laughing.

"He will know, and Lucius will come for me!" I threatened, making him clap his hands once more, before leaning forward and telling me,

"Oh, my dear, I am counting on it."

"Can I kill this fucker now?" Ruto said in a bored tone that told me he had better things to do.

"Fuck yes, please do!" I shouted, and the second this was out of my mouth Ruto let one of his blades fly straight towards the head of Matthias. I held my breath as I followed its path, one that would have flown true by embedding itself into his skull. But unfortunately, this didn't happen and instead, we were unfortunately rewarded with a slight taste of Matthias' power. For he raised a single fingertip, stopping the blade mid-air before he touched the tip and it turned to ash, just like the leaves that continued to fall from the Tree of Souls. In fact, it was exactly like that, making me question, was he the reason the souls had been infected?

Regrettably this was one question that was to be answered in the worst possible way.

With proof.

"Oh shit," I muttered, making Ruto look at me and say,

"You wanna try with a pencil?" Then he winked at me, and that proof of power I was afraid to see came after Ruto delivered first on his own. Because he suddenly erupted into his other form, surprising me with the sheer raw beauty of it. First came the bone structure of large wings that folded from his back, almost like some boned creature was trying to claw its way out.

Then as they stretched out, a silver energy worked its way up his body, like electricity slithering up over his dark trousers as if he was drawing it from some holy place that followed him. It continued to flow until it centred at his chest, building there for a few seconds before it shot outwards in a ball of light that consumed him. I blinked back the light, before what was left in its place was Ruto with a set of wings like no other. Thousands of metal shards, triangular in shape, now created a network of slatted silver feathers that forged over his bones, giving him a full set of metal wings. This happened in seconds before he lifted himself up in the air and shot his wings forward with an ear-piercing scream. This caused a blizzard of metal shards to shoot from his wings and head in the direction of Matthias.

But then suddenly the floor beneath us started to shake, as it turned out Ruto wasn't the only one with immense power. Matthias lifted his hands up and with this action, the roots beneath him suddenly broke through the slabs of stone. This meant that by the time the soaring blades came close to him, they were stopped by a line of defence protecting him and taking the impact from every single knife-edge. At least thirty of them were now embedded in the infected roots and with a quick twist of his wrist, these blades all too turned to ash, floating away like ignited paper.

My gaze shot up to Ruto, who was shaking his head in confusion as if he couldn't believe what had just happened. And for the first time, there was a dint in that cocky and confident amour he wore, and a real fear took over his features.

But then, as quickly as it appeared, it was replaced by pure rage. And in his fury, his young handsome features twisted into something frightening. Light behind his eyes burned white hot and with a vicious roar, he outstretched his wings one last time. This created another blinding light and this time, hundreds of feathers all rained down on Matthias like Heaven's wrath was falling from the sky.

"RAHHHH!" The echoing bellow of rage shook the Temple, making me fear for the cracks that travelled the walls, praying they would stop before they hit the ceiling and the entire place crumbled down on us. However, that deadly assault soon took precedent over my mind as I watched the flash of silver hurtling towards Matthias like a metal rain cloud.

But just when I thought Ruto would win the fight, as there weren't enough roots to cover every inch of Matthias, something happened. Suddenly the witch seemed to appear from nowhere and created a powerful dome of blue light that formed a protective forcefield around him. It was then that time seemed to slow down, to the point that even my own screams of panic seemed stretched and muted towards the end. This was because every single bladed feather that came from Ruto had hit this magical barrier and was now travelling back at him at even greater speed.

"RUTO, LOOK OUT!" I heard my next cry, but it was too late as soon he was attacked by his own force, hitting him with the power of the Gods that had made him!

This forced his body back against the stone wall, pinning him there like a broken insect. His eyes looked shocked, before they began to glaze over as they lowered down to take in our horrified faces, as if silently asking us how it had happened. His body was held suspended above us, stabbed by every single blade he threw, and the blood poured from his body as if it was being drained from him.

"NO! No, no, no!" I kept saying over again like this wasn't happening... *it couldn't be happening!*

I vaguely heard the demonic roars of anger both coming from Caspian and Clay, but it was drowned out by the pain at seeing Ruto hanging there as the life was pouring from him. But then he smiled down at me, and I could just see through the blur of my tears, as he mouthed something silently at me.

Then his head slumped forward as he lost the fight of life once and for all.

As those last words of his came too late…

Ruto was dead.

CHAPTER EIGHTEEN

A GERYON AND A MINOTAUR WALK INTO A BAR

"No... no... NOOOO!" I whispered, muttered, and then screamed in an angry flood of tears. Just the sight of him hanging there, as if he had just been sacrificed, had my heart breaking and tears barely drowning out the painful sight. But my anguish was drowned out by the roar of fury from Clay and Caspian at seeing their comrade die before them.

"YOU WILL PAY FOR THAT!" Caspian bellowed.

"His revenge will be seen this day!" Clay growled out with such depth the sound was born straight from Hell itself.

"Bring me the brothers!" Matthias suddenly demanded in response to these threats, and my early question of where the Keepers of Three were, was answered. As the witch waved her hand over a spot next to her on the wall, suddenly the broken and beaten remains of the Keepers appeared, chained against the stone.

"It is time I rewarded them with a promise kept, for they have served me well. But they will serve me better as the warriors they once were!" he said, before raising up his arms as roots shot up and took hold of the twisted limbs of all the combined brothers. The roots then started to literally pump some kind of Hellish essence right into them. It looked like liquid darkness being forced into their combined body and at the same time, the witch started casting a spell over them. I could see their mangled muscles tense, and the strain on their faces as they tried to contain the pain until it became too much. All three of them screamed in agony, something that only stopped when Matthias shot his fingers out, mimicking the actions of the roots as they stabbed each of the brothers in the heart.

"I have a bad feeling about this," I muttered as this spell the witch was casting seem to increase. It was as if she was drawing this power from the ground with one hand and casting with the other. She was forging it into what she needed and combining it with the power she gained from the poisoned roots, creating something new. A thick blue haze started to surround the broken bodies, until eventually it overtook the entirety of the rock wall. After this, all that could be seen was the rising shadows behind as if each of them was growing into something truly monstrous.

"Caspian, I think it's time we show Amelia here just what we're made of." Caspian nodded with a grunt in answer before bending over and curling in on himself as if drawing forth his own power, but he wasn't the only one, as an almighty roar of three bellowed from the veil of cloud that covered them.

"Go, my brothers! Take what is yours back from the Devil who stole it from you! FIGHT FOR ME!" Matthias shouted with a disconcerting, sinister grin on his face. This was all that was needed before three bodies erupted from the bellows of smoke that contained them and suddenly, we were faced with three giant men standing at least ten feet tall!

"Oh shit!" I cried, as each of them had been split from the confines set against them years ago. Now, as their own version of themselves, they ran at us across the vast space of the temple. Yet, despite this change in their appearance and giving them back use of their own limbs, it was still not enough to change them completely. As one was still blind, one was still deaf, and one could not speak. This was thanks to the damage that remained from where the hands of its brothers had once been forced to incapacitate the senses. The one who could not speak had his jaw hung useless and broken. The one whose fingers had once been embedded in its eye sockets, only had bloody holes left gaping and beyond use. The same went for the one who was deaf, as his ears had been completely torn off. However, each of them had their own monstrous bodies that were charging straight at us.

This was when all Hell broke loose.

Starting when Clay forced me back with an arm banded across my chest, one that had already started to change into something else.

"Stay back, little bird, let us handle this," he told me as his voice turned into one that became deep enough to have belonged to the Devil himself.

"But look! What are we going to do! There is only the three of us!" I shouted, knowing that I would need to get a grip and join in the fight. But then Clay took a step away from me and looked over his shoulder, telling me,

"Yes, *but I am not only one man.*" Then he winked at me as those unusual navy-blue eyes seeped into the whites of his eyes and the whites took over the iris. This swapped the two around and left something more demonic in its place. Then the rest of him started to change, as power rippled across his dark body like something was moving underneath his skin. He roared as he threw his body backwards as if his spine was being cracked back at an unnatural angle. His head was so far back that if he had opened his eyes, he would have been able to see behind him as his neck grew thicker and longer.

"Gods," I uttered, then as I briefly took my eyes off him, I saw Caspian had completed his change and was now running into the three brothers who now resembled demonic warrior giants. However, due to thousands of years relying on each other, their movements were subdued and shaky as they hadn't walked without the aid of their brothers. They banged and knocked into the sides of their kin like giant lumpy toddlers taking their first steps as they tried to charge towards us.

Their skin was like old baked leather that split at the increase of muscles beneath, and huge growths that looked like tumours mottled the surface all over their bodies. What little cloth was left from their change clung to parts of them in strips, reminding me of Bruce Banner when he changed into the Hulk. Although, purple pants wouldn't have helped in making these guys look any better or any less gruesome, that was for damn sure!

But these shaky steps then meant that Caspian had a greater advantage as he was more than steady… oh, and he was also a freaking Minotaur!

"*No way!*" I uttered, in complete awe at the sight of what Caspian was. Most of his body was covered in that same wiry silver hair that had looked so unusual in his mortal form. But not like this. Hair that was thicker at his back, running from the top of his head and down the centre of his spine. As for the rest of him, his arms were bulging with muscles under a light grey skin, speckled with the same fur. He also now possessed the massive head of a bull that matched the rest of him, as he had doubled in size!

I also now understood all the piercings, as even in this

form he was covered in them. A thick silver ring hung from his nostrils, along with rings in his ears and even one looked to have been drilled straight through one of the giant bull's horns. These thick horns stretched out from the sides of his head, and the one that wasn't pierced was decorated with thick silver cuffs. These were inscribed in demonic symbols that looked fused to the horn. He had the hands of a man but the hooves of a bull. These were thick and black, and currently stomped into the ground creating deep grooves as he charged towards the three brothers. Then, when he was close enough, he butted his head from side to side and his massive bull's head sent at least two brothers flying, thanks to his gigantic horns.

But in the seconds it took me to watch this happen was when Clay had started his own change, and the moment he did, I was left stunned once more. Because what Matthias had said was true, I was really in the presence of a Geryon.

But then I couldn't exactly say he was what I expected after reading about him in my parents' library. For starters, there were as many bodies as I had been expecting and as for heads, well two demonic skulls now sat either side of his shoulders that faced the sides. These also appeared to be alive as they snapped their jaws in sight of the enemy as if they wanted a bite.

Both were horned, and these framed the horns on top of Clay's head, making it look like two curled X's either side. Added to this new form was that of a scorpion's tail that ran down the centre of his back in large black segments, creating that of a new spine. Then, keeping with the scorpion theme, there were the two arms that came from his shoulder blades that were more animal. This was down to the hard black skin and large pincers that came with the moveable claw that snapped against the fixed one beneath. These rose up high above his head and reached out at the sides, ready for the attack.

As for his own arms, these doubled in size, and combined with these were two more arms coming from the back of his ribcage, that were purely demonic and full of claws. His legs also changed, becoming more like the hind legs of a beast and I soon knew why. This happened after he started walking towards Matthias, telling me,

"Stay here, I've got this!" Then he began running before dropping to his four arms and charging towards him with his tail and pinchers held high, ready to strike.

I pressed my body back against the stone pillar, knowing that I had to let them both fight without worrying that I would be caught in the crossfire. But I also knew I needed to be ready to call forth my own powers, despite my lack of experience, as making a single ball of energy in a make-believe field wasn't exactly what I could call pro level yet. But hey, it was all I had, so I tried to call it forth now so I would be ready.

Only for some reason… it never came.

"What the fuck is wrong with me! Come on!" I shouted at myself, now waving my hands in front of me as if this would help in kick starting them or something.

But an angry roar soon had my head snapping up to find the Keepers of Three, who had now been transformed into Hellish versions of their past lives as warriors, rising from where they had been knocked aside by Caspian's other form. The deaf one glanced at one of the many lanterns lighting the temple, before he ripped free one of the flaming discs. Then, with an angry war cry, he spun it through the air like a discus, with a tail of flames following it as the oil inside spun from the surface. This managed to hit Caspian in the chest, making that massive bull go crashing backwards into the stone.

"Caspian!" I shouted, unable to help myself, whereas for Clay, his Geryon side continued to go charging towards the man himself responsible for all of this. But Matthias drew forth the power from the roots of the Tree of Souls before he fired a long stream of dark smoke at him. This meant that he had to dodge the attack to get closer, which didn't look easy given his size.

Unfortunately, this was when the witch got involved, now drawing forth her own energy, one that shot from her hands like blue fire. But being attacked from both sides, Clay only managed to dodge it all for so long before one hit his chest. And he, like Caspian, was suddenly propelled backwards, slamming into one of the pillars closest to me and making a section of it come away. This was before the rest came crashing down over him.

"NO! CLAY!" I rushed over to him, not realising the danger overhead.

The danger that was about to…

Crush me to death.

CHAPTER NINETEEN

TRAPPED BETWEEN A CLIFF AND A MAD MAN

"NO! CLAY!"

I screamed over for him but just as I was about to run towards the rubble, I was suddenly grabbed from behind. Then I was spun quickly before being covered by a muscular arm bent over my head, as a rain of stone crashed all around us. Confused, I shook my head and forced my eyes open, despite the sting as tiny particles clung to my lashes from powdered rock. I instantly looked over to where Clay was buried and was just thankful that I saw movement, telling me he was still alive and trying to make his way out. I turned my attention back to my saviour, and soon found myself looking up into the face of a bull, as Caspian had saved my life as part of the temple roof had caved in. Not surprising after one of its pillars had been destroyed.

But then, in that very instance, I couldn't breathe as it felt as if something was lifted from my body. No, that wasn't right... lifted from my very soul! I sucked in a deep breath, wondering if like last time he would tell me to 'push past it'.

I saw him suck in a deep breath that was followed by a

deep grumble of his beast. But being this close, I could see the fine details of his face. Along with the wiry white hair that covered where his chin would have been, in a pointed beard. For some strange reason, I reached up and grabbed hold and shook it a little, before telling him,

"I think this just means you've got your soul back," referring to him repaying my life debt or whatever he had called it that day.

He grunted once and made me cringe as a bellow of air came out of his nostrils, making me hope that the damp splatted on my face was not Minotaur snot!

"Eww, you could have just said thanks." At this, he grunted with a jerk of his chin before I was spun again out of the way and pushed back to safety once more.

"STAY, HUMAN." This was his demonic order, and I said,

"Sure thing, soul buddy." He grunted like a bull once more and turned so he could continue the fight, one that started as he picked up one of the biggest pieces of the boulders that fell and used it as a weapon to throw to where the brothers were stood.

I have to say I was impressed with his aim, for it hit its mark in such a way that the one who was blind would not be coming back from. The other two had seen it coming and got out of its way, but the blind one was not so lucky. This was because it smashed into his body, pinning him between the stone and the rock face, which crushed his body on impact.

"Eww," I muttered at the sight of blood splatter that looked like a crimson star against the rock. Then I watched as the gory pieces of him that remained, fell to the ground, as if the limbs that hadn't been crushed had just been severed from his flattened torso. Caspian then picked up another boulder, deciding to try his luck again.

As for Clay, the rest of the rubble that had fallen on top of him suddenly burst outwards with a demonic roar. All six arms were thrown up in his anger as he erupted from the debris. He then pounded his fists on the ground and used this to propel him upwards, jumping from the rest of the stone and landing next to the brother who could not speak. He grabbed him with four of his arms and used the top two to cut through the brother's limbs with his scorpion claws. They both tore down the centre, tearing him in two as if he had been made of butter! Once he finished tearing apart his kill, he threw away the remains, now splattered and covered in the blood of the brother he had just ripped apart.

The one who couldn't hear the cries of death, was all that was left, and I didn't know why, but I had the sense that this might have been the way of things in his first life. But then he first looked to his brothers remains on either side, until finally his angry gaze brought his bloodshot eyes to mine. I could see it in his face. He knew he might not survive this but, in his determination, he wanted to destroy the one thing they were trying to protect…

Me.

This meant that he was soon charging my way, with an angry scream that shook the rubble from the mounds of stone left from the collapsed parts of the temple. Caspian and Clay both reacted but even I knew that they would be too late in reaching him before he could reach me. So, I braced myself, strangely feeling too numb to do much else other than wait for it to come. Because as much as I tried to draw up my power, it just wasn't happening!

I was backed against the wall with no chance at escape when suddenly something unexpected happened as, when he was only a hairsbreadth away from me, he was suddenly dragged backwards with his face moving further and further away. I half expected to see this was down to one of my saviours but in fact, was astonished when I saw the roots that Matthias controlled had been wrapped around the last brother's legs. Then he flung him into the wall of rock behind where he was stood, making him hit it hard enough to make a body sized imprint. Then he fell to the ground with an audible thud and into a useless looking heap.

Matthias had saved me, and now I knew there was only one reason why he would do such a thing,

He needed me alive.

As for the witch, with her powers she was already lifting boulders into the air and throwing them at Caspian's Minotaur form as he tried to get closer and closer to her. Which was proving difficult as he continued to find himself battling against the flying obstructions. Massive boulders of rock that he butted with his head, splitting the stone when hit right with the point of his horn.

Clay finally managed to get closer to Matthias, but with every intended hit against him, Matthias used his powers over the roots to prevent the blow. Then he would lash out at Clay, using this fuel of rage from the roots to make him stagger back by the force of it. I could also see the roots were entwined around his legs as if he needed that direct contact with them to help absorb its power.

It made me question even more if he had something to do with this infection in the roots? I even found myself questioning whether it wasn't an infection at all, but in fact some kind of power source that had been stolen from him. One that had somehow made its way into the very earth beneath his feet.

Was it possible?

But looking back to their fight, I saw roots shoot up from the ground all around Clay, momentarily keeping him locked in a cage that tried to cover him and consume him whole. But I could also see that as fast as they were covering him, he in turn was snapping out of their hold. He was breaking branches with all six limbs, kicking them and using his horns to snap the wood and his pincers to do the same.

Matthias looked as if he would soon lose this fight, as he was now being forced to dodge his own weapons, as roots were shooting his way. This was when he bellowed at the witch in another language. She then shook her head and looked fearful, trying to tell him no.

"But the last time it nearly killed me!" she replied in fear, yet he roared out, making the roots entwined around his legs shoot out towards hers making her scream.

"Your power is mine, do not forget that! NOW GIVE IT TO ME!" Suddenly the witch went rigid as if the essence was being sucked out of her this time, powering straight into Matthias. The force of this blew Clay back, until his body landed with a crash close to mine, as he went skidding along the floor.

Caspian also felt the force of it once he'd had his fill, as light erupted around them, forcing him backwards to the other side of the temple walls, separated from us. The witch slumped forward onto her knees as the ground beneath us began to shake.

Matthias looked beyond pleased with this added power as he grew in size and his eyes started to glow demonically. He then raised both his hands up and with an almighty roar, called up to the ceiling. He moved his arms outwards, creating a huge crack to open up in the ground.

"WHAT IS HE DOING!?" I shouted over to Clay, who stood about ten feet away, as the sound of the earth splitting was near deafening!

"STAY THERE!" he shouted back, a warning I only

barely heard as the ground continued to split further and further. This was until it became a giant chasm, forcing two sides of the temple apart. I screamed, falling to my knees, as Clay leapt towards me before I could fall down into the fiery depths below. It gave me enough time to see the river of fire I had once seen before, down in Hell when being on a boat and escaping the Hellhounds.

As for Caspian, he too only managed to escape its flow of lava, as the three of us were split up, with him on one side and me and Clay on the other. Matthias slapped his hands together and the earth stopped moving, and his demonic eyes simmered down to that of his usual colour of black.

The witch barely gained enough strength to lift her head, watching now as Caspian ran towards her, ready for the kill. However, Matthias saw this and threw one boulder after another at his charging form. The first he managed to dodge, along with the second, however with the third, he was not so lucky. Because this one hit its mark, and he was thrown sideways with such force he was knocked off the side of the cliff and into the fiery pits below!

"CASPIAN!" I screamed as pain tore through me at the thought of losing another friend. But as he went out of sight, I closed my eyes tight as the agony overwhelmed me. I thought of Liessa and the pain that she would go through, knowing that she had lost her husband, just the same as Ruto's husband would feel.

Clay saw this, and his demon reacted, growing even more in size before he rose up on his feet and engaged in battle with Matthias. Clay was clearly the stronger of the two as he barrelled towards him before he was close enough to hit his mark. But just as his stinger was about to lash its poison down on him, one of the roots snapped up and grabbed it an inch from Matthias' face.

Because strength didn't matter, as the roots he controlled unfortunately tipped the fight in his favour, for every time Clay moved one limb to punch in his face, it was grabbed from behind and held back before he tore it free and tried for another hit. His body was kicked back and with the aid of the rest of the witch's powers, was pushed even further until he hit the wall, and he lay slumped to the floor, unmoving.

It was at this point that I had hit my limit on being the protected one, as I could finally feel something stirring within me. My anger was growing and growing, as if something up to this point had been restraining it. But it was enough time that the force of the rage beneath my feet was something I could call forth and gain from. The same roots of rage that he was using.

A familiar anger was a welcoming sensation, as I could feel it in my fingers sparking now with an even darker intent, thanks to the Wraith Master's essence inside of me. And just like I had done in the void when testing my abilities, I lifted my arms up, and between my hands I created a force I knew had the power to kill him. Then, when it became too big to contain, I shot my arms forward and threw the power towards him.

However, my plan had backfired because as soon as it hit him, all he did was go back a step as he absorbed the darkness I had created. He actually looked truly shocked for a moment, as he tried to contain it all and tame it into something usable. The fucker then started to grow again in size and shuddered as if gaining pleasure from the sensation of being overwhelmed by even more power, even more than what the witch had been forced to give him.

"Oh no, this is bad," I muttered to myself as his eyes turned to that of burning coals, and lightning consumed his body. After he had transformed it into what he wanted, he then looked at me and grinned in the most sadistic way.

"Thanks for the upgrade." Then, before I could think of what to do, he used it against the last man standing. Because Clay had regained his strength and was now charging his way one more time towards the enemy. Something that lasted only seconds, as Matthias shot that same power I had thrown his way towards my friend, now hitting him with enough force that like Caspian, it threw his body off the cliff.

"NOOOOOO!" I screamed in horror, before running towards the edge of the cliff to see whether they had survived or not. But I never got there, as I was grabbed from behind by what felt like a band of iron. I was then roughly yanked back against the hard chest before a demonic hand found my throat and held me locked to the powerful being at my back.

"Now you're mine, and thankfully, I have more than one use for you." His other hand snaked up and grabbed a breast, giving it a painful squeeze, making me try and fight against him. He released it on a laugh and told me in a demonic whisper,

"Oh, I am going to have fun making you my Queen… *I love it when they fight back.*" After this sickening thought, he turned to the witch and demanded,

"Just in case they managed to survive the fall, seal it and raise the river… as I doubt they will survive the rising lava," he added with malicious intent and a sickening gleeful tone.

Then I watched as the witch cast a forcefield over the split in the earth, preventing them from getting free should they survive the fall.

"*Please… please don't kill them,*" I whispered against his gauntleted hand at my throat, making him band that arm around my waist and pick me up to his massive height. Once there, he then told me,

"Oh, they will burn, make no mistake. And as for you…" He paused his threat as he walked us both over to the portal in the Tree of Souls, and before stepping inside, he looked up and told me,

"So it begins, for I have the Eye, and now the one with the blood as its chosen Gaurdian to use it, for soon every soul on this tree will belong to me, and that flower up there means only one thing…

"Your soul included."

CHAPTER TWENTY

LUCIUS

THE FALL AND THE FAILURE

"Fuck... FUCK!" I roared in my fury, first doing so as myself and then as my demon side threatened to erupt. But this wasn't exactly surprising, not after hearing all the shit I had from my father about his fucked-up past!

But now I knew that trying to keep Amelia safe had been in vain, and breaking her fucking heart whilst doing it only made it all the worse! I should have fucking told her! I should have been honest and told her every fucking single sordid detail of my former life! But then, in my defence, it was one I didn't exactly think would come back to haunt me after 2000 years of letting it lie in the dust where it belonged. No, I thought I would have had time as I wasn't the type of person to be forthcoming in my mortal past... as fuck... it was too painful for me to even think of, let alone wanting Amelia to know it all!

This was made even more so after everything that had just happened with the fucking Wraith King and nearly losing her for good. Which meant that I hardly thought it would have been the best time to tell her. It wasn't like we didn't have enough shit going on! Hence why I wasn't exactly in a hurry to explain the reason everything had happened to her, was thanks to a wife I had kept from her. My bitch ex-wife who was now a witch with a fucking long grudge!

Okay, so technically speaking, I had never divorced her seeing as I thought death was pretty fucking final, first with my own and then hers, something I naturally believed had happened, seeing as she was supposed to be mortal and all. Now I felt like a fucking fool for not checking. But then, after my rebirth, I had walked away from everything associated with my former life. And for good reason. That bitch could have rotted in Hell for all I cared and well... this way I guess she would, as this time I would be the one to fucking kill the bitch!

As for Amelia, I was just trying to save her, but all I had ended up doing was pushing her in to more fucking danger than ever before! I'd fucked up and I swear if it ended up costing my girl her life, then I would never forgive myself!

Never.

And never was a really long fucking time for an immortal. Of course, it was also a really long time to spend trying to get her back because if Amelia was taken from me, it would mean only one thing...

War.

For I would start a fucking war unlike any other, and the first to die by my hand would be that fucking brother whose head I wanted to ground into dust with my hands!

"Hurry the fuck up!" I snapped at Dariush, who was currently creating a portal directly to the Tree of Souls, a place my father had told us Matthias would be. We had left our father's castle, as he had his own protective spells cast to prevent portals being opened inside, which meant we had to do so on the outskirts. At the very least he had assured me he would meet me in battle when the time came, but right now, going to war was the least of my worries!

"I know I usually make this shit look easy, but creating a portal to a place that's guarded by the fucking Fates themselves isn't fucking easy and nor was it the first time!" he growled in frustration, but it was nothing compared to my own, then again... *I had much more to lose.*

"Just get it fucking done, and NOW!" I bellowed with the demonic growl of words that couldn't be ignored. However, my brother continued to ignore me, intent on getting the job done as quickly as possible, for even I, in the midst of my rage, could see the struggle on his face. But then this wasn't surprising, as despite how powerful my brother was, the Temple of the Tree of Souls was forbidden for a reason. Yet clearly it wasn't forbidden to all, as my fucked-up brother had found a way in, making the God damn place his own!

Although Lucifer had explained the reason for this. As it was believed to be after I had unknowingly released his power from Tartarus, causing it to seep into the Tree of Souls and infect its roots. This had been what had allowed him access to the Temple. And in there, being so close to the powers Lucifer had drained from him, he would be at his strongest, until he was able to regain them back fully.

I was a fucking idiot!

I had led them straight into a fucking trap, and now I feared the fucking worst!

"*Dariush...*" I growled his name as my patience was at an end. But suddenly a crack in my father's realm started to appear, telling me that we were close. I gritted my teeth and clenched my fists to stop myself from barking at him again to get it done quicker, as I knew it wouldn't help matters. Thankfully, down here he was stronger, as back in the mortal realm he would first need the blood of whoever it was he wished to take with him through the portals he created. Because some portals had the power to rip a body apart. This was because, after my brother was charged with retrieving my soul and my new vessel, he was granted his promise. Lucifer turned him, but in doing so found in him something unforeseen. Because it was unknown at the time that Dariush was actually a descendant of Aeolus, the God of wind. This, combined with Lucifer's blood, turned him into something not even the Devil himself could have expected. Being the only one of his kind and possessing the ability of harnessing the power of his ancient ancestors.

For not only could he create portals, he also could summon a deadly vortex known as Aeolus' eye. A force that was originally created by Aeolus, the God of wind and Perses, the God of destruction. Yet despite having this ability, it was not something he could create at whim. In fact, it took most of his strength and he would likely be rendered unconscious after, for it drained him so completely, he would suffer from it for days later, trying to regain his power. Hence why he rarely used this gift, as he would inevitably be left vulnerable.

Lucifer had quickly recognised this new, successful creation of his and embraced it, making him a Great Marquis in Hell and King of the shifter portals. He was also granted thirty legions of demons under his command. However, Lucifer also feared his new 'weapon' would be potentially used against him, so at my request kept his ties to me unknown, after pointing out these facts to him. The true reason of course was that Dariush was my only true weakness… before Amelia that was. For I feared the same, and that Dariush could be used against me by my enemies, a list that grew from the very first moment I was turned… and growing, so it seemed, I thought with a barely contained growl.

"Alright, we are in!" he said, making me take in a breath before stepping through the iridescent portal without another thought. But then the sight that met me was one I had feared the most, as it looked like a fucking war zone!

"AMELIA!" I bellowed her name like a man possessed and ran through the large open space, only to find a fucking chasm that had been opened up on the floor of the Temple! Pieces of the ceiling had collapsed, obviously due to the missing column, as it looked as though something large had barrelled straight through it!

I scanned the space as quickly as I could, searching for her and my only solace came in the form that, at the very least, I could not scent her blood. Because I knew then that she had not been injured in the fight, but it also meant that she had been taken, for I could not sense her anywhere. No, only the barest glimpse of her still lingered, making me roar,

"FUCK! Fuck, fuck fuck! She is gone!"

"Fuck is right, it looks like a fucking battle happened." I continued searching to see he was right, and my eyes quickly found the casualties. First those I was glad to see dead, as I scanned the remains of the Keepers of Three. Brothers who looked as if they had been separated from the monster Lucifer had made them, which explained why they were dead now, as that power from the Devil would have been severed right along with the severing of their bodies.

Fuck me, but this witch was powerful. Forget about a level six, this bitch was off the fucking charts!

"Look for the others and I will… *oh Gods no!*" This

ended with a whispered cry of anguish as I first caught scent of blood… lots of fucking blood. Then my gaze shot to where it was and that was when I saw him.

Ruto.

I released my wings and shot upwards to where his body was pinned by his own making to the Temple wall. His head was slumped forward, and I knew before even touching him that there was no life that remained.

"*My second,*" I said, pushing past the emotion clogging my throat and choking me. I used my powers to release him from his razor tipped feathers, flying back to give myself room so I could pull them all at once from his body. Then, as he started to slip from the wall, I caught him, as the feathers rained down below. I flew us down and lay him down, before moving his dark hair from his young angelic face. I then lay my hand over his sleeping features and looked up, closing my eyes, and telling his passing soul,

"*Find peace in the next life, my friend, for I will avenge you.*"

"Luc, I found the others!" Dariush shouted, and I sucked in a quick breath, fucking praying for them not to be found in the same way. I wasn't sure how many hits to my fucking heart I could take in one blow!

"Dead?" I asked with dread, but he shook his head telling me no, and I took a breath of relief instantly, getting to my feet.

"Where?!" Dariush motioned with his head over to the side of the cliff and even before approaching, I could see the glow of fire reflecting on the jagged rock face.

"You'd better get here quick, they won't last much longer!" Dariush warned, and after the second it took me to get there, I soon figured out why. They were clinging onto the side of the rocks and even now, a small foothold crumbled beneath the weight of Caspian, making him grimace. I was about to ask why they hadn't yet climbed up when my brother circled his hand over the edge, as if he could feel something that I could not see.

"They sealed it off," he said with a glower of anger.

"How the fuck?" I snapped.

"Some kind of concealing veil or holding spell… look, you can see they've tried to get out many times only to slide back down." I looked to where he pointed to, and could see for myself the clawed marks in the stone. I could also see the rising level of flames as it looked as if the witch had created a rockslide to block the flow of the underground river of Phlegethon.

"Can you clear it?!" I demanded, but Dariush had already started, ignoring my bite of words and getting the job done. In fact, it was only when I began to see for myself the wavering of the air in front of me become something more tangible, did I know that whatever my brother was doing… it was working. Meaning that I could soon see the faint veil that spanned across the cavernous space between the two sides, like a distorted vision of what it should have been. But the moment Clay started to slide further down and closer to the river, I knew they wouldn't survive, I hissed,

"Hurry brother, for I do not wish to lose any more men this day!" Dariush paid my words no heed as he continued to concentrate on the job of saving my men, and looking strained whilst doing it.

"Fuck me, it's powerful!" he complained, as it was clear that this casting, whatever it was, came from a power that matched our own. A knowledge that made my fear double, for not only that of my men but for the knowledge that the woman I loved was now with them. Of course, I knew that they would keep Amelia alive, but in which manner they chose to do so, was another story. I also knew the inevitable by now, was that Amelia probably had discovered everything about my past and the full depth of my betrayal.

"Done!" Dariush shouted, as a blue fire ignited at the cliff's edge and travelled the distance over the veil as if burning it out. As for Clay and Caspian, by the time this power was extinguished, they weren't far from the top. Meaning they were soon climbing over the edge and back to safety.

"Unblock the river before it rises enough to fucking flood this place!" I ordered before turning now to my men.

"My Lord, we…" I cut Clay off with a hand before grabbing his shoulder and placing my palm to his forehead, knowing he would not fight me on this. Because I didn't have time for his explanation or his words, but instead needed to see exactly what happened with my own two eyes. Eyes that I closed as I let the recent memories hit me with a rush of images I had to try and put in order. Then, as I finally got hold of them, I started to reverse the effect and see it playing out from the beginning.

"*Oh, sweetheart… no.*" I felt myself whisper the second I saw it starting with Amelia's pain… one this time, *I had been the cause of.* She screamed and shouted and cried just as I knew she would, but right now it was a pain I deserved to endure. Because I had done this. I had fucking done this!

I deserved this pain, not her.

I had been wrong, and now that mistake had cost lives and all that was left for me to do was pray that, included in that loss, wasn't Amelia's life once more!

Something that had come close had it not been for my men who had been ready to sacrifice their own lives to save hers. Fuck, but I was so fucking proud, which was why, once

Clay's memories led to him clinging on for dear life back in his mortal form, I let him go.

"My Lord, I am so sor…"

"You fought with your lives to keep my Queen safe, and for that, I am forever in your debt," I told him, cutting him off and needing to do so once more when he started,

"But we…"

"You saved her life after I was the fool who put it in fucking danger! This is on me, Clay, not you… along with our loss," I said, looking back to where Ruto's body had been laid on the ground. Clay followed my gaze and did so with a pained look on his face, as he too felt the loss.

"He fought with strength and honour, my Lord," he informed me, and I placed a hand on his shoulder and told him,

"Yes, I know, and now it is time to avenge him and while I am at it…" I paused, looking back at the portal in the Tree of Souls that I knew Matthias had used, and vowed,

"It's time to kill my brother and…"

"…Get back my Queen."

CHAPTER TWENTY-ONE

LUSTFUL INTERRUPTIONS

Admittedly, the last fucking place I wanted to be was in the realm of lust, meeting with Dom's father once more. But if the shit hit the fan and Matthias managed to pull off his plan, then I would need all the help I could get. Because now he had Amelia, that meant he had the power to transfer every soul that was tied to me, onto him. Which meant that I would need an army, and one I didn't command. It was ironic really, for I had amassed the greatest army Hell had ever known, and the first time I was to see them in battle, it would be by the command of another and ordered to fight against me.

Hell was most certainly a brutal place and, in many ways, was one that mirrored the multiple realms that surrounded it, for greed and the need for more power was in the hearts that held the claim of ruler. Hence why I had amassed such an army in the first place. Because despite what my father had feared, being that of my ambition for more power than even he, I had not built my forces for that reason. No, it was solely done as a precautionary manner, so there were those that would not dare to try and claim what was mine by my supernatural birth right.

This, of course, included Lucifer himself.

But now my army and all the beings I had changed were in danger of becoming nothing more than a means to an end, for Matthias intended to make pawns out of each of them. And now Amelia was smack bang in the middle of it all!

My biggest fear of all wasn't actually losing control of my people or all my armies. But it was that Amelia would sacrifice herself before she allowed this to happen, something I knew her noble soul would do if she believed it could save her mother, my people and myself included.

After all, sacrifice ran in her family, I thought bitterly.

Thankfully, my brother was more successful in creating his portals now that none of them included trying to access the Temple of the Tree of Souls. Which meant he was the bearer of bad news as he found Dom topside… and with Clay and Caspian, had to explain to him what had happened. This was after I had him create me a portal to the Realm of Lust because I didn't have a moment to lose!

Because I also knew I would need the aid of another family member if I had any hope of getting Amelia back and well, Asmodeus also had a large army of his own.

With regards to Dom, I could only imagine his reaction upon hearing all that had happened to his daughter. After all, the blind fucking panic that turned to rage was one I knew well, for he would have no idea why his daughter was not now stepping through that portal into the waiting arms of her family. No, he would know something had gone wrong.

But sending Dariush was my only option, as he was the only one who could get to him in time and, at the very least, Dom would know my men so trust in what my brother had to say.

As for myself, I did not relish the idea of having to explain myself to not only one family member with a temper, but her grandfather also. As I doubted he was going to take this news lightly, not considering the last time I was here I had also lost her. But then, what other choice did I have... *fucking none!*

So, despite feeling the bitter sting of failure at not being able to protect Dom's daughter... yet a-fuckin-gain... I knew now that pride had no place in the decisions I was to make. In fact, my pride had gone to Hell... *literally!*

"Should I even bother asking why you are here, or should I go with the obvious, seeing as you're here now and still without my granddaughter by your side?" Asmodeus said, before adding,

"As I doubt very much you came to join in?" This then alerted me to the fact that my brother had created a portal directly into a room that unsurprisingly only seemed to have one agenda in mind...

Orgies and sex.

This was because the entire room looked like a mix between a modern sex club and some ancient harem. So, basically, what you would have expected when walking into the Realm of Lust. But I tore my gaze away from the sunken seating area and curtain of chains that hung over it. One that was currently being used as a giant bed for twenty plus bodies, all of which that were engaging in some sordid act or another, and most that went well beyond just sex. The walls were clearly being used as the 'play' areas, which looked closer to torture devices for those that craved the pain for sexual release.

As for the ruler himself, he was currently sat in the centre of it all, on a black throne that looked like an oversized chesterfield in its design. Of course, it was disconcerting seeing an older version of Dom whilst he was sat casually against the chair's high back and getting his cock sucked by three girls. A trio that all seemed to be close to fighting each other just to get closer to his... *fuck me*... but it had to be said... *his impressive fucking cock!* Oh yeah, I had to give the fucker that! Although, being the King of Lust, then what else was to be expected as it would have been a cruel irony to give him a little fucker.

But like he said, I wasn't fucking there to join in, so I pushed down the urge to growl in response to this question, and instead bit out a single word,

"*Privacy.*"

"Very well, serious business always was a cockblocker anyway... go... go on now, go indulge your sexual fantasies elsewhere, my pretties," Asmodeus said, waving his hand away as if he was sending off his servants. Then he rose from his throne and shrugged on a long black robe that fanned out along the floor, before walking from the room and leaving the orgy without its master. Naturally, I followed him and once we were out of the room, the door closed behind us and the sound of sex and debauchery was no more.

"And to what do I owe this unexpected prevention of pleasure?" he asked, morphing the usual saying so as to fit his purpose, that I had indeed cut short his pleasure.

"I need your aid," I told him, making him grin before telling me,

"But of course, you do." Then, before I could try and punch it from his face, I gritted my teeth and bore the annoyance, reminding myself once again that pride had no place in my life right now. So, I followed him down the long hallway that was lined with statues, all sexual in nature. Most of these were exact copies of the ones found in India, and mainly from the Khajuraho Temples, that were famous for their erotic sculptures. Carved figures that portrayed the concepts of Kama Sutra and tantric sexual practices.

But, as we reached the doors at the end, I realised that this theme was to continue into the next space, one that looked far less sordid than the last. It was a sitting room of sorts, that held a small library of books in one corner and an open balcony at the far end. In the centre, was a round table which was a mosaic of sexual positions that looked to match the star constellations. Tall arched chairs were positioned around it, in between each chair was a table with a bell placed upon it.

I could only imagine what ringing that bell brought you, and could only hope that Asmodeus would refrain long enough from using it until I had finished what I had come here to say. As for the rest of the room, its walls were a copy of those the Sun Temple in Modhera, being one of the ancient temples of Gujarat. Although, it made me wonder which came first, as the Sun Temple had been built during the rule of Solanki Dynasty during 940 CE and 1244 CE. Another temple where its walls celebrated the nature of mankind's urges and was covered in even more sexual figures in relation to the Tantric tradition.

"And as for the handsome devil who brought you here, and one so clever at creating portals at a mere thought, who might he be?"

"I am not here to discuss my people, Asmodeus," I told him, making him laugh as he made his way over to his table.

"No, and from what I hear, *your people*, may not stay that way for long," he said, taking a seat, and I followed his lead taking one of my own.

"So, you know what is happening?" I asked, shocked that he would.

"Don't insult me, boy, I am older than most Gods and know far fucking more than most, for don't let my wet cock fool you into believing otherwise... now, tell me what has become of my granddaughter this time, for you only recently made it from the Elementals' realms," he said and by doing so, proving his words true... he knew more than most. Although, I had to say, being called boy once more didn't fucking help my murderous mood, that was for fucking sure!

"Point made, Asmodeus, but we have more important things to speak of than the one who brought me here," I reminded him.

"You're right, it is not important, but the details of who took my granddaughter this time is, so I may cut their life short for the offence," he said with the barest hint of anger.

"As grateful as I would be for such a feat to be accomplished, I fear it is not as easy as you think. Besides, if it were, do you really think I would be here now seeking your help?" I said, stating the obvious.

"Perhaps not, young Prince," he said, making me grit my teeth at the title and for the first time in a long time, realising now why my own little Princess found the term so distasteful.

It was almost as bad as 'boy', because unless you were a King or Queen, being classed as anything lower had a juvenile sound to it that grated along my nerves. But then Asmodeus knew this, hence why he had purposely named me such. In truth, he was just as fucking annoying as my own father, and I could also understand why Dom often got frustrated when forced to meet with this particular half of his parentage. But speaking of Dom,

"And my son, what does he know of his daughter's capture?"

"Clearly not as much as he should do!" On hearing this answer coming from the man himself, I released a sigh and rose from my chair. Then I braced for what would inevitably come next...

An angry father.

"WHERE THE FUCK IS MY DAUGHTER?!" The sound of Dom's furious tone echoed around the large space, and was soon added to by the sound of an even angrier woman's voice, making me sigh even louder this time.

"Where is she, Lucius!?"

Then I turned to both of them after they had stepped through Dariush's portal, and said,

"Dom, Keira…"
   "I think you'd better sit down."

CHAPTER TWENTY-TWO

A KING'S CONFESSIONAL

By the time I had finished explaining to Amelia's parents everything that happened from the point of leaving the hotel in Jerusalem to now, I felt mentally drained.

In fact, it felt as if my chest cavity had been fucking ripped open. So much so that it would have been easier if Dom had just reached inside there, grabbed my heart, and squeezed until the fucker stopped beating! Because, in truth, it already felt as though it had stopped beating every time I had to admit how much I had failed him… *failed them both*.

But above all, how I had…

Failed my Chosen One.

In all honesty, I had been surprised he hadn't actually done this already. I think I would have preferred physical combat and have him go back to trying to kick the shit out of me. That way this torture of having to sit there and see the pain in his eyes every time I talked about how his daughter had been in danger, would have been cut short. By the end of it, I was almost ready to fucking beg him to, just so I could feel something other than anger and heartbreak, and anguish and worry… but most of all, to give me the slightest reprieve from the blinding fear. One only ever felt before when Amelia's life had been hanging in the balance.

I had contemplated sparing them everything that had happened, including the worst of it, which of course had been Amelia's death. Unsurprisingly, Keira had tears streaming down her pretty face that didn't seem likely enough to stop anytime soon, a sentiment I could understand. Dom took her hand, and I didn't know whether it was to comfort her or to gain comfort himself, for he looked as if his world had ended. But then came the moment when I had to explain how she had survived, and that offered both comfort and even more concern.

Yet, despite how I wished Dom would get up and knock me out with one punch, just to put me out of my fucking misery, I also knew that right now there was no fucking time for it. Which meant that my much deserved ass kicking would have to wait.

"I know you're angry, but all I ask is for you to hold back your need for revenge against me and all punishments you believe I deserve, until I have dealt with this and saved Amelia. For fighting now will achieve nothing other than wasting time in finding her," I said when coming to an end of my update, and looking at everyone who was now sat around the table. Which also included Dom's father and my brother, who had created a portal and brought them here. But as I felt Dariush tense next to me, I cut him a look and shook my head slightly, telling him not to act, no matter the bloody outcome. Because I knew that despite deserving their wrath, he would be at the ready to fight by my side.

Dom scrubbed a hand down his face and released a sigh before he stood from his chair, making me instantly do the same with my own sigh. I guess the answer was a no then, I thought wryly.

"Draven, please, please don't…" his wife begged him as she grabbed his arm, but he gently shook his head at her before shocking every single person in the room, and none more so than me. This was because he held out a hand to me and on a growl, demanded,

"Take my fucking hand, Luc."

"*What?*" I asked totally dumb struck.

"My daughter ran away from her home, she ran away from the safety of Afterlife, despite knowing everything that was going on. Despite knowing of the dangers. Yet you searched for her across the globe for two months. Two fucking months and I saw you. I saw you, Luc. I saw what that did to you, yet what did she do only days after you eventually you found her, and what happened when you did…?"

"*Dom, don't…*" I muttered with a wince as the reminder of events was like a verbal lash against my skin.

"What happened, Luc!?" Dom snapped in the depths of his own pain. So, I released a breath and gave him what he needed.

"She stepped into Hell." Keira sucked in a breath, this time trying to hold back another sob at being reminded of what I had only just told them.

"Something you tried to stop, yes?" Dom said, making me growl this time,

"Of course, I fucking did!"

"But she went anyway. She stepped into danger just like her mother did," Draven said, making Keira release her own growl, yet it was one he ignored.

"So, the way I see it, every time Amelia has made the wrong decision and walked down the wrong path, you have put yourself in front of her and tried to steer her right. You have saved her time and time again, and when many would have mourned her death, you refused to give up and you brought her back. Every decision you have made since then has only ever been made with her safety in mind," he said, making me shake my head and tell him,

"Dom, please, you don't have to…" At this, he placed a hand at my shoulder and stopped me by saying,

"Yeah, Luc, I do, for I may have not done right in the past when meeting my own Chosen One, but like you, every single decision I made at the time, was done so with Keira's safety in mind and that is all the power that we will ever have. Which means, as much as you are weighed down by guilt, this was not your fault, so I am not fucking blaming you." I swear, by the time he was finished I felt his words sink in and stay there, not realising until that moment how much I fucking needed them! Which was why I took this moment for what it was… monumental.

One I would never forget.

"So, take my hand as the comrades we once were, and will be again. For you will find me fighting by your side and this time, there is no greater cause, as we both fight for something we love. Now, let's go and get my fucking daughter." I clasped his hand and shook it, before saying,

"Just so long as I get to be the one to kill this fucker." At this he grinned, and I took that as his answer.

"I swear she is going to be so grounded, I don't care how old she is!" Keira piped up, making me want to point out how unlikely that was going to be.

"Yeah, good luck with that one, little Keira girl," I commented dryly, making her blow out air in an 'umpf' sound. This blew some of the blonde waves from her face, that were barely being restrained back in the plait she wore.

In fact, she barely looked a day older than the day I first met her and like then, she was dressed casually, this time in jeans and a dark red sweater that slipped off the shoulder and was tied with a black bow. As for Dom, he looked ready for action, and had forgone his usual suit for black combat gear. Even his longer hair was tied back from his face and he was sporting a shadow of worry across his it in the form of weeks without shaving.

"So, I take it you have a plan?" Keira asked after slapping her hands to her knees and getting to her feet.

"I do, but unfortunately it has zero finesse and mainly consists of us amassing every single being that will fight on our side, for make no mistake, the War of Souls is coming."

"Seriously, can't you guys ever think of a nicer thing to call it, we once had the War of Roses. But no, with you guys it's always the Blood Wars, the War of Souls, the War of Doom and Destruction... I know we're in Hell and everything, but even that guy has the Realm of Lust... hey, Pops," Keira said, waving to Asmodeus as if she had only just remembered he was in the room. At this, he smirked back at her and winked making Dom growl. Of course, his father simply laughed heartedly.

"Now stop that! For God's sake, it's not like I'm flirting with my bloody father-in-law here! And anyway, back to my point, if he has the Realm of Lust, then there has got to be hope somewhere," Keira said, making me smirk.

"Yeah, not sure it works like that in Hell, sweetheart," Dom said dryly.

"Fine, okay, so depressing war names aside here, what are our chances. I mean what are we up against exactly?" she asked, now making more sense.

"I have amassed the biggest army in Hell, so we're up against that," I answered honestly.

"Great, peachy. Maybe then it should be called the War of the Impossible and we should ask Tom Cruise if he wants to take a crack!" Keira said with a sigh, making Dom look as though he wanted to ask something, but she held a hand up and said,

"Seriously, thirty years, Draven, thirty years of making you watch movies with me, and you still don't know who people are." At this he pulled her close and told her,

"And I told you, love, you may be watching it, but whilst that is happening, I am watching something divinely better." At this she shot him an incredulous look, and replied in hushed tones,

"Seriously, can anyone say, 'like father, like son'." At this, Asmodeus chuckled and this time winked at Dom, who rolled his eyes at the gesture.

"You will pay for that one when we get home, little one," Dom threatened, and Keira smirked and muttered,

"Promises, promises, honey bunches." His look said it all before he turned his heated gaze from his wife and granted me a more serious one.

"So, this amassed force in Hell, want to explain exactly how you managed that?" he asked, making me shrug my shoulders and tell him,

"You know yourself, Dom, what happens when the most powerful beings pledge their loyalty to you."

"Whatever comes with them, also becomes yours," he finished off for me.

"Exactly, you know yourself just how many Legions of Hell one being can control, and with that, if one man is turned… that can then become hundreds," I added, making him nod in understanding.

"So, your sizeable army are souls you don't own but will none the less fight for the ones loyal to you."

"And then against me, once their masters' souls are owned by Matthias... hence you see my problem," I told him, making Keira jump in as it was clear she was falling behind in the conversation.

"Wait a second and back up a bit. Can we pretend for the last 30 years I haven't been a part of your world and haven't exactly read every book in our library yet?"

"Haven't exactly?" Dom muttered, making her hold up a finger and snap,

"Don't comment... now, explain this to me in layman's terms."

"My army is useless to me, for once there has been a transfer of souls, they will be controlled under a new master."

"Under this Matthias guy?" Keira asked, making me grit out,

"Yes." I did this, because this had been the only part I hadn't yet told them, who Matthias and the witch were with regards to me. Something I knew was coming even before Dom asked,

"And have you discovered who he is and why you are the target?" I looked back to Dariush, who granted me a knowing look that basically said, 'you poor bastard'.

"I am afraid this is when things get... *complicated*," I said with a wince, knowing it was time to reveal exactly who we were fighting against.

"This is when things get complicated... jeez, what were we calling it before exactly?" Keira muttered to herself, but this was when I told them the true depth of the situation.

"Before it was just an enemy to kill."

"And now?" Dom asked, making me swallow down the bitter truth and tell them,

"Now, it's my brother."

CHAPTER TWENTY-THREE

SHOCKING REVELATIONS

I realised my mistake the moment I said it, as Keira shot an incredulous glare at Dariush and said in outrage,

"Oh my God, what did you do, Dariush!?" It was in this moment that I winced, and my brother tensed, now sitting up straight and sending daggers my way. Because of course, she may have met him in another version of the past, but as for Dariush, he had never met the woman in all his life!

"What the fuck?!" Dom snapped, and I groaned before rubbing my temple as if a fucking mortal headache was coming on.

"Erm… I have a feeling I might have jumped to conclusions here," Keira said sheepishly, as she took in the sight of Dariush who was looking pissed at being accused.

"I think someone needs to explain, and now!" Dom snapped, making Keira mouth a silent,

'My bad' at me and that may have worked on a certain Imp, but it wasn't working for her.

"There are things even you do not know of me, old

friend," I told him, making him cross his arms over his chest and say,

"Then may I suggest you rectify that and start talking," with a nod towards my brother, making Keira look guilty and say,

"Yeah, and you may want to start with introducing your brother… hey Dariush." Keira finished this by giving my brother a little wave, and was purposely trying to ignore the astonished look her husband was giving her. Of course, ignoring him was only going to last so long, as he grasped her chin in his thumb and forefinger and turned her head his way, forcing her head back. Then he said her name in warning,

"*Keira.*" In answer to this, she shrugged her shoulders before telling him,

"What? It wasn't my secret to tell." His eyes narrowed down at her before expressing his thoughts on her excuse.

"We will discuss all the things you have kept from me once this is over, my dear, but for now, I take it what my wife says is true." This last part was directed at me, as he released his possessive hold on his wife and instead, began to run the backs of his fingers down her pale skin.

I released a sigh, and knew the time had come for keeping Dariush unknown from the world was at an end. But, out of respect, I looked to my brother and silently asked for his approval. Then when he granted me a nod, I continued with the truth.

"Do not be angry at your wife's good intentions, for it was my wish that Dariush not be known," I said, nodding down to Keira who was unsurprisingly biting her lip as was her habit when nervous.

"And I gathered this was something she discovered back in Persia?" Dom said, making Keira frown.

"I'm right here, you know, and am perfectly capable of

answering..." At this point, Dom covered her mouth with his large hand and then whispered down at her,

"*Quiet, little Vixen.*" I swear the angry look she tried to give her husband in return was about as threatening as a damn puppy and had me holding back a smirk.

"Yes, it was back in Persia."

"I see, and the reason you kept knowledge of him from me for so long?" he asked before clenching his jaw and making a vein there jump, telling me he was pissed. But then, this was understandable because, before there was Adam, Dom had been the closest thing I had to a friend. But now the time had come to reveal all, starting with the beginning. Of course, Dom knew how I had come to be, but he was surprised when he discovered it was Dariush who was told where to find me by the Devil. I then explained his payment for this was to be turned after me, which Lucifer delivered on and hence how Dariush was reborn.

"Dariush could create portals at a mere thought, and we believed this useful to keep to ourselves should it be needed. I didn't exactly trust you when we first met, and you know why." Keira looked at her husband at this and he just said,

"You don't know everything, sweetheart." Needless to say, she didn't look impressed.

"In short, Keira Girl, your husband basically handed me my ass in front of his throne and came close to killing me, which was when I discovered that my power of will could be exerted over more than just my own kind and that of humans. And it was lucky I did or that blade would have sliced through my neck that day," I told her, making her gasp before turning an accusing look to Dom.

"You tried to kill him?" she then shouted in outrage.

"Yes, well the cocky bastard wasn't exactly someone who

endeared himself to me the first moment we met." I laughed at Dom's reply.

"And when you say didn't endear himself, what exactly does that translate to?" Keira asked in a knowing tone. Dom folded his arms across his chest and said,

"The bastard walked into my throne room, killed a load of my guards and then demanded that I… what was it again you said…?"

"I think I said something along the lines of, you would be lucky to have me as your second in command or if you're not up to it, I could just take your throne… something to that effect." At this, Keira's eyes grew wide as if she too was remembering how Draven used to be back then, before commenting wryly,

"Yep, that would do it."

"Of course, the moment I was able to stop that blade of his from slicing into my neck was when he realised that I had been right, he would have been lucky to have me," I added, making Dom scoff,

"And still the same cocky bastard you were that day." At this I smirked.

"I thought you said the first time you ever used power over his mind was after World War Two?" Keira asked with a frown.

"She doesn't forget a thing, does she?" I commented to Dom, who shrugged his shoulders and told me,

"Rarely." Then he turned to look at his confused wife and said,

"That time doesn't really count, considering for a brief second it was like trying to push my blade into the walls of Tartarus instead of his arrogant neck." This time I did scoff a laugh before he continued.

"But in that fleeting moment, I knew I would have been

far better having him as an ally, than I would an enemy, and wouldn't you know it, years later this was proven correct."

"Yes, and now here we are, with me claiming your daughter who I intend to marry as soon as I can get her ass to stop running from me and back to a safe place," I told him, making Keira sigh,

"Good God, it's worse than Dynasty… maybe even EastEnders with a bit of Midsomer Murders thrown in… of course it would help if they had some Supernatural soap opera on Netflix that could wrap this up all in one," Keira muttered about things we had no idea about. However, Draven directed his gaze back to my brother and said,

"So, he is also the son of the Devil, and what about you, did you also know this?" Dom said, now looking at his father who had remained quietly watching this whole time.

"Son, there are many things my friend Lucifer does that you do not know about, yet one of them is common knowledge."

"And that is?!" Dom snapped.

"His quest for the perfect being. Yes, I knew there were others, yet I did believe that it ended with Lucius," Asmodeus said in an easy tone.

"Dariush was created shortly after me, but that is his story to tell, not mine."

"And will he tell it?" Dom asked seriously, and I couldn't' help but grin at my brother's reply, knowing it was coming.

"Fuck no and not a chance," Dariush said firmly, and truth be known, my brother had told no one of his past, not even I. Of course, I admit to being curious, but then knowing of my own past life's mistakes, then I knew that a person's story was his own. And often, if it is not a story you want to tell, there is good reason behind the secrets you keep. Because sometimes it was one so horrific it was better to be left in the darkness of someone's mind, than opened up and released to the world.

After all, knowledge was power, and that was being proven now more than ever. For my own history had come back to bite me in the ass in a way that could end my life. A woman's love scorned so badly that she was willing to eradicate all vampire life in her need for revenge. A brother whose hatred for our father ran so deep that he too despised all life that came after he was cast out by his creator's hand. A loathing that passed on to Dariush and I, for simply existing, for our only crime against him was that we lived. But that was the power of hatred, and what I had come to learn was the very essence that fuelled Matthias. But it was in this rage where his failure lay, for he let it consume him, even with his dying breath and admittedly, was the reason he was not the son Lucifer was hoping to create.

"So am I right in saying that the family revelations are to continue, for I doubt this is the brother you intend to kill," Dom said, pointing out the obvious after my statement made only moments ago, one Keira had obviously forgotten.

"Oh my God, don't tell me you've got another brother!" Keira shouted, as if this 'supernatural soap opera' of hers was getting more complicated by the second, when in truth, she had no idea just how much worse it could get.

"Matthias is our brother."

"Oh shit… and I thought I had it bad with my cousin, Hilary." Keira muttered, making Dom glance down at her with grin before his attention came back to me.

"And I take it this is yet another one of Lucifer's failed attempts?"

"It is, and a very bitter one at that."

"Yeah, I will say! I mean okay, I get it, be pissed at daddy for what he did but genocide and killing off an entire race? I mean what is he… the supernatural version of Hitler?! Jeez, don't you guys ever consider therapy or in your case, family counselling?" Keira said, making me laugh before I once again encouraged them to sit so I could replay to them what I had just discovered for myself.

After all, there was much more to tell and once I was finished with the history of Matthias, I knew the next family bombshell would have to drop when Keira asked,

"And what about this witch, is she like his wife or something?" I tensed at this, and heard Dariush mutter next to me,

"*Yeah, good luck with that one, brother.*" This was when I released a deep breath and said,

"No, she is not his wife…" Then, after rubbing a hand across half my face and closing my eyes a second, I finished that sentence and waited for the fallout…

"She's mine."

CHAPTER TWENTY-FOUR

SWALLOWING SORROW

"What the fuck!?" Keira cursed, which was unlike her. But then given the circumstances, it wasn't surprising.

"Come again?" was Dom's stunned reply, making Keira look side on at him and say,

"Really, that's all you've got?!" Dom raised a brow down at his wife, making her shout louder this time,

"He's got a bloody wife!" Dom then gave her a wry look and said,

"I have known him for over 2000 years and never seen him with a wife, which is why I believe there is more to this story, sweetheart." At this, she crossed her arms over her chest and made another good point.

"You also didn't know he had a brother but hey, look, Draven, there he is."

"Yes, and something, I may add, I would have known sooner had my own wife thought to tell me!" he snapped back, making her throw her hands up dramatically and say,

"Erm, hello, you've known him for over two thousand

years and me for thirty, be mad at him!" At this he knocked the spindled table that stood between them out of his way and dragged her seat closer, as the bell landed with an echoing chime,

"Yes, and I don't take Lucius to my bed every night and fuck him senseless, Vixen."

"*Thank fuck for that,*" I muttered, making Keira shoot me an evil glare.

"Yeah, well, that won't be happening for a while if you carry on being mad at me!" she threw back, making him growl and warn,

"Oh, we will see about that, heart of mine!"

"You know we could leave and just let the married couple argue it out, as I am not sure anyone would notice at this point," Dariush muttered, making Keira point a finger at him and say,

"You're going nowhere, Portal Man!" At this, Dariush held up his hands and said,

"I don't see a cape, but hey, your husband looks plenty capable of ripping my head off, so call me whatever you want, but can I point out that we don't exactly have time for this."

"I second that," I added, making Keira snap,

"You would, Mr Married to a Psycho!" I would have argued my own point when the double doors we had entered through opened and a long line of naked waitresses painted like gold statues walked in, in single file. Each carried a silver tray in front of them and as they drew closer, I could see that their breasts had been tied with golden rope. This was to make them swell and stick out in a firm way, as they still managed to walk with grace. A feat not easily managed considering that same length of rope had been used in between their legs to spread the lips of their sex wide open and on show.

"*Oh, you have got to be...*" Keira muttered as she covered her face with both her hands, and I could see she was getting more crimson by the second. Of course, it didn't help that each came to stand between us and lowered the platter at the same time. One that held a colourful array of sex toys, which included everything from rubber cocks ranging in size, cuffs, chains, clamps, and butt plugs. In other words, there was only one horny little Imp that I knew would have found a party like this appropriate, no matter the time.

"I *guess I now know what the bells do,*" Keira said, still muttering shamefully into her arm.

"This isn't fucking helpful, old man," Dom said with a growl of annoyance to his father, who was running a finger down the length of a cock as if getting ready to choose one for his next victim. This was also when my patience hit its limit, as I stood and demanded in a demonic voice,

"LEAVE, WOMEN!" At this, all the waitresses looked startled and to their master who nodded and with a wave of his hand, they all started running. Something that didn't look easy on their high heeled shoes that looked more like a punishment than just fetish footwear.

"Well, that was one way to do it," Keira said, after raising her heated face and checking she was safe to do so. As for Dom, I was happy when he got straight back to the matter at hand, reminding me,

"I have sent word to have my council and whoever else will aid us in this upcoming battle. As you know amassing our armies will take longer than this conversation, Lucius," Dom finished, and it was as he said, this was something I already knew. Hence why I had remained calm until this point, because I knew I was in no position to go searching all around Hell for Amelia when I was outnumbered and unprepared.

Something Dom also knew, as when I had Dariush create a portal to inform him of events, one of the things he was told was to get word to his council and the rest of the Kings. For everyone was need in this for us to have even a hope at succeeding. Because if Matthias managed to gain the souls and win this battle without being stopped, then what came next was him taking over the rest of Hell.

Meaning it wouldn't be long until the mortal realm followed.

Dom knew this.

"So, I suggest, before my wife reaches over this table and starts to try and strangle you to death, you start talking about this wife of yours… *before I let her!*" Dom warned, and I could see he was right, Keira was on the verge of wanting to mount my head on a spike. So, another sigh later and I finally told them.

"Dalene was my wife when I was Judas." After this, Keira's mouth dropped open, and Dom looked thoughtful a moment before he gave his own father a nod.

"Well, I'd best go and ready my own armies, for I do not need to stick around for this past tale of woe to know which side I will be fighting for. My dear, a pleasure seeing you blush as always," Asmodeus said, after rising to his feet and lifting a hand of his daughter in law to bring to his lips to kiss. Then, when she blushed further, he winked, making Dom growl,

"Did you say you had somewhere you needed to be?" At this Asmodeus chuckled, obviously enjoying being able to use Keira to get a rise out of his son.

"That I do," he said with a knowing smirk, before he too

left the room, leaving us with the privacy Dom knew I would want.

"So erm… getting back to the…"

"His bitch witch?" Dariush answered, making me scowl his way before I snapped,

"She is not my fucking anything other than the current bane of my existence!"

"Explain, Luc," Dom said, in a calm tone that managed to ease my anger.

"Dalene was my mortal wife, and one that grew inflicted as the years passed and in such a way, that as a mortal man, I wouldn't have ever truly understood at the time," I told them, being honest.

"Inflicted how, with like a disease or something?" Keira asked naively.

"No, but by a demon," I told her, after recently discovering for myself the true role that Matthias had played.

"*Oh, God,*" she muttered, putting a hand to her face.

"Matthias," Dom said, guessing correctly.

"Yes, by my brother." I nodded but Keira sucked in a quick breath again on hearing this.

"*Jesus…* eh, sorry, totally wrong name to say, of course I mean… Gods in Heaven… in Hell might be better," Keira said, slipping up and making me grant her a small smile, as at the very least she managed to lighten the mood for a short time.

"To what gain did he do this?" Dom asked next.

"Knowing the reasons why Lucifer believed him a failure, I believe Matthias' aim was to try and corrupt me enough so that I would be useless to Lucifer's plans." After this I then explained Matthias' history, keeping it as brief as I could until it brought events back to tie in with my own.

"So, basically, he turned your wife crazy?" Keira

surmised, and for her, this was something she had experienced first-hand after being kidnapped by a mad man who suffered the same affliction.

"Yes, he also became her lover, masking himself as nothing but a mortal man during those times, in hopes this would drive me into a jealous rage."

"To what end?"

"To try and kill my wife, I can imagine," I answered, making Keira shake her head.

"But obviously you didn't."

"No, in truth our marriage was done through a kindness and never out of love. Dalene had often before tried to manipulate deeper feelings from me but in this, only resentment grew."

"Then why marry her if you never loved her?" Keira asked, which was a perfectly understandable question but then this was also where things got more… *painful.*

"When I met Dalene, she was serving wine in a feast. Long story short, she caught my eye, as I caught hers and being of the determined type, she waited until I had succumbed to the wine she freely poured me and then…"

"Oh my God, are you seriously about to tell me that she seduced you!" Keira shouted, making me shrug my shoulders.

"I was a man, Keira, one full of alcohol and in front of me was a pretty girl leading me to a stable, willingly taking off her clothes."

"So, you were drunk and ended up playing hide the snake in the bush on some haybales," Keira surmised, making Dariush laugh.

"Oh, I do love how humans speak," he muttered, with a shake of his head.

"Something like that, only unbeknown to me at the time,

it was her first time and because of that, I did the right thing by marrying her," I said, making Keira frown.

"So, you're telling me because you popped her cherry, you had to marry her... jeez, is that how it went back then?" Keira asked, looking to Dom who frowned.

"I wouldn't know, Keira, considering as you well know, you were my first human. But despite this, I have a feeling Luc has more to add." Keira's gaze shot back to mine and looked at me expectantly. So, after a frustrated rub to the back of my neck, I told them the rest.

"I married her because I got her pregnant."

"WHAT!" she shouted in utter shock and well, it wasn't as though I hadn't been expecting it. I sighed again and told them,

"Dalene became my wife weeks after she missed her bleed and suspected she was pregnant. After that, she gave birth to our child and for a few years, life between us was sedate and well, naturally, mortal."

"Then what happened?" Keira asked in hushed tones.

"Matthias happened, and when the time for granting Jesus my aid came nearer, he took greater action against me. Because what Jesus had wanted me to do was something that, until that fated day, I had been unsure of, for I had a wife and a child to consider... that was until..." I paused, being unable to push past the emotion I felt myself near choking on.

"Before what... oh no, Lucius what happened?" Keira asked in a quiet voice, as she could only guess the horror that came next.

"Matthias convinced her to... to..." I swallowed again and pushed past the pain enough to finally say...

"To kill... Our daughter."

CHAPTER TWENTY-FIVE

LIVING NIGHTMARES

"*To kill… Our daughter.*"

The moment I said it, Keira's hands flew to cover her mouth as she cried in shock. Tears instantly filled her eyes as Draven's grew wide, for they were both pained and curious, as he was no doubt questioning if he knew his friend at all.

"You had a daughter?" Keira's voice sounded so small and for the first time, in many, many years past, my daughter's sweet little face came back as a memory, and I couldn't help but allow myself a moment to smile.

She had been perfect in every way.

Of course, I cared little that every parent thought this of their own children because to me, she had been the most beautiful being alive. I had never felt so much purpose in my life or been so proud until that moment I first held her in my arms.

In truth, until Amelia had come into my world, I had never allowed myself to love as I had done when I had my daughter in my life. I had never known what it was to love until the day she was born, for I did not even carry that love for my wife. No, I simply married her when she turned pregnant, for I did not want to condemn her into committing that sin. I did right by her but then again, in so many ways it turned out that I had done wrong.

"Oh, Lucius, I am so sorry for your loss… how old was she?"

"My daughter died when she was but three years old." Keira freely cried at hearing this, and Dom looked as if he was truly stuck on what to say, only getting out just beyond my name,

"Luc, I…" I shook my head at him and said,

"It is not needed." Then I rose from my seat in my desperate need to get away. Even after all of this time, the pain of losing a child never leaves you. Two thousand years and there were still things that reminded me of her. It was why I usually chose to distance myself from children as much as immortally possible, for those times were the worst. It was the memory of her hands that always stayed with me the most. The way she would wrap her chubby little fingers around my own, or the way she giggled when I would run my own finger around in a circle on her palm. The way I would run my fingertip down her nose to soothe her and rock her to sleep in my arms.

She was my greatest creation.

And she had been taken from me.

By the Gods, how I wanted to kill them both! I wanted to take the life of those who took my little girl away from me, over and over again until they felt only pain! But even then, I knew it would not be enough. Because the pain of losing anyone you loved was one that would always be eternal. I had lived with my pain for over 2000 years, and the hardest part was realising I would never follow them into the Afterlife.

I would never be reunited with them again.

This had been the hardest pill to swallow once I had been turned, for I knew even if I had died, my soul would never end up in the one place hers had. In truth, this was why revenge had never been on my mind when searching for the Lance of Longinus. The Spear of Destiny and Holy Lance that had pierced Jesus' side when he was upon the crucifix.

No, what I had wanted was what had been owed to me. What had been promised by Jesus himself. Because with the blood of God, then I would finally have the power to grant me my place in Heaven. I had made the deal with Jesus so that I may one day become an Angel and have the power to resurrect my daughter. That was the motive behind searching all of those years for the Spear's tip.

Ironically, the moment it happened I discovered I had no powers to do so, for I was not a full Angel. My deal with Jesus to bring my daughter back had failed. Because what no one knew, was that I had not only intended to sacrifice my life that day to Jesus' cause, should my action bring about my death. But after what happened to my daughter, I had intended to make the sacrifice with a promise made.

But his promise in death had not happened and with my own end on the horizon shortly after, I made my own promise, telling myself that one day I may have the power to bring her back. Unbeknown to anyone, it had been my very reason for living and had kept me focused for more years than not. Yet, after what happened with Keira and the Triple Goddess ritual, that day it all changed. The day I gained my Angelic side, was the moment that dream of bringing her back was long gone. It would then be years later that any chance at happiness was found once more and that was when my Chosen One finally entered my life.

Amelia was my gift from the Gods.

My chance at another life, and one not focused solely on the bitterness of my loss. I'd allowed myself to love again, and the moment that I had lost her, I had felt as though it was happening all over again. I had not wanted to admit it at the time to anyone, not even to myself. But since my rebirth, that had been the first time I had felt that hopelessness of death taken from my hands. A feeling I remembered all too well when it happened to me as a mortal father.

I left the table and walked towards the open balcony, needing to put space between the present and the past. I took in the view of the Realm of Lust, making out in the distance the black river that snaked through the land, barely visible through the eternal rage of the never-ending sandstorm. Another reminder of how love had the power to change us all. As the force created by Asmodeus the day his precious Sarah, Dom's mother, was taken from him, could be likened to the force of hatred my brother let grow, when his own loved ones were taken from him by the lightning of the Gods.

But as I took in the towering mass of carved black stone that was Asmodeus' castle, I thought about why I was never granted what Jesus had promised me. But then, deep down I knew why, just as I knew exactly what my failings had been when I was but a mortal man.

"What was her name?" Keira's soft voice asked from behind. This was before she came to stand next to me, mimicking my stance as she too rested her weight against the golden balustrades. Needless to say, each had been carved into the form of a naked, sexually bound girl that mirrored those of the waitresses that had walked in earlier.

I released a sigh and spoke the name I hadn't allowed to pass through my lips since the day I became something demonic.

"Her name was Kala." Keira smiled and murmured gently,

"That's a pretty name."

"How did she die?" was Keira's next question, and not one that surprised me. It was also not a question I quickly answered, as I confess to needing the moment to compose my emotions before I told her,

"She drowned." The moment Keira sucked in a shuddered breath, I turned from the view to take in Amelia's beautiful mother. The kind hearted soul of Keira had always struck me. It was not surprising then that at one time I foolishly believed myself to feel something more for her. Of course, it was not hard to know why, for Keira was both beautiful inside and out. But my connection with her was one that I knew had been fated from the start, because as the years passed, it would turn out that she would be the one to bring me the greatest love of my life. Yet, knowing what I knew now, it didn't diminish what we once had, it only morphed my fascination with her into one of appreciation and friendship.

"I'm so sorry, Lucius. Why didn't you ever tell me?"

"There is much of my life I walked away from, Keira girl, and as for my daughter, well she was sacred to me... besides, once changed, I also came to realise that memories could have power over you." Keira nodded as if understanding this more than I could truly know, and I respected that.

"Tell me what happened, Lucius." I ran a hand through my hair, holding its strands captive for a few seconds before letting them go on a held breath.

"Matthias, this unknown brother of mine, terrorised my wife and turned an already fragile mind into one of hysteria, for unbeknown at the time, she had suffered from prenatal depression. She confessed to me that she'd started to hear voices, but I didn't believe her. She had always been the type to try and gain my attention through lies, so I ignored the warning signs as they arose. To be honest, even after I changed and became what I am now, I didn't think too much about it. Too much pain had passed between us, and I blamed myself," I told her, making her suck in a breath before asking in disbelief,

"You blamed yourself... But why?"

"I left my daughter's care to a woman I knew was barely capable of taking care of herself, let alone our child. I was one of Jesus' disciples, unsurprisingly the title takes a lot of your time in spreading God's word. Yet, despite her struggles, I never believed her capable of... of what she did," I admitted shamefully.

"*What happened, Luc?*" Keira asked in a soft and soothing voice, one I knew was filled with emotion, both sorrow and regret on my behalf.

I closed my eyes, feeling my body tense as my fingers curled into fists at the very thought of going back that far in my memories. But yet, it was one that unsurprisingly I still held every single detail of. It was still there in my mind, locked away in the prison I had cast it to. Because you never forget moments like that. The moments where your life changed forever. It was as if your mind knew that it had just experienced a crucial point in life, and it held onto every aspect as though it would one day be needed. The birth of your children, the moment you get to hold them in your arms, or when you meet your soul mate for the first time. The first time you make love to them, or eventually are lucky enough to marry them. The crossroads of life were filled with moments like this and no matter how much you tried, those memories would not fade.

Not even after 2000 years of praying that they would. That one day you may wake up and suddenly find yourself free of the chains of pain that had entwined themselves around your heart.

Back when it first happened, the nightmares had been constant. I had been trapped behind the door, unable to find my way out. With nothing to do but claw at the wood like a madman, doing so until my nails tore off, for I could hear my daughter screaming. Then finally the door would open, and my wife would be standing there exactly the same way that I found her that day. That calm, serene look upon her face. It had sickened me even more so after I realised what she had done.

"Where is Kala?!" I had shouted in panic. Then with those dead eyes of hers she said to me,

"She's in a better place now, she's with your precious God."

In my nightmare, those same words were spoken as I pushed past her and ran towards the stream she used to wash our clothes in. Once there, I found the body of my daughter floating on the top as if she was merely asleep and enjoying the sun. She would look like an Angel looking up to the Heavens that awaited her.

I ran into the water and scooped her body up, holding her to me as I cried. Then my nightmare would end, and I would wake only to realise that the nightmare didn't end at all…

I was still living it.

CHAPTER TWENTY-SIX

LOST QUEENS

Always in my nightmares, it was the same.

And in them there had always been a door. For the reality was upon returning home early one day to find my wife void of emotion. Opening the door and hearing her say those same words about her being in a better place. That was when I knew. Then when I carried my sweet lifeless girl back to the house, Dalene threw in my face her reason. That she thought I would have been happy that now it could be just the two of us once again without anyone getting in the way. For she had known that after the very first second I held that little girl in my arms after her birth, I would never love anything as much. She became jealous, irrationally so, and this combined with Matthias winding his spell around her, convinced her that if she got rid of the child then my love would transfer back to her.

I told Keira all of this and once finished, she had tears once more streaming down her face and I had to keep my own locked back, refusing to let them fall.

"*Oh, God,*" she uttered again, as if she could barely imagine the pain I went through that day, just as I could barely believe that I had walked out of the house and let her live.

"He preyed on her weak mind because he believed that as soon as I discovered what my wife had done, I would kill her in my rage and therefore I would have sinned. Of course, it didn't happen this way, for I simply walked away and never looked back the day after I buried my daughter."

"And this Dalene, what became of her… well, other than bitterness and a recipe for a 2000-year-old grudge."

"I don't know, other than for some reason, Matthias decided to keep her around."

"And her powers?" she asked, making me shake my head.

"The fuck if I know, for she didn't possess a skill beyond pouring fucking wine from a jug and into a cup," I snapped in my anger.

"Well, she must have got those powers somehow, considering according to you guys, she's the most powerful witch that ever lived," Keira pointed out, ignoring my outburst.

"Something I intend to discover," I answered, fucking pissed that I didn't know already.

"So, what happened after that?"

"I played my part as the ultimate villain, intending to leave and live out the rest of my life until such time God saw me worthy enough to join my daughter in Heaven, should I not be granted her life being resurrected. But then I do remember seeing Dalene that day, she was speaking to the rest of the disciples. She told them things, things I can very much guess were told to her by Matthias. She showed them a bag of thirty pieces of silver that she found in our home, telling them that this was the price of my betrayal."

"Oh my God, she was the reason that they killed you... fucking bitch!" Keira suddenly snapped, outraged, and swearing because of it.

"I think it was Matthias' last attempt at trying to make me a useless vessel and no use to Lucifer. But it wasn't my body he was interested in. It was my soul. Now who my new vessel actually belonged to I shall never know, for I confess, I never found out. I had heard of the name Matthias before, only because he became my replacement as a disciple. A last 'fuck you' I suppose, but other than that, I mainly believed him just human and someone who was fucking my wife," I said with a snarl of words.

"You caught them?"

"I did. I believe this was yet another attempt on his part to get me to try and murder her, although now, I'm not so sure, for maybe they truly formed a connection, one psycho mind recognising another... or perhaps he just sensed some hidden power within her... honestly, who the fuck knows!" I said, after giving this some thought since all I'd discovered, yet was still coming up empty on why her.

"Wow, that's... that's a lot of history. No offence, I'm kind of wondering how you're not more fucked up." At this I couldn't help but laugh, telling her,

"I suppose all my little transgressions against you 30 years ago can now be overlooked." She gave me a wry look in return before nudging my arm with her shoulder and telling me,

"Don't push it." I laughed at this before Keira turned to me and wrapped her small arms around me, giving me a hug and forcing me to make the same gesture in return. Then I heard her whisper,

"I'm so sorry for the life you had to endure, and that precious little girl being taken from you."

"Thank you, little Keira girl," I replied softly, gaining comfort from her kind words. Then she released me, and swiped a tear from under her eye before she asked me the next painful question, one this time that was personal to her.

"I hate to ask, Lucius, I really do, but I've got to know… does Amelia know any of this?" I winced at this.

"No, she does not and before you say anything, yes I am now regretting all I have kept from her. As for her still being in the dark about my past, then I think it's doubtful!" I snapped on a growl aimed at those responsible.

"You think?" I gave Keira an obvious look and told her,

"Well, the bad guys tend to enjoy divulging pieces of information they know will inflict pain, so yes, I'm pretty fucking sure she knows."

"Yeah, good point… *my poor girl.*"

"Yes, well that poor girl of yours will no doubt be pissed at me for keeping this from her, and hurt and fucking heartbroken and every fucking thing else I deserve. But it matters not, as the most important thing is she is the one I'm trying to save… *again.*" Keira nodded in understanding and allowed me to hold on to my anger.

"Any idea about how we do that yet?" This question came from behind us, where Draven had now entered in on the conversation. Yet from the look on his face, then I would say he had been privy to this conversation for longer than I should have been aware.

"I would say the importance in stopping them is to first try and prevent them from gaining power over my souls," I said with a sigh wondering how the fuck I was to achieve such a thing, seeing as their means of doing just that was by using my girl.

"That would be good, as I don't particularly fancy the idea of becoming some sort of Vampire zombie," Keira said with a shiver, and Dom frowned at this before he tugged her to him. Then he kept her held at his side before tipping her head back with a hold on her chin.

"I won't let that happen, my love." As nice as that sentiment was, I wasn't yet sure it was something Dom could claim to have control of, which was why I said,

"I am not sure we will get that choice." Dom growled in response and gritted out,

"*Explain.*"

"Back in Tartarus…"

"Oh great, that place again," Keira muttered sarcastically, but I ignored this and continued to explain.

"As we both know, when I sacrificed my hand in Tartarus, it held in its veins the Venom of God. This acted as the key to keeping the Titans locked away. As it grew back, I kept that same Venom of God contained, so it could not do harm," I told them, knowing I was getting close to the part where I would need to confess to them both what I had stolen from them that day I was first introduced to their child. However, when the moment came, I found myself passing it by and continuing on,

"This meant that I possessed the blood of the Titans. but it also meant that in exchange, I left something of mine behind… that same key."

"Ewww, you mean your arm is still there… sorry, not important," Keira added quickly after Dom shot her a look.

"So, you believe he is trying to find the Keystone?" Dom asked, remembering all too well that day we defeated the Titans.

"But what good can it do, the Titans are all gone, and I should know, seeing I was the bad ass that buried them under a mountain that day," Keira added proudly.

"I am not entirely sure what his main goal is exactly, all I know is that when I sacrificed my hand, I unknowingly unleashed an infection upon the Tree of Souls," I said, then went on to explain to them of Lucifer's five-hundred-year-old punishment, and what began this chain of events.

"So, he wants to gain back this power… but won't he do that as soon as he transfers the souls onto him?" Keira asked, keeping track of all that was happening.

"I believe so, yes," I answered, making Dom ask,

"Then what does he need with the Keystone, and what does this have to do with the Titans?" I release a frustrated breath and said,

"In truth, I don't know what he plans. All I know is that he needs the power of the Crimson Eye, one that is now connected to Amelia." Keira sucked in a quick breath as Dom snapped,

"How the fuck did that happen!?" I explained the events I had left out, which I felt unimportant at the time, only now going through yet another time that Amelia had managed to get herself taken.

"Fucking Harpies!" Dom hissed, making Keira add,

"Yeah, they didn't like me all that much the last time I saw them and well, something tells me that Amelia might have paid for that grudge against me with that one." I didn't tell her that I agreed, but instead went on to tell them what came after and how the Eye had made her its keeper.

"It also meant that in doing so, it gave Matthias another means of gaining this power. For at first he would have needed me…"

"And this Crimson Eye, what is it exactly?" Keira asked.

"The God Janus…"

"Oh, I know that guy… he's actually really nice… well, eh… he was with me," Keira added this last part after Dom held the bridge of his nose in frustration, and I granted her a look. Of course, Dom's frustration came at being reminded of any time Keira went behind his back and took a trip through time. Thus, putting her life at risk and using the power of the Janus Gate to do this.

I opened my mouth about to explain, when Dom got there first, and thankfully did so quickly. He explained how the Eye was born through the rage of Janus, the God of Time and ruler of the Fates. It was even linked to Romulus, the first King of Rome who, like Tullus, had made a grave mistake in his rule and angered the Gods.

Janus in particular.

Of course, mass murder and kidnapping of woman would do that. So, Janus cried tears of blood that seeped into Hell and created the Eye through his anger at what mortal life had become.

Janus punished those responsible and left behind a piece of himself, a large red stone, sparkling in the ash remains of those slaughtered. One of the survivors, a woman who Janus had saved, was the person he deemed worthy enough to pick up the stone. Only when she did, she saw a glimpse of the future. A war that would kill many. So, instead of running away when she had the chance, she tried to change the future. Through her compassion, she put an end to the chance at war by marrying the King and changing his wicked ways. After this point, the God Janus thought it best to hide the Eye away, back to the depths of Hell, where it had been born from...

Tartarus.

Many years later, I was to become its keeper but now that guardianship had transferred onto Amelia, and in it the control of utter rage. For this was a by-product of its making, for it did not only show you the future, it also brought forth the power of your own rage, and one that was currently fuelling the Tree of Souls. This meant that the Crimson Eye also had the power to become a conduit to transfer those souls onto Matthias and with it, releasing the power that Lucifer had taken from him.

This was his plan, I was sure of it.

The only question left, was what this plan had to do with the last Titans?

"So, that's it then, it means we have no choice but to fight as Hell goes to war with itself," Keira said, making me agree.

"Yes, and if we lose, two things will happen. One, he will gain all control of Hell, overthrowing my father's rule... and trust me when I say, Lucifer may be an asshole, but letting Matthias take the throne is not something we want to see happen. Secondly, he will no doubt eradicate all vampire life, or make every single one of them his puppets to do as he pleases... including you, Keira." Dom roared at this.

"Not going to fucking happen!"

"So, you're telling me that this could be happening right now and the only way we're going to know if it has, is when all of a sudden I turn bat shit crazy and want to stab you both?" Keira asked, making me grit my teeth.

"I confess, I believe the reason it hasn't happened is that they need her alive and have very little in the way of forcing her to do this, as she cannot be controlled," I admitted, hating the idea of what they could be putting her though. Keira gasped, obviously thinking along the same lines as I.

"Oh my God! We can't let them hurt our daughter!" she cried out, grabbing on to Dom as if he had the power to do something other than looked pained by the idea.

"Hence why we need to gather our forces and meet them at Tartarus with our own armies at the ready!" I said, making Dom agree with a nod. However, Keira now looked as though she was ready to suggest something else but held back.

Instead, she continued to look worried and bit her bottom lip, until it looked close to bleeding.

After this talk, we found ourselves back around the table, with others joining us from Dom's council and mine. As Dariush had gone to the Temple of Janus where all the gateways and portals were found, and started opening up the ones needed to get as many of our people here as possible.

However, sometime later, after hours of planning battle strategies and logistics in bringing our forces together, I noticed that Keira was missing.

"Where is your wife?" Dom looked behind him over his shoulder and said,

"She said she needed some time alone, as I don't think she wanted the others to see her getting upset. She is worried, as we all are." I nodded at this but then after more time passed, I grew even more concerned.

"Dariush should have been back by now, for he said he was trying to locate Cerberus." Dom frowned at this and told me,

"That's odd, for he already told me that Jared would meet us in Hell as he was dealing with the outbreak of rogues in London." I narrowed my gaze and said,

"So, let me get this straight, both Keira and Dariush are missing... OH FUCK!"

"FUCK!" I shouted at the same time Dom did as we both bolted from our seats.

"Where did she go?!" Dom shouted at his father who didn't answer quick enough, so Dom grabbed him by his lapel and shouted,

"KEIRA! WHERE IS MY WIFE!" Asmodeus finally answered after shrugging Dom off, and we both ran in the direction needed. Only this was to prove useless as the moment we barged into the room he had directed us to, we found only one person left, now lay unconscious and bleeding on the floor.

Keira was gone and as for my brother, the blood seeping from beneath his clothes was from what I could now see clearly ....

A Summoning Hex.

CHAPTER TWENTY-SEVEN

AMELIA

PAST BEYOND ALL REASON

By the time I woke up, everything ached, and I felt groggy. It also took me a moment to remember the events that led me to this point, making me wonder where the Hell I was now... pun intended of course, seeing as I was pretty confident, I was still in Hell.

But pretty soon, I started to wish the memories hadn't come back to me. This was down to the pain that followed on seeing once more those that had been sent to protect me, die in their line of duty to their King. Ruto had been the first to lose his life but then Caspian and Clay had followed shortly after, being forced into that great chasm created by Matthias. After I had foolishly tried to help by firing my power at him and giving him what he needed to finish off my friends. It was of little wonder why I sat up now and covered my face with my hands as I cried over their deaths.

It was true, I didn't know for sure that Caspian and Clay were dead. But I was certain of one thing, and that was unless Lucius soon discovered his mistake in sending us to the Tree of Souls, then they both surely would have eventually fallen to their deaths. As I didn't know how long they would last before the rising lava consumed them.

Unfortunately, my hopelessness only continued as I questioned how on earth Lucius would come to know what had happened. I was starting to think that one of the biggest flaws in Hell was that there was no cell service, for communication was clearly the biggest difficulty we faced.

I lifted my head from my hands and tried to shake off the fogginess of the events that happened after being forced through that portal and back into Hell. I was surprised that this time it led to somewhere different and not the same place that I had found myself when stepping through it the first time. But then I vaguely remember Lucius saying something about that portal changing its destination after every use, which would make sense considering that Lucius hadn't followed me through like I foolishly thought would happen the first time.

But then again, I'd been foolish about a lot of things, and after what just happened, I knew I wasn't the only one to make this claim. In fact, all that seemed to happen with the both of us was making one mistake after another. Which then left us desperately trying to keep afloat and not drowning in our own errors, rectifying one mistake over and over again.

It was exhausting.

One thing became obvious, and that was I was in some kind of cell and after remembering the last time I woke up in one, I didn't think this promised good things for me. However, at the very least I was laying on a bed, despite the fact that it smelled mouldy and felt like the mattress was full of damp straw.

I remembered one thing after being forced through the portal, and that was finding myself in a barren wasteland with mountains in the distance. I had also been trapped in Matthias' arms, squirming to get free of his secure hold. However, something was soon blown in my face, and I found my mind going blank and quickly giving way to unconsciousness.

This meant that I had no idea where I was now and no recollection of how I even got here. The one thing I did know for certain, and that was I could not use my powers against Matthias. No, it was as if the power I held was somehow connected to his own and instead of it being used to fight against him, I only ended up powering his own abilities and making them stronger.

I got up from the bed and hated the fact that I was forced to use a bucket in the corner to relieve myself, only thankful to see it empty. The skirt of my dress was a tattered mess, so I tore the longer pieces off that trailed along the floor to make it easier to walk... or should I say, fight. A thought that came to me once I heard the scathing voice of the witch.

"Oh, that's a shame, I was hoping that I would be forced to wake you up, as I had thought of some painfully, inventive ways of doing so." I took this opportunity to piss her off by hiding my true reaction of anger, knowing that looking disinterested would be a hit to her ego and hurt her more. So, I faked a yawn and stretched out my arms,

"You know I think I needed that rest," I said, and I could see from under the red hood she always wore, the grimace of annoyance at my easy manner. I allowed myself a knowing grin to stretch across my face, because in situations like this I enjoyed nothing more than pissing off the enemy, and well, as for this one, she most certainly deserved it.

After this she demanded that I go with her, and knowing the strength of her powers, I decided it was best to try and get there with my strength and body intact. I had a feeling that I was going to need both for the fight that was to come.

So, after having only moments awake in the cell to get my bearings, I was walking out of the solid door that had been used to lock me in. I followed the witch who silently led the way and instead of provoking her further, I too remained silent. We looked to be in some kind of remnants of a Castle, very similar to the one that I remembered being in after I was kidnapped by the harpies.

I had so many questions, the main one being, where in Hell was I this time? But the witch was hardly the one I wanted answering them.

I was led down a stone corridor before the witch was pushing open one of the doors, and instead of being led out into a bailey which would have been my first guess, I was led out to that same barren wasteland that I had seen when first stepping through the portal. A vast sand coloured field where only long thick blades of grass grew and nothing else. No trees, no bushes, nothing more than a light orange grass and the crumbling stone remains of the building I walked from.

I turned and looked behind me to see that it had indeed been a Castle, but one long abandoned, for only pieces of it were left, one of which had been the prison that I had been locked in. However, this sight only held my interest for a moment, and that was until I heard Matthias' voice as the witch walked me around the side of the ruins. He emerged from behind what looked like some kind of sacrificial stone, a large slab stood upright that was the height of a house.

Just past this, were tall giant rocks that looked as if they had fallen from the sky and landed in a perfect circle surrounded another rock, only this one had fallen on its side resembling an altar. Each upright rock stood like stone sentinel's with no features, reminding me of Stonehenge, without the slabs across that bridged two stood close together.

Matthias now walked to the centre altar and, with a grin on his face, gestured for me to come forward.

"I must say you are looking well rested, my dear," he said in a smooth tone, unnerving me with the strength of it. Once again, I didn't know what to say, so I decided to say nothing at all. But because I didn't want him thinking that my silence was a sign of weakness or that I feared him, I did as he asked and stepped closer. Once there, he lifted a familiar looking bag from behind the altar where it had been hidden and lay it on top of the stone. Of course, the instant I saw it, I knew what it was…

The Eye.

This was when I decided to speak.

"I don't know what you're planning or think you will get me to do, but if it's to help you in any way by touching that Eye, I'm telling you now, it's not going to happen."

"Is that so?" he said with a smirk, and I wished I had the power to punch it off his arrogant face.

"You're going to have to kill me," I stated in a firm tone, knowing this was no idle threat. And as much as I hated the idea of never seeing Lucius again, breaking my heart at just the thought, there was no way I was going to put his life, or that of my mother's, in jeopardy. At this, he clapped and laughed the once like it was all very amusing to him.

"Ah, but such spirit, such courage, I'm starting to understand and see what it is my brother finds appealing in you and well, after that impressive show of power back in the temple, I most definitely know of the good uses he must get out of you..." He then paused to drag his gaze up and down my body, making me feel sick and nauseated. His eyes homed in at the rips at my legs, as if he had the power to tear them open further with his mind and expose all of me for his sick pleasure. The sight of his sinister grin and obvious lust in his eyes, made me shiver and in all honesty, this time I threw up a little in my mouth.

"Yes, well I think he's going to get a lot more use out of your head when he tears it from your body and presents it to me as a trophy," I replied with a sneer.

"But you have such faith that such a thing is even possible," he said amused.

"Why not get him here and find out by fighting him for yourself, because isn't that what this is all about, some kind of revenge against him, and for what exactly?" I said, ending this as a question I wanted to know the most.

"Oh, I have my reasons, just like Dalene does, don't you, my dear?" Matthias said, as the witch came to stand by his side like a good little Red Riding Hood who worshipped the Wolf.

"As fun as this is, listening to your egotistical mind claim how great it all is, can we just skip to the part where you tell me what it is you want, because clearly, it isn't a fair fight between you and your brother," I said again, trying to sound bored as it had worked on the witch.

"Oh, but you're wrong, for that fight is coming, my dear, make no mistake about that but before it does, I want to make Lucius know what it feels like to go through exactly the type of thing that I was put through," Matthias said, partly answering my question but yet holding enough back. It also made me wonder if Lucius had discovered anything of his brother's motives since I had been pulled back into the Temple.

"Yeah, and what's that?" I said, now keeping him talking and hoping he would give me more. Because it was like that age old saying went, knowledge was power and right now, it was all the power I had!

"To know what it's like when everything you ever had, that you were given and gifted, is then taken away from you. In short, I want back what was owed to me," he said with a flash of annoyance, making his dark eyes glow for a few seconds.

"Which is?"

"Ah, but all in good time, my dear. No, first I want you to tell me where the Tartarus gate is," he said, making me remember the first time he asked, when I was being held by the harpies and they were using Nero as bait against me.

"And why would I tell you that? I have no reason to, as it's not as if you have anything to hold over me anymore and I don't see any bait hanging around," I said sarcastically, reminding him of the time that he had Nero hanging over a well and threatened to drop her to her death and drown her. But then he grinned as if he was counting on this very thing, and just like it always did, a bad feeling shivered its way up my spine. Because Matthias hadn't got this far by not planning for every eventuality. As it seemed as if he was always one step ahead of us, in every direction, and had been ever since we came into Hell.

"You know, I could torture you, chain you up and use you. I could have you beg me for mercy, all of which, as you should know, my dear, I would enjoy immensely," he said, now getting closer to me, and I tried to stand my ground and not let his presence, or his sickening words intimidate me.

"Oh, but to take just a taste of what you gave my brother

on a regular basis, how I would enjoy seeing his face when he realised that his precious Chosen One had been tainted by the hands of another son of the Devil," Matthias said, and as much as I hated to give him the satisfaction, I couldn't help but react from the revulsion his words enticed in me. Of course, if such a thing were to happen, I would probably die fighting him. Anything rather than give myself to him freely, despite knowing that I wouldn't come out of the ordeal unscathed on the other side.

"But quite frankly, I don't really have the time. Now, once this is all over with, then I intend on making you my Queen and fucking you until you beg me to stop, and then continue as I please." At this, I laughed in a mocking way and told him,

"Like I said, Dickhead, I would rather die." His grin turned a deeper depth of evil.

"Yes, but death is not something I class as a punishment… but now as for being forced to live out your life in a way that you feel is a living nightmare, well then, that is a much more fitting end. Besides, I have a feeling that once I've had a taste of you, I will not be so eager or so quick to give you up. After all, there is a reason my brother keeps you around." I was once again about to hurl abuse back at him, when he stopped me by saying,

"But where are my manners speaking in such a way in front of his wife." This was said with utter glee, and I frowned at him, before responding the way he no doubt wanted,

"Yeah, well I'm sorry to burst your bubble, but I'm not yet his wife." At this he started laughing, once again clapping his hands, which seemed to be his habit, and said,

"Oh no, no, no, my dear, you have mistaken me, for I was not talking about you." This was when I swallowed hard and shook my head a little, before trying to force myself not to give him what he wanted again. Which of course, was a reaction. But then this was near impossible, when his words had the power to affect me so much. But surely, he could not be implying what he seemed to be.

Surely it couldn't be true!

But then his eyes brightened in utter joy.

"Oh, I'm sorry, my dear, for I was not aware that Lucius would ever keep something like this from you," he said, faking his astonishment.

"Something like what?" The unsure words were out of my mouth before I could stop them, and his grin widened because of it.

"But you two have met so many times now, that I'm surprised it never came up, or that Lucius never mentioned it… ah well, no time like the present after all, so please let me have the pleasure of introducing you now… Amelia, say hello to Dalene…" he paused in this pleasure as he reached out and ran a cold finger down my cheek, making me turn my head away. Only he grasped my chin in a painful hold and snarled down at me, finishing his sentence,

"…Lucius' wife."

"No! No, no… No, that is impossible… Lucius would never keep something like that from me!" I snapped, hating that I felt the tears start to cloud my eyes.

"Oh, would he not, are you so sure about that? After all, I did witness that very touching moment between the two of you in the Temple. Don't you remember it just before you stepped into Hell? Only moments after you first found out that Lucius had taken a piece of your soul, the very essence you were born with and yet, he kept that from you." At this I ripped my chin out of his hold, despite the pain it caused.

"But I am surprised that you have never wondered what

else he had kept from you. The knowledge of a wife perhaps, or even that…" He paused, bent his head closer to mine and whispered in a menacing way…

"…of a child."

CHAPTER TWENTY-EIGHT

A MOTHER'S HAND

The second I heard this, I couldn't help but stagger back a few steps, as if I had been shot in the heart. It couldn't be true… it just couldn't be!

"You lie!" I shouted, unable to hide my reactions anymore. Because it couldn't be true. Lucius would never keep something like this from me! But then, even as I thought this, Matthias' words played over and over like a weapon against me. Because I never would have thought that Lucius could have kept something as important from me as what he stole from me that day. Yet the truth was, I could not deny that he had. That, in fact, he had kept it from me all of my life. He had also lied and broken my heart purposely, making out as if I was nothing more to him than just some silly little girl with a passing fancy. That I was some spoiled little Princess trying to bag herself a King.

It was through these lies that my insecurities could not rule out what Matthias was saying as being true, even though I was near desperate to. I loved Lucius and I wanted to defend him and his honour in every way. But I also had to question out of all of the things that Matthias could say to me that he could lie about, why would he choose this? Why would he choose what seemed like an impossibility?

But then, the doubts on both sides burrowed further in my mind, because I had seen visions of the witch, I had seen her past.

She had been a little girl.

Which could have only meant that Lucius would have made her his wife after she had grown into this witch. It didn't make sense and my face must have shown as much.

"If you do not believe me, go ahead and touch the Eye and ask of it what you will, for you will see the truth as the Fates cannot lie," Matthias said, playing on my doubts and I started to shake my head.

"This is all a trick, it's just a game to you! A game that you're playing to try and get me to touch the Eye and tell you exactly what you want to know. It won't work, I do not believe you!" I stated more firmly this time as I backed further and further away from him.

"It is of little matter to me what you believe. For, know this, you will touch that Eye and you will tell me what I want to know," he said with his tone becoming more insistent.

"I wouldn't count on it, asshole," I snarled back. Matthias looked unfazed by this, and instead turned to the witch I knew now was named Dalene.

"Call forth the hex and summon her through." I frowned in question, wondering who it was he was talking about now.

"Yes, my Lord," she said, bowing her head. Then, as she raised up her arms, I watched as an eerie green glow emitted from beneath her hood, and the burning white of two eyes shone from the shadows of her face. A power then radiated down her arms to her hands, a pair that she started to move as if creating a portal herself. Yet this time it was different, for it looked more like she was yanking at the very fabric of time! Like she was making the space in front of her warp and twist as she dragged the very landscape out with her hands, stretching it as if she was trying to drag something through.

But then, of course this was exactly what she was trying to do and the moment an image appeared, one being yanked through, I couldn't help crying out at the sight of…

My mother!

"Mum!" I shouted, and she took about two seconds to take in the scene around her before my mother's wrath took hold. A blinding light was all any of us saw as Matthias and Dalene were suddenly blown backwards from the force of the power bomb that had erupted from my mother. I felt the strength of it myself, going back a few steps as if a powerful wind was trying to push me back. So, I threw an arm up over my face, to protect myself when trying to continue to watch what was happening.

As for what I found, then by the Gods, it was nothing short of magnificent! As there my mother was, stood in front of Matthias and Dalene as they tried in vain to fight against my mother's power, as she raised up both her arms. This made them both rise up in the air before she stretched out her arms to pin each of them to the upright stone slabs.

"YOU DARE HURT MY DAUGHTER!" Her demonic voice roared at them until the rocks they were pinned to, began to crack. She became nothing more than a glowing, white-hot figure of fire, as it consumed her body. The sparks of immense power licked out angrily at the air around her as it crackled and hissed with her movements. She still had both her hands out towards them, holding them in place as prisoners to her will.

She was utterly stunning, and a beautifully terrifying image of a mother's wrath come to protect her daughter.

Because my mother's powers were a force to be reckoned with, and this was the first time I had ever seen them, making me gasp in shock. Of course, if I hadn't been so surprised and rendered speechless, I would have been whooping in the air with my fist up like some demonic cheerleader! As my mum continued to hold Matthias suspended, along with the witch, she walked slowly over to me. This was so she could stand in front of me in a protective way.

"Stay behind me, Faith," my mum warned in that demonic voice that I had never heard before this day.

"I'm going to get you out of here," she said, but even I could hear the strain in her voice as if this power of hers would only last so long. Of course, what we really needed was a portal, but it was clear neither of us had the power to create one of those.

However, in the end, none of it mattered, because it turned out that history wasn't the only thing that was coming to bite Lucius in the ass, it was also going to come round and bite my mother too. I knew this the moment the witch started to whisper, despite still held paralysed against the stone by my mother's power. As the moment she did, was when my mum's power started to fade. Both Matthias and the witch were released and fell to the ground, but this was along with my mother who landed on her knees and started holding her head as if in agonising pain.

"Mum! Stop it! What are you doing to her!" I shouted in panic, feeling helpless as I could do nothing to help her other than take her in my arms and hold her to me, as she started to shake uncontrollably.

"Stop it! Stop it, now!" Neither of them listened as Matthias got back to his feet and brushed himself down as if nothing had happened. Then he walked closer to us both and told me,

"Why would I stop it? When I had this all put in place 30 years ago."

"*What?!*" I hissed, shaking my head, trying to understand.

"I knew one day I would need to control her." Again, I started shaking my head as if trying to make sense of what he was telling me.

"*What… what do you mean?*" I whispered, now with every single shred of attitude gone from me and only panic taking its place.

"Your foolish lover believes that all I've been trying to do is get to you both all this time, when in reality, it was never just about the two of you." At this he paused to look down at my mother, still cradled in my arms and shaking, holding her head, and muttering about letting go of something.

"What are you saying?!" I snapped.

"I only ever wanted a few things in life, things that would aid me in my quest for revenge and my ambition for more… *for the things that were taken from me!* You think this plan started with you? Don't be so foolish, the box was something you were always meant to find. You have all been puppets in a very elaborate game, and one that brings us all to this point… where I fucking want you to be! And now there is only one piece missing… but first, I will kill your mother if you do not give me what I want," he said, gripping my arm and dragging me away from her, before clasping a hand around my throat forcing me to look up at him.

"You can't kill her!" I cried out.

"Oh, but I think you'll find that we can. You see, Dalene over there visited your mother once. Years ago, she put herself in a cell deep under Afterlife. But of course, you know of it… your father's prison, of course." As soon as he said this, I was assaulted with the memory of the vision I had seen. Of my mother when she was only human and had not long before met my father. She had found her way down into the prison trying to help a girl she thought trapped.

It had been Dalene.

"She fooled your mother into believing that she needed her help… ah, but I see you've already seen this story before, I can see it in those pretty wet eyes of yours. What you may not know is there, in that very moment, she whispered a spell, one easily cast on her mortal soul. One that would stick there and stay there forever, even long after her transformation into what she is now," he told me, making me cast my eyes down at my mother who was suffering and shaking on the floor. I felt the tears slip down my cheeks at how powerless I felt in trying to help her.

"This was so that one day when we were ready, we would have the power to control her. For it is not your blood I am after and it never was… *it was always your mother's.*" Hearing this, I gasped in shock.

"But why… why my mother's?! I don't understand! It's Lucius' blood you need," I told him on a cry.

"That's where you are wrong, it is the Venom of God I need, and my plan originally was to use you as bait to force Lucius into granting me the use of the Eye. But since it transferred its guardianship over to you, then I believe it has worked out more in my favour, for there is nothing like the love a daughter has for her mother…" Oh God, he was going to force me to do this!

"…And well, today, we get to put that to the test and see just how deep that love goes… so, tell me, my dear, are you willing to save her life? For I assure you, I do not need her alive to gain her blood, but quite the opposite." After this Matthias nodded to his witch and, as if to prove a point, my mother screamed in pain and I tried to yank myself free to go to her, only to be tugged back by my neck, making me choke.

"Uh huh, not without your answer, little Queen," he said calmly. He was clearly enjoying the show when my mother tipped over onto her side and circled herself into a protective ball, as if this would help as she gripped her head so tight. I could see her pulling her hair out as she screamed in utter agony. Tears were flowing freely down my face, knowing that I couldn't stand it much longer. I wanted to take her pain away so badly that I broke down and told him,

"Yes! Please, I'll do anything you want! Just please stop it! Stop her pain!" Matthias yanked me back harder against him and whispered in my ear,

"As you wish, *my Queen of Sins.*" Then he motioned with a flick of his hand over to Dalene and soon my mother's screaming stopped, as it was obvious the pain had been taken away from her. I was then let go so I could run to her and scoop her back into my arms to cradle her against me. Her face was wet, soaked full of tears and sweat dripping down her cheeks.

"It's okay, Mum, it's okay... I've got you... it will all be okay," I soothed in soft voice as I brushed back her damp hair with my palm, wishing I could do more. Wishing that my dad was here and knowing that he would scoop her up into his arms and whisk her off to somewhere safe. Because all I had the power to do to keep her from harm was by doing something I promised myself I wouldn't do. Because I knew now, that to save my mother, I had no choice but to do whatever Matthias asked of me. Even if it meant giving him control over the souls! Because at least that way there was a chance of maybe getting them back. I knew he could have tortured my mother for hours or even worse, he could have killed her outright and still got what he needed, which was her blood.

Suddenly, I was dragged upright from my mother again,

and this time pushed over towards where the Eye sat waiting for me on the stone slab. It was still in the bag that I had put it in before we had left the Tavern, which seemed like an age ago now, making me wonder how events would be playing out now had I not allowed the witch to get the Eye before pushing me through that portal into the Fae realm.

"Now you have a job to do, so I suggest you get on and do it, before I show you what real pain looks like, for I assure you, your mother had only a taste of it. Now, tell me where the Tartarus gate is!" I was shoved so hard I fell into the side of the altar, feeling the edge hit my pelvic bone, making me wince. Of course, I already knew where this Tartarus gate was, having seen it before, the second time I touched the Eye. It was the one that led to a crumbling pyramid, and some kind of temple of sorts that looked as if it had been destroyed in a battle fought against the Titans.

I saw the massive Keystone laid on the floor, and I knew that something needed to be done for it to once again be put in its place.

I would have been able to lead him straight to it, but right now that wasn't why I touched the Eye. Because in my weakness, there was one more thing that I wanted to know.

So, I placed both my hands on the Eye, closed my eyes and let the power surge through me with its sole intent of looking to the past and finding out once and for all the truth.

Which meant the sob soon tore through me the second I realised that what Matthias had said was true…

Lucius… had a wife.

CHAPTER TWENTY-NINE

PAST LIVES

After touching the Eye and letting it show me the past, I had to admit my heart sank when realising that Matthias was right.

He hadn't lied.

This witch, this Dalene, had once been Lucius' wife! I didn't understand why or how or really any of the details, for the flashes of the past that were shown to me, half of them didn't make sense. But what I was certain of, was that Lucius had lied to me yet again, and that knowledge broke my fucking heart!

I had been numb when Matthias had started drawing from the power he had gained in the Temple of the Tree of Souls. One I had only helped with by foolishly adding to it. A power he now used against the monuments of stone as a way to create a portal. As soon as it was finished, he grabbed me, yanking me from my mother once more. I cried out in pain from the bite of his fingers and his rough treatment, before he stood me in front of the portal and placed a palm on my forehead. Then he demanded,

"Show me the Tartarus gate, show me where the Keystone is!" I swallowed hard, and did as he asked before he could hurt my mother again. Then, I closed my eyes, seeing for myself once more what the Eye had shown me, because I knew I had no other choice, he would kill my mother.

By the time I opened my eyes, a large portal that spread out between two of the stones appeared, and was one big enough that you could have driven a car through it. A portal that was now showing the place I had seen in my mind on the other side of a veil of shimmering air.

"Excellent," Matthias said, after walking me through the portal and telling the witch,

"I cast the portal on the outskirts of Tartarus, for the Keystone will have to wait until after I am reunited with my old resting place... bring her mother," Matthias said to Dalene, who bowed her head at her master.

"*Tartarus,*" I muttered in awe the moment we stepped through. As what faced us now was what was left of a once colossal mountain that looked as if an eruption had happened years ago. An eruption that had made half of it collapse back in on itself. We were stood on the side of a cliff that surrounded the landscape below, giving us an unrestricted view of the barren land hundreds of feet beneath us. Because the mountain was surrounded by the dry, open plains of a desert, one that looked like a bomb had gone off and wiped out all life. Like a dark wasteland, and one that looked like every depiction of Hell that had ever been painted, for all it missed was a river of fire snaking through the landscape. It sounded strange, but it was the most Hellish place I had come across yet in the entire realm.

Behind me, I heard my mother cry out as she was thrown through the portal and landed on the floor in a heap.

"Mum!" I shouted taking a step towards her, after first yanking my arm free. Then I crouched down closer to her as she lifted her head to look up at me.

"Both of you get up, it's time to get walking... but we have one more stop to make before we reach the Keystone," Matthias said, in a stern tone that told us both we didn't want to see what he would do if we didn't obey his command. So, I helped my mother get to her feet and placed her arm around my shoulders to steady her.

And we started walking.

We were about half an hour into making our way down a deep canyon, using the jutted rocks like stepping stones. I was making sure my mother stayed on the inside, as I could see her fear of heights was making it difficult for her.

"Seriously, you've been married to a guy with wings for how long, and you're still scared of heights?" I teased, in hopes of cutting through the tension of our dire situation. She gave me wry smile in return. At the very least, she was walking easier and no longer needed my help having gained her strength back. As for Matthias and the witch, they were well ahead of us, knowing that we wouldn't dare try and run. For starters, the distance they put between us meant only one thing, that they could control my mother and didn't need to be close to do it. This meant that we were on an invisible leash.

At the very least it gave us time to talk, even if at first it was difficult to even know what to say. So much had happened between us since the last time we saw one another, there was so much to be said and yet I knew if I started, I would probably end up in tears. Something that was soon confirmed when I said,

"Mum, about what happened, I..."

"You don't need to say anything, Fae," my mum said,

cutting me off and giving me a squeeze around the waist, hugging me to her side.

"But I do! Please, let me just say this." My mother looked thoughtful a moment before she nodded ahead of her, telling me to go first when a slight narrow part came up on the brutal mountain path. So, I grasped her hand behind me, knowing she needed this as we made our way through. Then, when it widened once more, we walked side by side again, and I started my apology.

"Back in the library, when I saw what I thought I saw... well I freaked!"

"I know, Fae," my mother's soft, understanding voice said, making me feel even more guilt for my past actions.

"I got scared and I ran... and I blamed you... and I blamed Lucius and well, I shouldn't have. I should have trusted you," I said, rambling on until my mum squeezed my hand again.

"Oh, Fae, I don't blame you for your reaction. Trust me, kid, I have overreacted many times because of your father, and I have run from him even more. You might not believe this, but before you came along, I made a lot of stupid mistakes, a lot of foolish decisions that got me into dangerous situations. Believe it or not, you are not the only one who came into Hell believing that they could save the one they love," my mum said, explaining then of the time that she too came to this very place in order to try and save my father.

"I had no idea of all the things you did, why did you never tell me? There are all these stories, these amazing things that you and Dad did together for the prophecy, to save the world, and you never told me any of them," I said, unable to keep the accusing tone from my voice.

"Maybe one day you'll become a parent, and you'll realise that you want to protect them, and sometimes that means lying to them or not telling them about the whole truth by keeping things from them. I'm not saying that it was right, and I also know that in a lot of ways we pushed you away by doing it… by not including you in your father's world, *in our world.* I know you felt segregated, sweetheart, but you have to know we have never ever stopped loving you and sometimes, when you love something so much, you can suffocate it with your own protection."

"I get that, I do, but it wasn't easy, especially not when Theo came along," I said, not mentioning my other brother as I knew that would only remind my mother of the hurt she still suffered over Thane, so I tried never to mention him for that reason.

"Look at you, you're so grown up now, you're the one protecting me," my mum said, patting my cheek and looking nothing but proud. I had to admit it warmed my heart. It also gave me enough courage to ask what we both knew needed to be asked.

"I need to know, Mum, I need to know about Lucius… did you…?" I paused for a second as I tried to push past my fears and swallow them down like the lump caught in my throat.

"Did you know he had a wife and a…" I paused again, unable to say it this time, and the second I saw my mother's face fall, was when I had my answer.

"It's not what you think it is, Fae," she said softly, as I wiped the tears from under my eyes that I couldn't have stopped from falling if I tried.

"Oh, honey."

"I know it's irrational, but I feel like he trusts you more than he trusts me."

"That's not true, Faith. I'm not sure why Lucius kept it from you, only now that I know his past… honestly, it's so painful I could barely stop myself from crying just listening to it. But, Fae, you have to know, I only found out about his past moments before I was pulled through that portal."

"What?!" I cried out in shock, astonished by what she just said.

"It's true, and the only reason he told us was because he had no choice. He knew he had made a mistake the moment he went to see his father. He discovered that it was in the Temple of the Tree of Souls that Matthias was waiting for you." I covered my mouth with my hand and sucked in a quick breath.

"Oh, my Gods, does that mean Clay, Caspian?"

"They survived, yes," my mum told me smiling.

"*Thank the Gods!*" I muttered into my hand, now closing my eyes a second as I let that knowledge take hold.

"And… Ruto?" At this my mom shook her head, the pain easy to see in her eyes, telling me that no, he hadn't survived. I felt the heartache in that, yet deep down I'd known there had been no coming back from what he'd endured.

After this, my mom explained the things I didn't know from the point of Lucius getting word to them via Dariush. She also explained to me why it was she felt as if they had the power to control her. When her and my father had only recently first got together years ago, she had been staying in Afterlife and heard the cries of the girl desperately begging for help. It drew her down into my father's dungeon and she had found the witch posing as a mortal girl trapped in a cell. My mum, being the kind hearted soul she was, became easily convinced and tried to help her. This ended up being a mistake as we now knew the girl had cast a spell on her without her even knowing it. One that would lie dormant in the mortal part of her soul, until such time it was needed, today being that day.

But the moment that the spell had been called to the front of her mind, was when years of dreams of the future assaulted her all at once, making her mind feel as if it would explode. It was then that she realised that the spell cast had something to do with being able to see glimpses of the future, and realising this had manipulated the choices my mother had made that all led to her own prophecy.

Of course, her telling me this, made me realise that same prophecy led to Lucius releasing Matthias' power to the Tree of Souls, starting the infection to slowly take hold of its roots. Years later, the first of the rogues became infected not long after I opened the box, making me wonder if doing so didn't somehow speed it up?

My mother also explained everything that Lucius had told her, that had to do with both his past and that of how Matthias came to be. She explained her own reasons behind keeping the knowledge that I was Lucius' Chosen One, was because Pythia, the Oracle, had asked her to do this. She told my mum that it was fate, that if Lucius and I got together too soon, that it could mean that our own prophecy would be in danger. She also admitted how much she regretted not being there for me when she knew that Lucius had broken my heart. She felt helpless and understandably so, because the Fates had made it so that she couldn't help me.

But this led on to what she believed was all fated, and that the box had always been destined to bring us together. Lucius told her that Pythia had been the one to hide the box, knowing that fate would bring us to this point.

"To this point?" I said, questioning that statement with a nod of my head and reminding her where we were.

"Well, maybe not to this point," she admitted sheepishly.

Despite what my mother believed, I didn't trust this. That was because I knew the witch and Matthias had used the box as a tool to get me and Lucius together, and everything had been orchestrated up until this point. Which begged the question, had my mother been played by the Fates?

"It's all about blood, all of it. He said he planted the box, what if it isn't just Lucius' blood that can open it, what if it's actually the Devil's, something all three of them have?" I asked, thinking back over time.

"But Luc said he took it back," my mother added, reminding me of the Devil taking back his blood from Matthias.

"Yeah, well, I don't know, what if he didn't get it all? I mean, they have known everything, every move we have made, what if it was because of the box. But then really, who the fuck knows...?"

"Oi, language!" my mum snapped, making me give her a disbelieving look.

"Really, Mum, we are in Hell, about to get our asses handed to us and cause a war in Hell... and you're telling me off about my language!"

"I'm a mum, sweetheart, even when in Hell," was her crazy reply.

"Yeah, and speaking of Hell," I said, as I nodded ahead when we finally came to the end of the climb, and there in front of us was Mount Tartarus... or what was left of it.

The vast space in between it was where I knew the battle would take place, as it made the most sense. It was also one I knew would not be the first to see blood spilt upon its sand, as my mum explained to me what happened that day she took down the Titans.

I had to say it was difficult, knowing that my clumsy mother, who usually tripped over her own feet and would fall by putting jeans on too quickly, could have the ability to take down the Gods. Of course, she explained about having the blood of Pertinax, and using this to be able to accomplish the task, for only a God had the power to kill a God.

Well, it was just a shame then that Lucifer had taken this essence from my mother, making her once more who she was before. Which was part vampire thanks to Lucius turning her, and also, what my father's essence had also made her. My mum joked, calling herself Heinz 57, saying there were lots of ingredients that made up her mix. Or her natural brand of crazy as Pip would call it.

But then, after this, and with that long way to go still ahead of us, I asked her,

"I know it is not your place, but I need to know. I need to know his past." My mum released a deep sigh and told me,

"I understand, and even though it is not my story to tell, I also know it's one he regrets not telling you himself, as he told me this."

"He did?!" I asked in a hopeful tone, making my mother smile and then she grabbed my hand and gave it a squeeze.

"Would your mother lie to you?"

"I think you just admitted to lying to me, quite a lot actually."

"Okay, so good point, but I wouldn't lie to you now so… yes, he said that." I laughed a little after this, and it would be the last time I did for a long while. As soon after, came one of the hardest conversations I've ever had in my life, as I forced myself to listen to the heart-breaking story of Judas.

I should have been hurt that he had told my mother this before me, but then it's like she reminded me, you often kept the hardest things to say from those you loved the most. And it was true, he had wanted to protect me from the truth, just like my mother and father had. He had protected me from the past that had been too painful for him to want to recall to the person he loved the most. To the one he knew it would affect the most. Because the pain of someone you loved affected you deeper than someone who was there to just listen.

And by the time his story had been told, pain was all I felt.

Because, as my mother told me of those horrific events that led up to the death of Judas, I took every word in and felt it like a slice against my soul... against my heart. And suddenly, the weight of the world that had once solely been on Lucius' shoulders, I had now taken a piece of it upon my own, as I listened to the heart-breaking tale of the death of his child.

One I now knew was named after his mother's favourite flower.

Kala.

CHAPTER THIRTY

SOULS UNITE

I didn't know how long it was that we continued to walk, but by the end of it, both my mother and I were grumbling, vowing together that if we made it through this, then once it was all over, we would go to the gym more… as in, more than never.

"I mean, it's not like we don't have a good excuse, both Lucius and Draven have their own, although admittedly I much prefer to sit on the side-lines and watch your father topless, getting sweaty with a sword in his hand."

"Mum! Come on, not a picture I need to see right now!"

"What, you think just because I'm your mum, I am immune to that man's sexiness and raw hotness?" she said, making me shake my head.

"You spend too much time around Pip."

"You can never spend too much time around Pip, you know that." I smiled at her reply, and would have said something witty in return when suddenly my mum's mouth dropped open, and she said,

"Forget Tartarus, I think we just found Mordor!" I turned my head to see what she was talking about, and she was right, it looked like we had just come across the entrance to Mount Doom!

It also looked as though it was some forgotten entrance into the very mountain itself or at least, what remained of it. We had just been travelling around a collection of fallen boulders the size of office buildings, which were massive chunks of stone that had clearly broken away from Mount Tartarus.

Behind this was a stone staircase carved into the base of the mountain and had, at one time, led across into an enormous open archway. In fact, it made me question if giants lived in the cave, as its entrance was certainly big enough to accommodate them. But how Matthias expected us to access it, I had no clue, as it was clear the bridge had crumbled to the ravine below when the mountain had fallen.

A massive structure framed the archway which had been carved into the rock, creating the appearance of giant pillars either side of the opening. These protruded from the rock face and rose up to the top of the arch, which looked covered in oversized cobwebs. This pale grey webbed blanket then bridged the gaps between the jagged rock and the smooth carved pillars. One side was completely intact, whereas the other had given way to the landslide, losing half of its design. This being the elaborately crowned mouldings, with Ram's horns on top that curled down. Then, in the centre, was a huge statue of a demonic and monstrous face with its mouth open. Its long tongue hung down, with its top row of teeth, sharp and dagger-like, spread out in warning.

Above its head was something I recognised, as I had seen it before. A crown of serpents, that the Harpy Queen had once worn, sat above the head of this carved demon, telling me it had something to do with Matthias. Its face must have been the size of a house, for it sat above the very top of the arch. This was as if threatening all those who approached, silently warning them, that only death would find them should they be foolish enough to enter inside.

I wondered if this was Matthias' own tomb and the place that I now knew Lucifer had imprisoned him for over 500 years. Well, I was soon to find out, as my mother and I followed him up the steps after we both looked at each other, reading the dread on each other's faces.

I watched as Matthias stood at the very top of this stone staircase cut into the rock. Then he held out his arms, and I became amazed to see another glimpse of his immense power. It was the same that I myself could build up inside of me, as he too channelled it to his chest. Then when it grew too big to handle anymore, he threw it outwards and cast it like a glowing cannon ball into the dark and empty cave.

"What do you think he is doing?" my mother asked quietly.

"I don't know... but at a guess I would say it has something to do with that," I said, changing my answer when we started to feel a rumbling beneath our feet. It was as if his power had finally hit whatever target it was meant to. Because seconds later, a fiery glow started to illuminate within the cave and travelled outwards at speed, making it glow brighter and brighter. Then soon we discovered why, as lava started to flow from within before it fell like a waterfall of fire from the edge and into the abyss below. We both looked over the edge to see that this part of the damaged mountain was no longer surrounded by darkness, but had started to fill with a river of lava.

"Dalene, if you would be so kind," Matthias said, looking back at his witch as she approached from behind and took his place at the front. Then she too used her powers against the incredible force of the lava that continued to pull from inside the cave. She moved her hands around as if she was manipulating something right in front of her, and it was then that the flowing lava started to lift.

"Gods," I muttered as she started to drag it closer towards them, making it look as if it was now being forced to flow over an invisible bridge. Something that only stopped when it made contact with our side. Then, once it was done, she waved her hand once more and cooled the molten rock, turning it once more into coarse stone.

Once it was safe enough to step on, Matthias took the lead once more and made his way across the centre of the cooled lava that now acted as a solid bridge. I only wished that there was some way, once they made it to the other side, that we could have destroyed the bridge, turned around and ran away. This was because I knew that whatever was inside that cave, meant being forced to do something that could potentially change the world forever.

One look at my mother and she knew this too, which was why she said,

"Amelia, I want you to listen to me now…" I knew the moment she said my name, one she only reserved for serious and important times like this, what was coming next.

"No, Mum, don't even say it," I told her in a stern tone, but as I started to walk past her, she grabbed me and pulled me back. Then she placed a hand on my cheek and told me,

"I love you, Fae, and I know you love me, but what you are about to do in there is not worth saving my life, not when so many others will lose their own if you do." I started to shake my head, but she placed her other hand on my cheek, ceasing my movements,

"Fae, listen to me, listen to me now, sweetheart… the sacrifice of one to save many, is a rule which we live by." I tore my face free and said,

"And Dad, do you really think he would live by that rule if it meant saving your life…? Or Lucius, do you think he would sacrifice me to save everyone else? Because, if you can look me in the eye and tell me that you honestly believe that, then we will both sacrifice our own lives to save the rest." The moment my mum closed her eyes and I saw a single tear fall from beneath her lashes, I knew my words had rang true.

"Please… we can't allow this to happen," she said, still with her eyes closed as if she couldn't stand the idea of her life for so many. I nodded once and was about to say something else, when the angry demands of Matthias came from ahead. So, we continued moving and I held my mother's hand as we made our way across the bridge and to the other side, before stepping into the once resting place of Matthias.

The long cave continued to flow with lava, only this time it remained at the sides, in the channels created by the cooled rock in the centre. Then, once inside, I could see it was very similar to the Temple of the Tree of Souls. This was because it looked like a massive cavern had been carved right out of the mountain. Its space was lit by flaming medieval sconces, that were hammered metal strips, and held flaming rocks in their half-moon shaped baskets. These were riveted to the rock walls, making the pale stone glow and cast shadows beneath the light above. The river of lava was flowing from the great hole at the centre of the room, telling me this was where Matthias' power had taken the hit. It travelled up, overflowing from below until it then cut off into two streams that made their way out of the cave.

Then, in the very far end of the cave, stood a lone structure, like a small temple, the size of a single-story building. It was all carved from stone and reminded me of the roman temples you would find built to house a single statue and a place for you to worship the Gods. However, there was a very distinct difference, and this was down to the entwined network of black infected roots that lay over the roof of the temple like a blanket of thick black snakes.

This root system then flowed down to the foundations below, that spread out and nearly covered the entirety of the cave floor wherever the lava didn't flow. This naturally made it difficult to walk across. Especially for clumsy people like me and my mum. As for Matthias, he made short work of getting across the vast space of the cave, quickly getting to the temple, and snapping out his orders for us to hurry, something neither of us wanted to do.

I also noticed that the witch was hanging back slightly, and it seemed as if she was muttering to herself, making me wonder if she was casting spells. She also kept making erratic movements with her head, suddenly shaking it. Her hands would then come up by her sides with her fingers curling into tight fists. I nudged my mother and nodded to the witch so she too could take in her strange behaviour.

"HURRY!" Matthias roared out again, following up with a threat to drag us there by our hair if we didn't hurry. So, as we climbed our way through the intertwined roots that only got thicker the closer to the temple we got, it only became harder. Then, when my mum slid down one, I quickly shot out and grabbed her hand, preventing her from falling.

I tugged her up to where I was close to the top, letting out a relieved breath when we made it. Eventually we made it the rest of the way until we were at the temple steps. Then, as I walked through its open doorway, I found the reason why Matthias had named it to be his resting place. A large sarcophagus sat dead centre of the single room and one that too, was covered in roots. This meant the carved design on its sides was long gone and entirely consumed. In fact, it looked as if some tree monster had tried to swallow it whole and left only the lid askew, with a gap big enough for Matthias to have escaped from.

A lid he suddenly kicked off the top, making it crash backwards and slide down the raised dais it was sat on. If I hadn't been in my right mind at that point, I might have made a joke about vampires and their coffins, telling him that this looked like a fixer upper for sure. However, thankfully I refrained.

But it was clear now that what Lucifer had told Lucius had been true. Somehow these roots led straight to the Tree of Souls and had become entwined with Matthias. An infection that had taken years to spread, and one that had been released by Lucius the moment he'd lost his hand, sacrificing it to the Titans Keystone. It all made sense now and was why he brought us back to this place, for this would be not only where he would gain that power back that had been drained from him for 500 years, but where he would also take much more. Draining the souls from the tree itself, gaining every single one tied to Lucius.

And now came the point where I was the one that was to be forced to do this. It felt like the ultimate betrayal I had no choice but to make.

"Now, you will use the Eye to transfer the souls and give me back my power that is owed to me!" Matthias said, handing me the bag with the Eye inside.

"I have no idea how to even do this!" I snapped, but he

growled back at me like an angry animal that was so close to consuming its meal,

"Lies! For what you speak of is lies. I know you can use the power of the Eye, I saw it for myself. Just like I know you transferred power from it to others, like that witch you call friend," he said, referring to Nero, and I had no idea how he knew I had done that when we were about to be eaten alive by Hellhounds. The important thing was that he knew I was bluffing.

"Now, put your hand inside the sarcophagus and spill your blood on the roots, and hold the Eye... do it, or your mother dies!" he snapped, making me look back at my mother. But then by doing so, I also saw the witch, and this time she looked different.

Unhinged. Afraid. Horrified.

"Don't do it, Fae, think about what I said! It's not worth it!" my mother said, pleading with me with her eyes, before falling to her knees and crying out. I shot a look to Matthias to see his eyes glowing as he had that same power his witch had over my mother. But how? Was it being back in this Temple that gave him that strength?

"NO!" I cried out, about to run to her, when Matthias grabbed me by the dress at my back and yanked me from her, before throwing me towards the sarcophagus. I bent double over the edge, looking inside and seeing now the bed of spikes. It was as if soulweed had been used to keep him trapped there, keeping him imprisoned. Of course, I knew of soulweed, and being impaled upon the spikes would drain you of your essence. Which was how Lucifer had Matthias' powers sucking the life from him and keeping him in a weakened state.

"AAAHHHH!" My mother screamed again as I hesitated too long.

"Please stop! Stop it now... I'll do it!" I shouted, as my mother's cries grew louder and the horrific sound vibrated off the walls and seemed to spin around me, consuming my thoughts. I just had to save her, I had to make her screaming stop. I had to end her pain!

"Good, now do it!"

So, with a deep breath I took out the Crimson Eye from the bag, squinting against the bright red glow that grew in intensity as I held it in my hands. I could feel its power and the pull where it wanted me to look inside. To delve into the very core of it and get from it what I required. It had the strength to drag me under and never let me return, for this was what I knew happened to anyone else that touched it. Its power overwhelmed those that it didn't deem worthy. It consumed them with the power of its rage before it killed them, destroying the very essence of what made them.

"No... don't... Fae." My mother's weak voice was barely a desperate whisper as she reached out a hand towards me, trying once more. The pain on her face was an unbearable reminder of what I was about to do. But what choice did I have? Was I really going to sacrifice her life, when I knew that Matthias would only bring more people I cared about to take her place? Because how many would I be forced to lose before I did as he asked. He would take their lives one by one, because he would never stop. This grudge, this revenge, and this bitter rage he had consuming him had lasted over 2000 years, and it was only getting stronger. No, Matthias would stop at nothing, and the only hope that we had was that once I transferred these souls, he would be defeated in the war that Lucius would bring down on his head. For I knew he would not be fighting alone. He had the other Kings... he had,

My father.

So, I reached inside and did what I was being forced to do.

"DO IT!" Matthias bellowed, and just when I was about to grab one of the roots was when something unexpected happened. Because suddenly there was a high-pitched scream, and this time it didn't come from my mother.

"NOOOOO!" The witch shrieked, before power shot through me, sending me staggering backwards against the wall of the temple with the Eye falling from my grasp. I looked towards that cause to see the witch with a bloody dagger held high in her hand, and blood running down over her chest. She had torn the side of her cloak to one side and exposed the scarred skin over her collar bone. Gods alive, but the girl was covered in healed symbols carved into her skin. Just like the one now, which was from the new symbol that she had just cut deep into her flesh. Her head started shaking, as ancient words spilled from her scarred lips. Her hood fell back, and the haunting face of scarred features started casting another spell. This was when Matthias started to look worried,

"Now, what did I tell you, girl? Get back inside where we cast you into the shadows of your own mind!" I couldn't understand what Matthias was saying.

"I won't let you take the souls! I won't let you kill him!" she shouted, making me realise that now she was talking about Lucius. I didn't understand what was happening, other than the fact that his wife was obviously having a change of heart.

But none of it made sense!

"It is too late, child, it is too late to stop us, now give her back to me!" Matthias shouted.

"NO! Not this time, Matthias, I won't let her take over

again!" she shouted, shaking her head and as she raised the dagger closer to her own heart, Matthias reacted by roaring out and shooting power her way before she could do it. This force knocked her backwards and as she hit her head against the stone, it quickly rendered her unconscious. Then, what followed was my mother screaming even louder than before, holding onto her head as she dropped to her knees. Matthias was again forcing his will upon her. Then I watched in horror as one of her arms reached out and grabbed the dropped blade that Dalene had once again tried to use against herself.

I could see my mother struggling against her own will, trying not to let her own arm curl inwards so that the blade may be placed against her own neck.

"NO!" I shouted as soon as it got closer and closer to her skin, now held taut as her she stretched her neck up as if ready for it. She then looked at me and managed to mouth the words,

"I... love... you... Let me... go."

I cried out for my mother before making the quick decision. Because I knew that I now had no choice, for this was it! So, I quickly grabbed the Eye from the floor and ran over to the sarcophagus. Then before he could say another word, I plunged my hand inside, stabbing my hand and impaling my palm on one of the large thorns, knowing that I needed to make a blood connection, because the power was in my blood, I had known that from the moment that I had created it in my father's vault. I held on as tight as I could as the Eye started to vibrate in my arm, where I had it tucked tight to my chest.

"*Gods, aid me.*" I whispered this prayer as my whole body shuddered through the immense power that consumed me. A power that started to flow up from the roots, through my hand and to the Eye I held in my grasp. It was a sensation I had never known before. It was as though every single soul was passing through me, one after the other, thousands of them, hundreds of thousands in fact, all within seconds.

I couldn't breathe. It was as though my own body was suspended and frozen in time, my mouth open, my eyes wide and startled, as if I was nothing more than a conduit. I was just a means to an end, for when the time was right, Matthias took hold of me and placed his hand over mine that was touching the Eye. He then sucked in a shuddered breath before roaring up to the ceiling as every single one of those souls connected with his own. Each one carried with it a slither of his power that had been stolen all that time ago.

It was the most incredible feeling I had ever known and with it the most frightening. I didn't know how long it lasted but as soon as Matthias finally released me, I knew that he would have gained from it all that he needed. I yanked my hand up from the root in sight of what I had done. But then, as I cradled the Eye even tighter to my chest, telling it I was sorry for what I had done, I realised it wasn't yet finished with me.

It had something more to show me, and this would be more shocking than anything that I had ever learned about Lucius' life, because it was something that even he didn't know.

A secret so horrendous that a silent scream tore from me the moment every single vision assaulted me. Every memory that showed me the horrifying truth!

Because Dalene had never been the witch.

She had never been the source of great power.

She had only ever been a prison for the true strength that they kept locked inside her. Two souls fused together and forced to live in one vessel. A vessel that belonged not to Dalene, but in fact to a promise made by Jesus.

A promise he kept.

The resurrected soul of Lucius' daughter,

Dalene was…

Kala's prison.

CHAPTER THIRTY-ONE

BROKEN AND SEVERED SOUL

What had I done?
   I fell to the floor, as the pieces of my life started to crumble around me.

Nothing seemed to make sense anymore, like the parts of my soul that no longer felt like my own. I could barely keep conscious as my eyes failed to open, doing so for only seconds at a time. Barely even more than flashes, and not really enough to take in what was happening. I don't know how long I had been this way, as my mind was too hazy to process the details.

All I could focus on was the images of that little girl being made to stand there and watch as her mother burned at the stake. Something I now knew Matthias himself had been the cause of. I knew in those few moments of being shown her life, that he had tried to manipulate her, doing so with her mother's help since the day she was born.

Because what he found in Dalene when she was pregnant with Kala's reincarnated soul, was a power of the likes he had never known. In fact, I knew, thanks to the knowledge the

Eye had given me, that he had been about to rid himself of Judas' wife, the day after his death. The day after his plan had failed and Judas became the King he always wanted to be. But then, in his rage and as the knife drew closer to her neck, he paused in murdering her, when he felt the power of the life now growing inside of her.

So, he waited until the child was born and as he thought, it was a power that only increased with time as she grew. But this supernatural force inside her was of a Heavenly one. One gifted from the Gods as promised by Jesus. So, Matthias drew from this power and used it to keep her mother alive so she could control the girl. But then, as the years progressed, she grew even more suspicious and rebellious against them. She started having dreams of her father, Lucius, who they had tried to turn her against. She started to understand their evil intent and that Lucius was not the evil tyrant as she was led to believe.

So, Matthias knew something had to be done before her strength grew too much for him to contain. So, to spark her hatred of vampires, he decided what better way than to use her mother. He manipulated for her death to be carried out by being burned at the stake as a witch, by villagers who he veiled as vampires.

Then with it, he used the last of his power to merge their souls into one vessel. However, the moment he did this, Kala saw every evil intent her mother possessed, including the knowledge that she had been the one to end her first life. She saw that day through her mother's eyes as she watched with distaste and jealousy as her father cried over her death. In that moment, it was the first time she truly knew what it meant to be loved by someone.

But 2000 years was a long time to be manipulated and finally, when she grew into a woman, she discovered a way to escape. But this came at a price, as each time she would have to carve a releasing rune into her own skin, allowing her some time to be in control. Matthias used her for her powers, locking her will away and allowing her mother to take full control.

It was a prison of flesh she was forced to endure. Forced to watch as their plans grew closer and closer to fruition, knowing that Matthias' plan was so much more than just simple revenge against her father and against his own. But then, as my mother's existence came to light, Matthias knew it was only a matter of time. But first he needed to get an angelic soul into Hell, and there was only one way to do that.

My father.

So, they manipulated Layla, and used her obsession with Lucius, planting her with him to watch his movements throughout time. Then, when she was needed for more, they had her stab my mother in Afterlife, knowing she would be cast down into the dungeons. Once there, a summoning hex brought Dalene to be caught trying to break her out and she was put exactly where she was needed. Because I had been right about one thing, she had needed my father to kill her and send her soul into Hell, for she could not take Kala there freely.

This then turned her powers into something darker and gave Matthias the darkness he needed. But in his quest for revenge, Kala still tried to stop him. There were moments when she tried to keep me and Lucius apart, thinking this the way to prevent the future she was plagued with. Even when she tried to steal the box in that winter garden. Of course, her hatred for me was one of blame, for I was to be the cause of her father's fall. I remember her shock at finding out I had already taken his blood. Something she knew would have the power to open the box and discover the map.

Matthias had been the one to send the Hellhounds, and their intention was to find Kala, but they found me instead. But then the answer came as to why even after I had opened the box, they still needed it back. Which was when I realised the box held so much more than just a means to get us into Hell.

It was a key.

A key he still needed.

"Ah, but finally, here is the last piece of the puzzle," I heard Matthias say, and this time it forced my eyes open. This was when I saw a lone figure step from the shadows. Another soul he now controlled, and one that I knew was powerful enough to destroy everything!

And this was not because of what he carried with him, but because he was someone who knew how to get into Lucius' vault, someone who was acting against his own free will.

The one with the power to rip Hell apart. All he needed was a single command from his soul's keeper.

"*Adam.*" I felt my lips move but no sound came out as I watched my uncle hand over the box to Matthias.

"Well done. Now we will go to the Keystone and once there, my plan will be complete, as I finally get to meet my brother for the first time on the battlefield."

I shuddered on the ground, knowing what this could mean as Adam handed the box over to his new master. But then I heard another voice, one I knew better than any other, for it was the first I'd ever heard.

My mother.

At first the relief hit me in my chest, thanking the Gods that she was still alive. But then, when she too was at the ready to do Matthias' bidding, I knew that her soul was like that of Adam's... *it was lost*.

Just like all the others.

Gods, what had I done!

I looked to the ground to see that the witch was still unconscious, and I wondered who she would be and which version of herself would I find when she awoke.

And as for me, well I could feel myself falling under, with my own soul soon to become lost to the control of another.

I also knew, thanks to these visions, what would happen the moment Matthias finally found the Keystone. For his ultimate goal was not just to get his powers back and to claim every soul that Lucius had once owned.

He wanted to kill his father and take over Hell.

He wanted to become…

A Titan God

CHAPTER THIRTY-TWO

LUCIUS

ELYSIAN FIELDS

It had begun.

I knew it the moment I fell to my knees, crashing to the floor as the crushing impact of having every soul leave my own, rendered me unconscious. It was like suddenly finding myself breathing for the first time all over again after my death, only now this was in reverse as I opened my eyes and saw the sky above me. I felt the blades of grass surround me, questioning where I was this time.

"Judas… Judas… come on now… we have to go." I heard a sweet soft voice I barely even remembered, but one I did all the same. As though it had been but a glimpse in my memories and somewhere buried deep. I sat up, squinting and holding my hand up against the sun from blinding me. Then I blinked away the dark spots in my eyes, and focused on my surroundings as that enchanting voice still called for me.

"Mother?" I questioned the moment I recognised it fully

this time, but I had been only a boy then. That's when I glanced over to the figure moving in the field we used to play in. She was holding out a hand to me, telling me to go to her. I found myself trying to think back to a time before this. Trying to recollect something I needed to be doing... something important, but then she grinned at me, such a beautiful smile. I remember my father telling me once that he fell in love with that smile and everything else after that followed. He hadn't been the same after she was taken to the next life.

But then again, neither had I.

"Judas, come on Judas... your father will be wondering where we are," she called to me again.

"I don't understand," I admitted, the sound of my voice feeling strange, as it too was one I didn't recognise. I then looked down at my hands and saw for myself a pair I had not seen in a long time... so many lifetimes ago. For they were not the hands of Lucius, the vampire King, they were the hands of my mother's son...

The hands of Judas.

"Now, haven't you got somewhere else to be?" Suddenly this was a new voice, and I spun around as this time it was one I knew well. I then took in the beautiful face staring back at me, a face I would never forget. Gods, she was stunning. She looked like some fallen Goddess, in a white flowing dress with her dark hair spilling over her shoulders in a carefree way.

"Amelia?" I said her name in question, surprised that she was here too.

"We're all waiting for you, Lucius... *I am waiting for you,*" she added, and this time when I looked down at my hands, they were back to being those belonging to the lover she had called me. I knew now what this was. It was a test with two choices to make. I could go with my mother as Judas, or I could go with Amelia, my Fated One and fight for her and for a future where we may be together.

"Amelia, where are you?" I asked, wondering now if she had some kind of connection to me and this was her way of holding on.

"I am in Tartarus waiting for you. The Keystone is waiting... don't let him get there." The moment she said this I sucked in a startled breath, knowing what this meant. Matthias wanted the blood of the Titans to change him into a God. Which meant that we had to stop him before that happened!

I already knew that if I was here in the Elysian fields, that all the souls that had once been a part of me, were now lost. Amelia must have had no choice but to use the Eye to transfer them into Matthias. But that didn't mean that all hope was gone, for if she was able to reach out to me here, then there was still something left to fight for.

And I knew I would rather die fighting, than just give up and turn around to walk towards a memory that was long since dead and buried. Because I was not that man anymore. Judas had died not long after my daughter had taken her last breath. Lucius was who I was now, even if I had to fight to keep the name. For I would rather die with the memory of me falling on the battlefield than dying the moment my souls were taken from me.

So, I took one last look at my mother as a way of goodbye, and then took the only hand that mattered to me...

I reached out for my Queen.

CHAPTER THIRTY-THREE

QUEEN OF SINS

"He's back!" I heard someone shout, the moment I came back into my body with a start. I opened my eyes and found a hand slowly come into focus. It was one held out to me and the moment my vision finally cleared, I clasped it and was swiftly pulled upright by Dom.

"What happened?" he asked, and even I could see that he had clearly been concerned for me. But then no one would have known what possible outcome there would have been for me once the souls had been taken. At the very least I could feel my demon still clawing at me, ready to take control. I released a frustrated growl and told him,

"The war has begun, he has taken the souls and is making his way to the Keystone."

"Fuck… and Keira, Amelia?" he asked in a desperate tone, one I too felt deep in my core. For it was so strange, this feeling of sudden… *emptiness.*

I shook my head, telling him I didn't yet know if they too were under his control… however, I didn't want to add that the outcome of their souls being any different to the rest, was highly unlikely. So instead, I looked around the open space to see that we were on the edge of Tartarus. Then, with narrowed eyes, I saw all of our people and our armies amassing behind us. There were legions of them and none, not a single one, was loyal to me. I had to admit, it was a bitter pill to swallow for a King.

For I was now a King with no Kingdom.

"Fuck, how long was I out for?" I asked, knowing then it must have been a while for all of this to have happened.

"A few hours at least. Turn around, for we haven't been the only ones busy," Dom said, and I did as he suggested, now walking closer to the edge so I could see for myself what we were up against.

Fucking thousands!

I sucked in a startled breath when I saw before me an army that was once mine, and the greatest ever combined.

"Fuck me," I muttered under my breath, a curse Dom heard.

"My sentiments exactly, although I will say our own is shaping up nicely." I turned then to see our own forces, and it was true, for despite us not having the numbers, what we did have on our side was strength. All those of a demonic nature had been pulled together from both sides. With the exception of a few that Dom explained were the ones left behind to try and prevent any more of the rogues entering Hell at the portal gates. This was because Matthias was calling forth every soul that belonged to him to fight in this war. Sigurd, Ragnar, Vincent, Seth, and Takeshi had all been leading Dom's Enforcers in creating their own army to prevent the vampires from returning. Theo was naturally in charge of this, using his own council to aid him. For if the vampires from the mortal world also managed to get through, then we would be looking at hundreds of thousands, and a force all of Hell would not survive against.

"And my brother?" I asked, tensing and bracing myself for the outcome.

"Still unconscious, and I hate to say it, but in all likelihood he will remain this way unless the hex is removed or the one who put it there is killed," Dom told me, fearing what I already knew, because his body and his abilities had been used against his will for the last time. As he had fought so hard against this summoning, his body had tried to reject the hex and as a countermeasure it had tried to consume him. His power and the power of the spell were fighting one another, and Dom was right, soon one of them would have to die.

So, as I looked behind me now, I knew the time had come for the battle to commence, as I could already hear the battle cries from below. Matthias' forces were growing restless and ready for the fight, great hordes of them, all in their different ranks. Demons, monsters, shapeshifters and everything in between were all down there. The ghostly figures of the Dybbuks and the wild beasts of the Chimera. This along with the pounding hooves that created their own war drums from the herds of Centaurs. And of course, there were the hordes of Gorgon leeches, and all of these creatures came with their own masters that had once been loyal to me.

As for our side, we consisted of many demonic forces, with a few exceptions. Like the Aqrabuamelu, these scorpion-men of ancient Mesopotamia, or the red-faced demons of the Oni. Giant ogre-like monsters of Japanese descent, the Oni are man-eaters who carry with them their heavy iron clubs, ready to do damage.

Speaking of which, Matthias' first wave had been released and were currently making their way up the cliffside.

These were none other than a pack of hundreds of Hellhounds.

"Excuse me, I think this is where I come in," Jared Cerberus said, rolling his shoulders and taking off his jacket, throwing it off to one side to a girl known as Smidge, who caught it on a growl. But then he always acted as if this was his prized possession, one he didn't want to get dirty... or should I say, almost ripped to shreds when he finally changed into the Hellbeast King he was. The large members of his council shoulder barged their way through the line of people coming to the front, his own brother, Orthrus, included. The guy was about the same size as Clay, who I knew we would now be fighting against. Him, along with every other member of my council, I thought bitterly, as I loathed to imagine meeting them face to face on the battlefield. Fuck, but these men would be a formidable force on their own!

As for Cerberus' army, one by one, each of his Hellbeasts changed into their other forms, with skin cracking and joints popping, as they fell to all fours and gave way to their Beasts. This was just in time, as they leapt from the cliff face, taking with them the first line of Hellhounds that had reached the top.

I closed my eyes and called forth my other form, welcoming my demon and with it, the armour I knew would protect me. However, I knew it would be no match for that of a Titan... should we fail, and it came to that.

I released my wings, watching Dom do the same, now embracing his own demonic side of his nature. But then, just as I was about to command the army into battle, I heard my name being called by a familiar sound,

"Luc! Oh, thank a Gods ball sack! I can't find Adam! We were on our way here through the portals and then when I turned around, he was gone... well, after the bastard pushed me through that was, but I thought that was some kind of new foreplay before battle type thing!" Pip looked frantic, and it was not a usual sight I could say that I'd ever seen her in.

But then, after this, an almighty roar tore through the battlefield, shaking Mount Tartarus and causing parts of it to cave in on itself even further. Suddenly Abaddon erupted from the inside and jumped, landing on legions of men below, killing those that were on his own side.

"Oops, my bad, never mind, found him!" she said, wincing when she saw him kick an overly large Aeternae out of his way, a creature with bony, saw-toothed protuberances sprouting from its head. I released a sigh, knowing now that we had even bigger problems on our hands. I looked down at Pip to find her chewing on a painted nail that look like it held a small dick in the centre. Naturally, I didn't ask, as was the way with most things to do with Pip. It was always better not to ask.

She was also dressed in some cosplay warrior outfit that made her look more like a cartoon character. This was complete with a green cape attached to massive golden shoulder pads, that would have even been too big for the 80's, and a gold helmet with pink wings glued to the sides. And I had to say I didn't think the white strip of material across her tits that said Candy Coated Hell, was going to cut it. Nor did I think the fake fur, and bright pink skirt, complete with furry boots was going to do much in the way of protection either. I rolled my eyes and stormed to one of the nearest warriors. Then I ripped his shield out of his hand, thrust it her way and said,

"Be safe, Imp, and remember, your husband isn't under your control or mine anymore, he is under the control of Matthias, so shaking your tits at him is not going to work this time, little squeak."

"Gottcha, boss man!" she said, giving me a salute.

"Any ideas what we can do about that?" Dom asked nodding towards Abaddon, making Pip pop her bubble gum and push back the riot of green curls that were currently in bunches at the top of her head.

"Hey, I will have you know that's my Hubba Bubba you're talking about," she snapped, before popping another bubble in her mouth. Then, this Hubba Bubba of hers started on his rampage, picking up a centaur and throwing it at us, forcing us to all sidestep as it went rolling through our army like a cannon.

All three of us followed its path of destruction before we looked back at Pip.

"Okay, so yes, anger management might be on the cards when we get home, that or tantric sex with me dressed as a kitten... one of the two," she replied, painting an image I really didn't want before a battle... or ever for that matter.

"Right," Dom said, looking as if he held the same thoughts as I had.

"Leave him to me," Lucifer said, after landing next to us in his demonic glory and looking like a demonic God we, most definitely, needed on our side. He was followed shortly after by Dom's father.

"Leave him to *us*... you know you can't take him on your own, besides, who helped you get his ass into that pit the first-time round?" Asmodeus said, making Pip huff,

"Hello, if you're all gonna talk smack about my husband, the fight's gonna start right here! I don't care if you're the Devil and I don't care if you're the King of Lust... although, just so you know, you're my favourite out of all the Kings... big fan... just saying."

"I don't care who deals with him, I just need him out the way. Dom and I are going to get as close to Matthias as possible, for we need to prevent him from getting to the Keystone as I know now that this battle is only a distraction to his end goal," I told them.

"Zagan and Sophia will lead our armies," Dom said, and at this Sophia slipped through her husband's legions with him behind, both of them clearly ready for battle and in full armour.

"Hey, old man," Sophia said in a sweet tone going up to her father and kissing him on the cheek in a loving way. Then she walked over to Pip and they exchanged a fist bump,

"Hey, girlfriend, you ready to get our last Titanna back?" I didn't know what this meant but I was pretty sure it was referring to Keira in some manner. Dom must have thought so too as he interjected dryly,

"Leave Keira to me, I will get her back, even if it's kicking and screaming and trying to take my head off." And I was of the same sentiment with Amelia. Although, I had to say, I think Amelia was going to be a little easier to handle, unless, of course she had mastered the use of her powers, because if that was the case, then I was screwed. Or should I say royally fucked, and not in a good way!

"Any ideas on how he's going to resurrect this Keystone, last I remember we destroyed it for good reason?" Dom asked.

"He's going to use the box," Lucifer informed us, making me grit my teeth as a growl of frustration made its way through.

"Come again?"

"I might not have been completely forthcoming with you regarding the box," he admitted, making me want to punch the fucker!

"But of fucking course not!" I growled, stopping myself from dragging a gauntleted hand through my hair and tearing every fucker out, leaving me to go into battle with patches of hair fucking missing!

"The box was not just a way for me to communicate with Pythia, but it was also a weapon."

"So that's the real reason he took it," I replied with a sneer.

"It cannot be used without the Venom of God, for when that blood is poured inside, it will open up and become a key."

"A key to what exactly?" Dom asked, as he could see I was on the edge.

"It enables you to reverse the effects of the Venom of God, something used to both release and bind the Titans to their prison. The box makes it so that the Keystone grants the power of the Titans. This is how he will use it," Lucifer said, making me clench my jaw as I knew he was fucking keeping more from me.

"Oh shit, that's why Adam was mumbling something about a box before he pushed me through the portal," Pip said, now remembering this, and obviously explaining to us who in fact had retrieved the box for Matthias. Because, of course, he would fucking know that Adam would know how to get into my vault, being my second!

"Fuck!" I hissed, before snapping,

"You didn't think that this would be an important bit of information to tell me when you had the chance, like when I had the fucking chance to say, bury the fucking box a mile underground!" I snapped, making Lucifer shrug his shoulders and as usual take not a fucking shred of responsibility for his fucked up actions!

"Dom, I think it's time we go get our girls," I said, before I started the fight right here.

"Lead our armies into battle, and may the Gods be on our

side!" I said, before launching myself up into the air and taking myself over those that were already making their way across the battlefield. Thankfully, both Dom and I knew where the Keystone remained, and were heading that way now. However, unfortunately this was when we found ourselves with a new foe to fight.

Minokawa.

This was a giant demonic eagle, a hundred times the size of Dom's pet bird, Ava, who she had in fact been created from. Its lava filled veins heated up each feather as it headed straight for us, meaning we had no choice but to try and fight the fucking thing in the air! However, the moment this beast started to release what I knew would be a poison, I shouted to Dom,

"Look out!" But then I also knew this would come too late as it opened its large beak, ready to let out this poisonous mist. One that the second it touched our skin, would make our wings useless and we would fall to the depths of the army below. I shouted again, as I could see its energy building up and just as I believed it was too late, a stream of ice came from nowhere before I saw the body it belonged to.

The McBain brothers.

Their combined beasts rose up in the air like a mighty force, taking down the Minokawa as easily as if it was nothing but a common bird. The ice scorched the creature before it let out a high-pitched cry, and then fell crashing into the thousands below. I nodded my thanks to all three of its heads before watching as they swooped down low, becoming an army within themselves. Now grabbing large groups of the solders with all six of its feet before throwing them against the mountain it circled around.

Dom and I carried on now that the skies were free of enemies, as those with wings now wisely stayed on the ground, no doubt not wanting to chance a death like they had just witnessed. I turned when I heard a battle horn blow, as this was the signal for our own armies to rush into battle. We had the advantage from above as legions were charging down the slope, using arrows and streams of power and magic to throw down at the infantry below. Yet, despite this advantage, I also knew that as it stood, it would not be enough for we were far too outnumbered. This was because Lucifer and Asmodeus had no choice but to take their own forces and try to deal with Abaddon. Because if he was to allowed to escape into the rest of Hell, then it would not take him long to destroy its entirety. Matthias and his Titan power be damned. For nothing could stop Abaddon.

Already he had split parts of the land, making sections of it come away so that the armies were split. Of course, Dom had his legions, Sophia hers and also her husband's, but seeing as mine was reduced to zero, it still meant we were outnumbered.

"LOOK!" I turned my head when Dom nodded in the direction that would flank our forces. Carn'reau and his army had just appeared, bringing with them some Dragons that belonged to his brother, along with some of his own army.

"Thank the Gods," I muttered as aid had come after all, for I could see them already charging into battle. Thank fuck, for the Fae were beautifully swift and brutal and with each swipe of their blades, they took down ten of our enemies. Already I could see them hacking down wave after wave of demons. As for Jared Cerberus and his council of Hellbeasts, he too was making headway through the packs of Hellhounds. Someone new was leading the Hellhounds and controlling them. I had never seen him before and I got a glimpse of him, now coming head to head with Jared himself.

I wanted to be down there charging into battle and taking

on as many of our enemies as possible, but right now I knew there was only one enemy standing in my way, and until the very last breath had left my body, then I would fight him until I had crushed his black dark heart in my fist!

Dom and I landed in the part of Tartarus that used to hold the temple of the Titans. But because everything in the land had shifted when Mount Tartarus had fallen, it could not be seen in the rubble. This was why Matthias didn't know where the gateway was anymore, and we were the only ones with that knowledge, for I remember Amelia telling me that this had been one of the things that Matthias had demanded to know from her when she was captured by the harpies. I had believed it pointless at the time, seeing as there was no way to bring back the Titans, for they were long gone. But I had underestimated him, and so had our father.

"Any ideas?" Dom asked,

"MATTHIAS, COME AND FIGHT ME!" I bellowed in rage.

"That would do it," he responded dryly when he heard the furious roar of my brother in response. Then suddenly he appeared behind the formation of rocks that I gathered had once been the temple entranceway. He was not at all like I remembered but then, that had been when I believed him to be merely a mortal. However, I could already tell the power he had gained, for he was at least seven foot tall and now wore a demonic amour like most warriors of Hell.

"Ah, but we meet at last, for I confess I have dreamed of this day for over 2000 years," Matthias said with his demonic voice echoing.

"Funny that, because I only knew I had an asshole brother not long ago and really didn't give a shit about your existence," I replied in a dull tone, knowing that this would get to his ego.

"Yes, well as much as I would enjoy fighting you, I have two people here that would probably enjoy it more. Ladies, if you please." At this, Keira seemed to come out of nowhere, and started attacking her husband with a ferocity of the likes I had never seen from her before. One kick and he was on his ass, sliding along the floor. It was as if she had been consumed by rage, and that was when I realised that his control over the souls now fuelled them with hatred and the darker parts of his own soul.

But unfortunately, I didn't watch him getting his ass kicked for long, as I had my own Hellcat to deal with. Something that started when she walked up to Matthias, and curled herself into his side, as he draped his arm around her. Then he grinned at me with a knowing smirk that I wanted to rip off his face.

Because that's when I knew that my nightmare was quickly coming true, and Amelia had indeed fallen under his control.

"Why, how rude of me, let me introduce you to..."

"My Queen of Sins."

CHAPTER THIRTY-FOUR

ALL'S FAIR IN LOVE AND DEATH

I had to say that when I finally came to rescue Amelia, I was not expecting to find her as a Hellcat Princess intent on kicking my ass, and fuck me, she was strong! I thought her powers would have increased, and unfortunately this was proven right when she fired balls of energy my way. Thankfully, these had been off target by quite a lot, giving me enough time to get out of the way. Which meant, she may have been strong but, thankfully, she had a shit aim.

As for Keira, she too was giving Dom more than just a hard time. Of course, this was made even more difficult seeing as the two of us didn't exactly want to fight back, and every move we made was done just to survive. It was in one moment that I found myself thrown back by the force of Amelia's kick, and landed close to Dom when he too had found himself with his face in the dirt.

"Was this what you had in mind?" Dom asked through gritted teeth, making me backflip to my feet and tell him,

"Not exactly."

So far, neither girl had said anything, but I had to say, out of the two of them, Keira was the one who seemed more out for blood. I knew this the moment that Dom was picked up by the blinding white force that consumed Keira's body. She looked like an avenging Angel and threw him into the side of the mountain we were fighting against. As for Amelia, she seemed to be enjoying herself, and I had to question why.

As for the battle, it continued on behind us, with a deafening sound of battle cries, demonic bellows of anger, and the screams of those that were moments away from being slain. This was combined with the ear-splitting sound of Abaddon trying to break his way out of Tartarus, where Lucifer and Asmodeus fought to keep him. It had to be said that Lucifer could lay one hit on such a beast and the force of it managed to knock him back a step. But, then again, a single punch from a God had the ability to do much more damage than just break your nose. Now, as for Amelia, I felt my blood trickling down my face more than once, and like Dom, we spent our time trying to block and pin them down to catch a breath.

But then I also noticed that Amelia kept looking back at Matthias, and this made me furious.

"What's the matter, sweetheart, looking for the pussy whipped asshole that has girls fight his battles for him?" I threw at her angrily, trying to tell myself that it wasn't actually her fault, but feeling the irrational need to say these things in my anger. Then, as soon as she saw that he was out of sight, obviously having enough time to enjoy seeing her trying to kick my ass, she suddenly threw herself flat against the rocks. Then, I watched as a darkness overtook her, and this was when my fear doubled.

"Amelia!" I shouted her name running over to her, and as soon as Dom was thrown this way, like some fucking winged ragdoll, he managed to ask,

"What's wrong with her!?" This was before Keira was at him once more, punching her fist into the rock he just managed to move his face from in time. Thankfully, he was the only one that she wanted, and she snarled his way, once more engaging in the fight. So much for a happy marriage, I thought wryly.

But back to my girl, who was now looking more demonic in nature by the second. Her skin was starting to look grey, and her veins looked to be filled with a black poison. Was this the work of Matthias?!

"Amelia!" I shouted her name again, this time braving taking her by the arms and giving her a shake, bracing myself for her wrath for doing so. A few moments later, she seemed to snap out of whatever had consumed her, before punching me in the face and knocking me flat on my ass. I groaned, getting back up to my feet after spitting the blood on the floor, then I cracked my nose back into place so it would heal without me looking like a dickhead.

After all, my girl liked me handsome, and I would have preferred to stay that way.

"That was a sneaky move, sweetheart," I told her, but then she ran at me, jumping at the last moment to wrap her legs around my waist and propelling her body round, taking me off my feet. It was in this moment that she landed on top of me, then she pinned my arms to the ground, and said,

"All's fair in love and war, lover boy." Then, as I was still left stunned beyond words, she lowered down and kissed me quickly, before whispering,

"Remember, you're not the only one who can act." Then she slapped me on the chest and demanded,

"Now, get your ass up, handsome, we have an asshole to kill!" My mouth fell open in shock as she spun out of the way. I finally got to my feet, grabbing her hand and pulling her back to me.

"You were faking it?" She smirked at this and said,

"Don't worry, honey, the battlefield is the only place I would do that." Then she winked, making me fucking laugh, the last emotion I thought possible of emerging during this time!

"Good to know... and your mother?" Amelia looked towards where her mother had just kneed her father in the balls, making him fall to his knees before she kicked him in the face. Amelia winced, but not as much as I did knowing exactly how it felt.

"Oh no, she's actually gone bat shit crazy, vampire zombie style, speaking of which, we don't look like we're winning," she said nodding to the battle, and I had to agree with her. In fact, we were close to having to fall back, because despite the added help from Carn'reau, what had once been my own forces were just too great of an army set against us. I could see now in the distance the likes of Caspian, charging in his minotaur form, taking out groups of Fae soldiers.

"No, the only chances of us winning are for me to gain back the souls... if such a thing is possible." At this she winked at me and said,

"Oh, it's possible, and as for our chances of winning, I decided we may need a little help in tipping the scales in our favour." I was about to ask what she meant when Amelia nodded behind me, and I turned around in time to witness the impossible.

"*Wraiths.*"

"I knew I said I wouldn't do it, but I felt like I had no choice and besides, they were pretty good about it. They even seemed a little excited... at least, that's what I thought they meant when they started trying to grin," Amelia said, and I watched in utter awe as a swarm of black ghostly warriors swept over the opposing army, outnumbering them now three to one. Engaging our forced enemy in a never-ending fight, for the Wraiths could not be beaten.

"You're a fucking genius," I muttered, unable to help myself, making Amelia chuckle behind me. Then I felt her lean into my back, get up on her tip toes and tell me something even better,

"You wanna know the best part?" I looked down over at my shoulder at her and nodded.

"I told them not to kill anyone. All they have to do is keep fighting and keep them busy long enough until we can find a way to get you their souls back." At this, I couldn't stand it any longer, so I twisted my body and banded an arm around her waist so I could lift her up to my lips. Then I kissed her with so much emotion I felt like I was going to burst.

"You're fucking perfection," I told her, making her blush, and then she said with a grin,

"I seem to be a lot of fucking good things today." I nipped at her lip and growled,

"You're my fucking hero." She giggled and then I put her down.

"Well, let's not get ahead of ourselves, because we still have one big problem."

"I know, but he will not get my blood." At this she winced, and said,

"He already has it, don't forget you're not the only one with the Venom of God in their veins, and he already took my mother's blood." At this, my gaze shot up to see if he was any closer to opening that fucking box!

"I have a plan, but you're gonna have to trust me." I looked down at my beautiful Chosen One and told her,

"From now on, I will trust you in anything, for I never should have thought that I could have done this without you." After this she raised her hand to my cheek and gave me her soft loving eyes, before she reached up, kissed me on my other cheek, then she told me,

"In the words of Han Solo... *I know.*" Then she patted where she'd kissed, took my hand, and explained her master plan.

"It's time to fight your big brother, and while you do that, I'll get the Eye." As far as plans went, it wasn't the most elaborate, but nevertheless, I shrugged my shoulders and said,

"Yeah, that'll work." She grinned at that before telling me,

"Time to see how good your acting is, because you're gonna have to hit me." My eyes narrowed.

"What!"

"Come on, you have to make it look believable, we get closer, you then hit me, I fly across the floor, and he pays me no attention, so you start fighting him and then I am free to sneak and get the Eye... you see where I'm going with this, right?" she said with a rush of words.

"Unfortunately, yes," I conceded.

"Oh, come on, don't be a baby about it, I mean I'm not asking you to break something, just make it look believable," she said, making me grit my teeth.

"Fine, but I'm not punching you, and nothing in the face... you're too pretty for that," I said with a smirk.

"Oh, you are so smooth for a guy about to hit his girlfriend... kidding, kidding," she commented with a wink, and I hung my head with a sigh and let her lead me over to the perfect place. One, so that when she was to fall, he would see. Meanwhile, as we walked past Dom and Keira, she was currently holding a boulder suspended in front of her.

"Now, put that down...! Keira, I mean it, put it down...

don't you dare throw… don't you… *dare… fuck*!" This ended the moment she threw it and it hit him in the chest, making him fly backwards… the poor bastard.

"Jeez, I really hope they don't need marriage counselling after this," Amelia commented dryly before getting into position. So, I grabbed her by the top of her arms and whispered,

"You ready?"

"For you, always," she said sweetly, before screaming in my face,

"DIE VAMPIRE!" I raised a brow at her and mouthed 'really?' and she rolled her eyes before I did something I really didn't want to do. I swung around and threw her bodily through the air, knowing that the landing was going to fucking hurt. However, she went flying past the point where Matthias would see and as soon as I saw that she'd hit the rocks, I winced, bunching up my shoulders as if I could feel her pain. The glare she shot me was most definitely not acting, that was for sure.

Then it was time to face my brother, so I let the length of my sword, Excalibur, be summoned to my hand. It had been a long time since it tasted blood, and I swung it around, rolling my wrist as I shouted,

"COME OUT AND FIGHT ME, YOU COWARD!"

I stepped around the rocks to see just in time as Matthias was spilling the blood he had obviously collected from Keira onto the centre of the box. Then I watched as it started to open up, just like it did that day I discovered how to read the map. Only this time it folded in on itself, spinning and creating a pyramid. It became an exact replica of the Temple of the Titans. Then it started to sink into the ground as if melting, becoming liquid stone.

I knew then, that unless I kept him away from it, we

would all be dead. Upon hearing my voice, he snarled at me over his shoulder, before concentrating back on his task at hand. I could see now the rocks starting to rumble, as if something was coming.

I was running out of time.

"Okay, I guess that didn't get your attention, so let's try this." I released my wings and flew over to where he stood and when I knew I was in position, I folded them in and let myself fall, holding my sword at the ready. I expected to see it slice through his torso, but the moment I was within an inch of him, he spun quickly and grabbed the blade.

"Oh fuck!" I muttered, before he used it to swing my body round and propel me into the rocks. Needless to say, it fucking hurt. However, instead of just letting my body slump to the ground like it almost begged me to do, I shrugged off the hit and pulled myself from the Lucius sized imprint in the stone, shaking the rubble off my wings. At least I managed to achieve one thing… *I got the fucker's attention.*

But then, as I got myself ready for another attack, I could see the Keystone was building back up from where the box had unlocked its power. This time becoming something different than when I had sacrificed my hand.

This was the demonic snarling face of Zeus, the son of Cronus, who had managed to defeat the Titans the first time. His mouth was wide open and ready for a willing sacrifice to gain the blood of a Titan. But just as Matthias was about to reach in and gain the power, I threw my sword like a spear and this time it hit its mark, embedding itself into his shoulder. He bellowed with rage and reached round to rip it from his body, for no matter how much armour he wore, my sword would cut through anything.

Then he released his own weapon, a long spear that with

one twist of his hand, extended in size and released a curved blade each side of the spear tip.

"I thought this would be a fitting weapon, considering one similar took the life of your precious Jesus!" He threw it at me as if it would be an insult.

"He is not my precious Jesus, asshole!"

"No, not even after what he gifted you?" he said confusing me, as I had no fucking clue what he was talking about.

"Let's drain that gift of yours for I have no need for her anymore," he said, suddenly slashing a hand out towards the witch and making her scream as I saw her essence flowing from her suspended body, one now held taut like a bow. He took the power and transferred it into his weapon before coming at me and engaging in battle. I had to say the fucker was quick and he was strong, but this was even more so now that I was lacking my own power, for since the souls had been taken from me, I knew now that it had weakened me significantly.

Hit after hit, nothing got past him! Whereas I could not claim the same for my own body. But then I could also see that Amelia was reaching for the Eye, gathering it up to her chest, and trying to sneak away with it. She would have been successful too, except in that moment another bitch from my past appeared from fucking nowhere! Layla emerged from the shadows and shouted,

"She's trying to get the Eye, master!" Matthias turned around and snarled in her direction.

"YOU DARE GO AGAINST ME, GIRL!" he roared at Amelia, and I knew, despite her powers, she would not have stood a chance against him. However, the moment I went to stop him, he lashed all of his power at me, and I flew back into the rocks, this time the force embedded me far deeper, as I felt bones crack and snap like kindling on impact.

But then I heard her screaming my name, and I forced myself and my broken body out of the hole I had made. The sight that met me made my blood run cold. Because this was when I had to make a decision. One I knew might have been my last. For just as he grabbed Amelia and was about to swing a dagger from his belt her way, I threw my sword towards them both.

Because my aim was not shit, it flew in such a way that it spun in the air and ended up slicing through his arm. One that had been holding her. Being released suddenly, she fell to the ground and dropped the Eye, making it roll towards me.

I made a dash to get to it, but then suddenly an impact threw me backwards, with a force so powerful and painful that it tore through me… *literally.*

For I looked down at the same time I felt my body falling backwards, when I realised what the cause was. Because now I was looking at his spear, that had now punctured my heart, travelling straight through my chest.

It was a hit I knew I was not coming back from.

Meaning the last thing I heard was my name being screamed in agony and anguish, from the girl that I loved.

Then death made me close my eyes, with only one face in my mind and one name from lips said in prayer…

"Amelia."

CHAPTER THIRTY-FIVE

AMELIA

BECOMING GODS

"NO!" I screamed the moment I saw that spear hit his chest and pierce his heart, feeling as if it had been my very own. For it was in that moment that I realised, what Lucius had gone through when seeing me die. It was in that moment that I realised the pain... the *fucking agonising pain that was unlike any other!*

"And now there is no one left to take their souls from me!" Matthias said with booming laughter, before going back to the Keystone. I knew that I should try and stop him, but what good could I do? I knew I wasn't strong enough, for my power would only be absorbed by him. I needed something more, but there was nothing left!

An agonising cry ripped through me as I ran over to Lucius, knowing that I wanted to spend my last moments with him. But then I was grabbed roughly from behind and I saw it was that bitch, Layla! She was the reason. She was the fucking reason!

"Now it's my time to kill you, bitch!" she screamed at me as she tackled me to the ground. Then the blade came from nowhere, one that was just about to come hurtling down into my own heart, a death by the same cause. But suddenly she was pushed off me by a force and when I saw where it came from, I knew then that I was looking at the face of Kala not Dalene.

She had saved me!

She nodded to the Eye that was still in between Lucius and me, left there now that Matthias believed that nothing could stand in his way.

"The Eye, Amelia... quickly both of you, use it now!" she cried desperately, but then the moment that Matthias saw her aiding me, he backhanded her, making her fall backwards with a sickening thud. Then, before he could reach out to stop me, I scrambled to my feet and ran towards him, leaping at the last moment. Then I pushed the other side of the Eye into Lucius' outstretched hand. One that looked as if he had died trying to reach for me, and the pain I felt in knowing that cut me to the core!

But it was like Kala said, *I had to try!*

So, I pushed it the last inch that was needed to touch his fingertips, which was when the connection was finally made. I sucked in a startled breath, as I knew now that I had the power to gain back the souls. Souls that had travelled through me, and the essence was one that still lingered. I was the anchor to drag them back. Which was precisely what I did. And just as Matthias was about to reach me, he fell suddenly to his knees as I tore every soul from him. I closed my eyes and forced all those souls back into the Eye, and pushed them between myself and Lucius.

Then I open my eyes and watched and prayed for him to open his own, for just even one flicker of his fingertips would be enough. Anything to acknowledge the power and know he had accepted it. I didn't know where he was in the world right then, in which realm, be it Heaven or Hell or some other afterlife, but wherever he was, I suddenly screamed his name,

"LUCIUS!" Then I closed my eyes and forced the power of the Eye to do my bidding. I cradled it closer to me and placed his palm on the other side, so he was touching it even more. Then I let go of all my tears of love and loss, allowing them to fall and drip onto the very essence of Janus. This was when I finally felt its power and this time, it wasn't one of rage like the Eye had been made from.

It was a power that could defeat the roots of rage and cleanse them of all the hatred that Matthias had powered into them.

And in this, it was also what had the power to make a vampire's heart beat again.

Suddenly Lucius sucked in a deep breath, and then he took in another, before finally his eyes opened… and we stared at each other over the Eye that we both held. At first, he looked confused, but then as if it all started to come back to him, he looked down at the spear still in his chest and suddenly ripped it from himself. He then healed instantly as if the Eye had the power to do this.

"Gods, Lucius!" I threw myself into his arms, and he cradled me to him, and it would have been the most perfect moment by being reunited, that was until Kala screamed,

"THE KEYSTONE!" This was when the whole mountain started to shake, and I looked back to see that we had been too late. Matthias had plunged his hand into the Keystone and was now absorbing all that the Titans had left to give him. He was becoming a God, one I knew no one would have the strength to fight! Then I looked up to Lucifer and found him being held and about to be crushed by Abaddon, because it no longer mattered that all of the souls were now transferred back into Lucius. There was only one thing that would manage to calm him down, and that was his Pip.

"What are we going to do?" I questioned as Lucius dragged himself into a sitting position, obviously still affected by what had happened physically.

"Only a God can defeat a God, Amelia," he told me, and I started to wonder at those words. Started to wonder at what exactly had made a God. The Venom of God seemed to have transferred into him and made him into the beast he was becoming behind me. My mother too had made herself into a God, and this was with the blood of Pertinax, for she had told me the story.

It was all about the blood. It had always been about that life force the Gods themselves could not live without.

"What is it?" Lucius asked as if he could see on my face, it was all starting to make sense.

"I think I know how to stop him," I told him on a whisper.

"Good, because we're going to need something."

"You're gonna have to trust me again," I said.

"I will always trust you," he told me after a few moments of looking at each other, for words weren't needed. But I nodded and then told him,

"Okay… then it's time you give me back what you stole from me, Lucius." Then, before he could react, I ripped his gauntlet off his hand using the strength of my power left and before he could stop me, I raised his Hellish hand up and bit into it as hard as I could.

"Amelia, no!" he shouted, but it was too late, I overpowered him, holding him still with the energy I had left in me. Doing so now as I sucked the essence he had stolen from me, combined with the Venom of God that he had kept locked away in this part of his hand. Then I didn't let go until I felt as though I had consumed it all, until the hand beneath my hold was transformed back into that of a man once more.

"Amelia!" Lucius shouted, as my body suddenly flew backwards and landed hard on the ground. For a moment I felt stunned, unable to move, as if some piece of me had just been slotted back into place and my whole soul was now taking the time to absorb it and accept it. Something that had always been mine and yet, had always been missing. But of course it had because Lucius had been taking care of it for me.

Suddenly I placed my palm flat on the ground and my entire body started to shake, because I heard the roar of anger… the roar of a Titan behind me. Then I took in a deep breath and felt myself rising from the ground. Rising upright to then find myself surrounded by a red fire. But I didn't stop. No, instead I continued to rise, wondering when this serene feeling would end. Almost as if I was no longer a body but more like a ghost. It was strange because I felt weightless, and then when I brought my hand in front of my face, I felt its movements and focused on that feeling. Suddenly I felt my entire body come back to me as power started crackling around, making me feel warm and safe.

It was when I looked down that I saw I was still floating in the air, suspended there by my own doing. It was then that I realised it had worked, for this must have been how a God felt.

But then I was in control, and my mind was free and calm. For I no longer felt the rage that I needed to be able to use the power I gained in Hell. I flicked my wrist around and spread out my fingers, now commanding more flames to appear in my hand. A ball of red energy started to spin, and it took no effort at all. In fact, the same amount of effort you would need to catch a ball.

It was incredible.

With this power surging through me, I had never felt so alive, so strong... so unbeatable. Suddenly the rest of my senses started to come back to me. I became aware of what was going on around me. I heard my name being called by a voice I knew. A voice I loved. But he sounded so worried, so scared, yet he didn't have anything to fear, for I wouldn't let anything happen. Though, perhaps he didn't know that. Perhaps none of them knew. But then suddenly more started to come to me, like the clashing of swords, the scream of my mother... my mother... who was hurting my mother!?

Then my father called my name, but yet he was fighting... who was he fighting? Suddenly these questions started to come with answers as I remembered what had happened, or more importantly why it happened.

What had been my reason for taking back this piece of me, along with the Venom of God.

"Matthias." The name escaped my mouth like I was spitting out venom trying to kill me. But nothing could kill me, nothing but another God. And as for Matthias... he didn't have what I had. For I had been born half Angel, half Vampire, and now I had the blood of a God added to that, no one was more powerful.

Lucifer had finally found his perfect creation. But then I knew that this was what he had always intended. It was why he allowed that blood to make its way down into my mother's womb. He hadn't taken it all from her, the pure blood of Pertinax... no, instead he gave a piece of it to me, for I was to be the first God born. My mother with such a mix of supernatural blood, and the Venom of God in Lucius' hand, had been the only things strong enough to contain it for me, until I had been ready. Until I had been strong enough to survive it. I knew now that if he had never taken it from me, then it would have ripped me apart as time went on. The power would have consumed me and turned me into something purely dangerous.

But I had grown up with love. I had grown up into being the nerdy funny, clumsy mortal that I was always intended to grow up to be. Otherwise, this power would have consumed me long ago, and now I was using it in the right way.

And it was time I started doing that.

For I was not the Queen of Sins, I was the Queen of Blood, and now I had the right one running within my veins!

This was when I finally came back to myself and looked around, seeing my father fighting Matthias. Someone who had grown in size and now looked like a demonic giant version of himself. But even my father was not strong enough, for Lucius too was trying to fight him but both of them kept on getting knocked back. My fear for them both, the two men I loved most in this world, and I could not stand the pain I would feel in losing them. So, before they could hurt themselves, I held them back with the thoughts in my mind.

They couldn't understand what was happening. I could still hear Lucius calling my name as if trying to get me out of this suspended state surrounded by red flames. So, I calmed my powers and let my body float down to the floor and as soon as my feet touched the ground, I felt centred. My body was back so that I could feel every aspect of it once more. I even shuddered and tried to suppress a giggle at the feeling.

Then, so no one else could get hurt, I created a barrier between us, and I could vaguely see that the war in the background had now ended. That the souls had been returned, meaning there were no more enemies left to fight other than this one.

Matthias would pay.

"Amelia?" Lucius said my name in question, and I walked closer to him and picked up the sword that he had dropped. Then I engulfed it in pretty blood red flames, and told him,

"I've got this, handsome." Then I turned around and started to walk towards my enemy.

"Amelia, no!" Lucius cried my name in panic. So, I paused, stopping long enough to tell him,

"This is my destiny… it is… *who I was born to be.*" Then I walked towards Matthias, now seeing him controlling the ground and splitting it up, so that lava poured out. Then, when he saw me coming, he threw it my way but with a single hand, I lifted it up and the molten liquid stopped before it could touch me. I gathered it all up in my own hand without even needing to touch it, before I yelled over to him,

"Hey, dickhead, try absorbing this!" After this, I threw it at him, combined with my own energy, a power that hammered into him, knocking him back enough to bleed.

"Oh, wouldn't you know, Gods can bleed after all," I said, making him angry.

"IMPOSSIBLE, YOU ARE JUST A WOMAN!" he roared at me, in his demonic voice that cracked the stone beneath my feet. Then I smiled at him, lifted my sword, and spun it around before answering,

"No, I am a Draven!" I shouted back, and then used my powers to force him back to his normal size! After this, I kicked up his spear that he had used to try and kill Lucius, and threw it his way, until he caught it. Then I told him,

"And we never stay down… now fight me!" Then I ran at him, and raised my flaming sword high before it came crashing down over his head. A blow he barely managed to defend with his own weapon, cracking it in two. Then he threw away the broken end and started to fight once more. He managed to break away from my brutal assault, now deciding to use his powers after I kicked him so hard in the chest his rib cage shattered, and he fell back against the mountain wall.

"Yeah, how did that feel? Not so hot, eh?" I said with a laugh, knowing that he'd done the same to my boyfriend and well, this was payback. His entire body started to glow, and I knew he was pulling in his powers. Suddenly, he picked up all the boulders within his demonic reach and threw them at me. I could have simply made them all disappear. I could have made them crumble at a thought. But the truth was I wanted to look like a badass. So, I used my sword and sliced through every single one before it hit me, doing so in a series of moves that I had learned from my father. So that by the time I fell to the ground and landed on one knee, I held my sword down in front of me as all of the pieces of rock I had cut through, rained down around me.

As far as badass moves went, I knew it looked good. Especially when I heard Lucius mutter behind me, still trapped behind the veil I had locked him behind,

"Fuck me."

But then my head shot up the moment I realised I had got cocky, for Matthias was not done yet.

"NO!" This scream came from Kala, as I saw now he was draining her of all of her power, screaming down at her,

"GIVE ME MORE!" I knew I had to stop it, so I severed the connection by picking up all of the stones that he had thrown at me, then I propelled them at him like bullets from a gun… big fucking bullets! One after the other they hit into him, but it did not matter, for with this extra power he decided to go straight for the person I loved. The veil behind me crumbled as if someone had set fire to it, and before I had chance to do anything, I saw all of the power he had gained from the witch now travelling towards Lucius.

"NO!" I screamed, but this ended with another. For Kala threw out her hands towards it, making it come hurtling back to her. The moment it hit her square in the chest, I knew then it wasn't something she was coming back from.

This was when I finally gave way to rage.

I lashed out at Matthias in such a way, that he could not heal fast enough. But then when he finally fell to his knees and his weapon fell from his hands, I picked it up and threw it in front of him, demanding,

"Pick it up!" He tried but he couldn't, being too bloody and broken.

"I SAID PICK IT UP!" I roared down at him, making him try again. Then I told him,

"I will not kill an unarmed enemy, for your heart of darkness will stop beating by your own fucking blade!" Then, when he finally picked it up, I used my will against him, forcing his own hand to hold his weapon dead centre at his chest over his black heart. Then keeping my control over his will, I kept it there as I walked away a few steps, turning my back on him, and now looking at Lucius. Then I told him,

"This is for you and your daughter." I never waited for his reaction, but instead I turned and kicked at the end of the broken spear, so it entered Matthias' heart, making him roar in pain. Then I twisted my blade in my hand before delivering his sentence,

"As for your head, that I will sever with my own!" Then I spun on a heel, and swung my blade whilst landing on my knees with my back to Matthias. Then with my head held down, I waited for the sound of his head as it rolled from his body before landing on the floor beside me. I lifted my gaze to find only one pair of eyes I needed to see in that moment.

Lucius.

But then I remembered as he came running towards me, that there was someone more important in that moment.

His daughter.

Someone who had just saved his life.

I ran towards her, skidding on the ground as I got to her battered body, one full of scars. Each one became a badge of honour, and a symbol of just how hard she had fought to free herself from the clutches of evil.

"Take care of... of my father..." she forced out through bloody lips.

"Just hold on and I will try..." She reached out for my hands and took them in her own.

"No, no... it is time... please... it is time for me to go home and be free." I closed my eyes at this, feeling the tears fall once more.

"Just promise me... love him like... like she never could." I tensed before nodding, telling her,

"I will, I promise you."

"Tell him... I am finally going where I was always meant to be."

"No, please... please hold on, so he can..." I said frantically, giving her hands a shake that gripped both my own.

"My power dies with him... it was always meant to be this way," she said, with barely more than a whisper of breath now as the life was leaving her for good.

"Amelia?" Lucius said my name in question behind me before telling me,

"That is not my wife." I swallowed down the emotion I

knew I needed to get past in this moment, so that I could finally bring them both the closure they needed.

"No... sweetheart, do you trust me?" I asked him, making him say,

"I told you, I always would."

"Then come, come here and say goodbye." He frowned in question but lowered himself to the girl he would never know. Then I closed my eyes and told him the painful truth,

"She is no longer your wife... she is... oh Gods, Lucius, I am sorry, but she is Kala, she is your daughter, and you need to say goodbye," I said with tears falling now without being able to stop them. Lucius looked too shocked, too traumatised to move. But then I took his hand and told him,

"I am here... I am with you." Then as I watched his own tears started to overflow, I knew then that he saw it. He saw the truth. He quickly fell to his knees beside her.

"Could it be... could it really...?"

"I am sorry, I tried to stop her... I tried to beat her back but..."

"Ssshh now, ssshh... now drink." Lucius was about to bite into his arm when she reached out and placed her hand in his to stop him.

"It won't work... for it is not meant to be this way."

"Please... I cannot... I cannot... lose you again..." Lucius said breaking down.

"God did not forsake you. He granted you your wish and now I have mine, for I finally get to tell you... I... love you... my father."

"My daughter..." On hearing this, she released her last breath and let go of her life with a small smile gracing her lips. After this, all the scars on her body suddenly faded as if being absorbed back into her own flesh. But then, when a witch dies, so does the spells she casts.

Lucius then gathered her up in his arms and my heart broke for him, when he started saying,

"My little girl... no... no... please." Then, just as his tears started to flow down on her beautiful face, he gazed down at her. He then ran a single fingertip down along her nose as if this was his way of saying goodbye. Then her entire body started to glow, before it burst into a heavenly white light, and suddenly Lucius, transformed into his angel side.

Glorious white wings erupted from his back before he stood with her glowing form cradled in his arms.

"Wait for me," he told me, placing his forehead to mine.

"Always," I answered softly before suddenly, he looked up at the Heavens and then...

He was gone.

To be Continued
In Lucius and Amelia's
Happy Ever Afterlife

Please note that the
Story will continue from this point on.
Date to be confirmed.

ABOUT THE AUTHOR

Stephanie Hudson has dreamed of being a writer ever since her obsession with reading books at an early age. What first became a quest to overcome the boundaries set against her in the form of dyslexia has turned into a life's dream. She first started writing in the form of poetry and soon found a taste for horror and romance. Afterlife is her first book in the series of twelve, with the story of Keira and Draven becoming ever more complicated in a world that sets them miles apart.

When not writing, Stephanie enjoys spending time with her loving family and friends, chatting for hours with her biggest fan, her sister Cathy who is utterly obsessed with one gorgeous Dominic Draven. And of course, spending as much time with her supportive partner and personal muse, Blake who is there for her no matter what.

Author's words.

My love and devotion is to all my wonderful fans that keep me going into the wee hours of the night but foremost to my wonderful daughter Ava...who yes, is named after a cool, kick-ass, Demonic bird and my sons, Jack, who is a little hero and Baby Halen, who yes, keeps me up at night but it's okay because he is named after a Guitar legend!

Keep updated with all new release news & more on my website

www.afterlifesaga.com
Never miss out, sign up to the
mailing list at the website.

Also, please feel free to join myself and other Dravenites on my Facebook group
Afterlife Saga Official Fan
Interact with me and other fans. Can't wait to see you there!

facebook.com/AfterlifeSaga
twitter.com/afterlifesaga
instagram.com/theafterlifesaga

ACKNOWLEDGEMENTS

Well first and foremost my love goes out to all the people who deserve the most thanks and are the wonderful people that keep me going day to day. But most importantly they are the ones that allow me to continue living out my dreams and keep writing my stories for the world to hopefully enjoy… These people are of course YOU! Words will never be able to express the full amount of love I have for you guys. Your support is never ending. Your trust in me and the story is never failing. But more than that, your love for me and all who you consider your 'Afterlife family' is to be commended, treasured and admired. Thank you just doesn't seem enough, so one day I hope to meet you all and buy you all a drink! ;)

To my family… To my amazing mother, who has believed in me from the very beginning and doesn't believe that something great should be hidden from the world. I would like to thank you for all the hard work you put into my books and the endless hours spent caring about my words and making sure it is the best it can be for everyone to enjoy. You make Afterlife shine. To my wonderful crazy father who is and always has been my hero in life. Your strength astonishes me, even to this day and the love and care you hold for your family is a gift you give to the Hudson name. And last but not least, to the man that I consider my soul mate. The man who taught me about real love and makes me not only want to be a better person but makes me feel I am too. The amount of support you have given me since we met has been incredible and the greatest feeling was finding out you wanted to spend the rest of your life with me when you asked me to marry you.

All my love to my dear husband and my own personal Draven… Mr Blake Hudson.

Another personal thank you goes to my dear friend Caroline Fairbairn and her wonderful family that have embraced my brand of crazy into their lives and given it a hug when most needed.

For their friendship I will forever be eternally grateful.

I would also like to mention Claire Boyle my wonderful PA, who without a doubt, keeps me sane and constantly smiling through all the chaos which is my life ;) And a loving mention goes to Lisa Jane for always giving me a giggle and scaring me to death with all her count down pictures lol ;)

Thank you for all your hard work and devotion to the saga and myself. And always going that extra mile, pushing Afterlife into the spotlight you think it deserves. Basically helping me achieve my secret goal of world domination one day…evil laugh time… Mwahaha! Joking of course ;)

As before, a big shout has to go to all my wonderful fans who make it their mission to spread the Afterlife word and always go the extra mile. I love you all x

Also by Stephanie Hudson

Afterlife Saga

A Brooding King, A Girl running from her past. What happens when the two collide?

Book 1 - Afterlife

Book 2 - The Two Kings

Book 3 - The Triple Goddess

Book 4 - The Quarter Moon

Book 5 - The Pentagram Child /Part 1

Book 6 - The Pentagram Child /Part 2

Book 7 - The Cult of the Hexad

Book 8 - Sacrifice of the Septimus /Part 1

Book 9 - Sacrifice of the Septimus /Part 2

Book 10 - Blood of the Infinity War

Book 11 - Happy Ever Afterlife /Part 1

Book 12 - Happy Ever Afterlife / Part 2

Transfusion Saga

What happens when an ordinary human girl comes face to face with the cruel Vampire King who dismissed her seven years ago?

Transfusion - Book 1

Venom of God - Book 2

Blood of Kings - Book 3

Rise of Ashes - Book 4

Map of Sorrows - Book 5

Tree of Souls - Book 6

Kingdoms of Hell – Book 7

Eyes of Crimson - Book 8

Roots of Rage - Book 9

Heart of Darkness - Book 10

Wraith of Fire - Book 11

Queen of Sins - Book 12

Afterlife Chronicles: (Young Adult Series)

The Glass Dagger – Book 1

The Hells Ring – Book 2

Stephanie Hudson and Blake Hudson

The Devil in Me

OTHER WORKS BY HUDSON INDIE INK

Paranormal Romance/Urban Fantasy

Sloane Murphy

Xen Randell

C. L. Monaghan

Sorcha Dawn

Sci-fi/Fantasy

Devin Hanson

Crime/Action

Blake Hudson

Mike Gomes

Contemporary Romance

Gemma Weir

Elodie Colt

Ann B. Harrison

Ingram Content Group UK Ltd.
Milton Keynes UK
UKHW041506120723
425001UK00001B/16